Cullen X
Cullen, Jonathan Michael
The ranks of Jody Brae /

34028074539256
CYF $22.95   ocn449858957
05/25/10

P9-ASK-493
3 4028 07453 9256
HARRIS COUNTY PUBLIC LIBRARY

THE RANKS
OF
JODY BRAE

THE RANKS
OF
JODY BRAE

By Jonathan Michael Cullen

A Block Island Book

Published by Bryant Park Press Inc.

BLOCK ISLAND BOOKS

An Imprint of Bryant Park Press Inc.
100 Park Avenue 16th Floor
New York, NY 10017

Copyright © 2009 by Jonathan Michael Cullen

Published in the United States by
Bryant Park Press Inc., New York, NY
www.blockislandbooks.com

All rights reserved. No part of this book may be reproduced in any form or by any electronic or mechanical means, including information storage and retrieval system, without permission in writing from the publisher, except by a reviewer who may quote brief passages in a review.

Cover design by Burnt Sky Media.

Interior design by Val Sherer,
Personalized Publishing Services

First Edition

ISBN: 0-9796816-6-9

ISBN13: 978-0-9796816-6-0
LCCN: 2009928145

12 11 10 9 10 9 8 7 6 5 4 3 2 1

Printed in the United States of America.

"Fire is never a gentle master."

—*Proverb*

BOOK ONE

CHAPTER ONE

The fires raged every night that summer. Sirens echoed through the streets like devils warning of the apocalypse. Driving to work the next day I saw the aftermath. One morning it might be the ruins of a forty year-old apartment building. The rows of windows were stained with black soot like the mascara on a prostitute; chunks of burned roof shingles fluttered in the wind. Another day it might be the charred remnants of a "triple-decker," the sort of massive multi-family houses that dominated Boston's neighborhoods. With no brick shell to hold them together, these monsters often collapsed in on themselves. The scenes were ghastly.

There had been some chatter around the department about the spike in fires. But most of the cops and their families were safely distant from the epidemic. The regular officers lived on quiet streets in the tidy blue-collar neighborhoods of South Boston or Hyde Park. The higher-ups raised their families in the leafy sections of West Roxbury, Brighton and further beyond in the suburbs. All the while the fires devastated the rundown parts of Dorchester and Roxbury, consuming brick apartment buildings and multi-family homes with the ferocity of a cyclone. If it hadn't been for complaints from local Black civic leaders, the outbreak might have been ignored altogether and an entire neighborhood would have turned to ash before City Hall or the State House took notice.

As for me, I lived on the edge, in a cramped third-floor apartment in the Mission Hill section of Roxbury. I discovered the rental years before, an ad scribbled on torn paper and taped to a public bulletin board in the Park Street subway station. The house was an old three-family building, situated along the steepest face of the hill, built into the ledge like an ancient Incan dwelling. On windy days, the entire structure creaked and swayed. During storms, water seeped into the walls and made the paint bubble. The landlord, Demetrius, was an old Greek who lived in the basement either to maximize rental income or because he feared heights. He seldom left his cave, except to collect rent on the 1st of each month. From what little conversation we had, I learned he had bought the house sometime 'before the war,' although I never was quite sure which war he meant.

Nevertheless, it was a comfortable place, an anonymous little corner of the city, threadbare but reliable, and gave me solitude without isolation. From the bedroom window, facing north, downtown spread out before me in a crowded peninsula of winding streets, church spires, gated parks, office towers and apartment buildings. With the Charles River to the west and Boston Harbor to the north and east, the city seemed embraced by water like a peaceful floating metropolis. To the east, my kitchen window looked out across all of Roxbury, a dense jungle of triple-deckers, workers cottages, vacant factory buildings and public housing complexes. The homes were decrepit, with sagging porches and rotting roofs and everything was gray, but for a few infested oaks trees and gnarled elms that sprouted from the asphalt in suffocation. Even in summer, the area had the bleakness of a dying seaport.

On sleepless nights I sat in my underwear, sweating in the summer heat and stared out to Roxbury. With a cup of tea in one hand, I searched the landscape for the smallest spark or glow of flames because I knew somewhere out there a house or building was burning. If there were sirens, I stretched my head out the window and followed the flashing lights until they faded out of view. As I gazed into the darkness, I imagined screaming children, a smoldering couch, a flaming china cabinet, burning photo albums, perhaps a white wedding dress, neatly stored in a closet besieged by flames. I knew that even if the occupants escaped, a part of their past and history was obliterated. My midnight surveillance, the search for fire, became a minor obsession and provided relief from an almost crippling insomnia. If someone had asked the last time I slept through the night, I could have given the exact date and duration—ten months and five days.

Since I could remember, the dreams had been a part of my life. As a child I was terrified of the night. I would stay up late, wide-eyed and angst-ridden, with my chin propped on the pillow and staring through the window at streetlights and passing cars. Sometimes I hung over the side of the bed knowing that, if I fell asleep, I would fall to the floor. Other nights I would shake my arms and legs and work myself into a sweat to stay awake. Regardless of the method, I always succumbed to exhaustion and later awoke, breathless, disoriented and shivering like a wet dog.

In my early twenties the dreams were more of a nuisance than curse. They might haunt me for a week straight and not return for months, sometimes years. From the day I entered boot camp in '49 and up through my two-year stint in Korea, I didn't have one sleepless night. I thought I was cured. The guys in my platoon were amazed how soundly I slept while huddled cold and hungry in a foxhole or pitch tent. What they didn't know was that years of fearful, restless nights made the deprivation of infantry life seem like a cakewalk. After I returned from Korea and joined the force as a street cop I had forgotten about the nightmares entirely. Maybe I had gotten cocky. The moment I felt at ease, the moment I could put my head on the pillow without the slightest hesitation, the dreams came raging back into my life like a psychotic ex-girlfriend.

The alarm rang. I sprung up and threw off the bed sheets. For a flash moment I was unsure of where I was. My heart pounded in my chest and I struggled to breathe, although there was nothing to constrict me. That was how I lived much of the time. Once I got out of bed and started to dress the nightmare faded into the backdrop of morning routine. A pot of tea, a few slices of toast and I was myself once again. Something about physical movement kept me focused on the moment.

Tonight I was finally taking out Ruth. I remembered the first time I saw her, the winter before, sitting nervously behind the front desk at headquarters, taking instructions from an older secretary. When I came to the top of the stairwell she looked up and smiled briefly, but a millisecond longer than necessary. From that day on, I thought of nothing but meeting her. Ruth arrived at Forensics as an intern, still wet behind the ears and aglow with confidence. Like many young interns before her, she came in with high expectations that were soon dashed when she discovered she was a glorified secretary. In a department that was controlled top-down like a Soviet bureau, no manager was willing to give up an inch of responsibility for fear of losing control. As a result, Ruth wasn't given any serious forensic work and spent her days processing document requests, answering phones and providing the front lobby a pretty face.

Since Forensics and Internal Affairs were on the same floor, Ruth was the first person I saw when I came into headquarters. I had laid the groundwork with small-talk, a light-hearted compliment, meaningless question or remark about the weather. Over the course of the summer I learned a little more about her each day. I was surprised to learn she had been born in Boston. But since her father worked for the State Department under Roosevelt, the family was in constant motion, which explained her generic, almost exotic, American accent. Ruth spent her formative years in San Diego when it was still a small and undiscovered backwater along the Mexican border. An entire childhood spent outdoors in the hot California sun had given her skin a soft, permanent tan and her personality a bubbly optimism that at times made me cringe. She left home at seventeen, never to return, and obtained a degree from some state school in the mid-West. When she decided to start a career, she chose to move to Boston after seeing a postcard of the Public Gardens during springtime. She was that impressionable, or so I thought.

By August, at the height of the fires, I wandered into headquarters daily to pull records, review case notes and check in with the brass. I almost subconsciously arrived early so I could stop and talk with Ruth. If she was focused on the typewriter or had her nose in a file cabinet, I caught her attention with a forced cough or exaggerated stomp on the floor. Then she would look up from her work, never straight at me, but always from an angle with her eyes gazing cutely from behind a wisp of hair. Although I never admitted it to myself, I usually stopped in to see her whether I had business at headquarters that day or not. Her smile brightened my day more than a cloudless summer morning. A few casual words from her would put a little skip in my step the rest of the afternoon. That was Ruth.

"Hello there."

She looked up from the typewriter with a girlish grin, her hair pulled back and thick-rimmed glasses magnifying great blue eyes.

"Hi Jody. Did we oversleep?"

"Let's just say that me and the alarm clock aren't in agreement."

"I can't imagine anyone...or anything...not being in agreement with you."

"I have my enemies."

"I am sure you have more friends. Want a cup of coffee? I just brewed a fresh pot."

"No thanks. I have to get over to see Jackson. He wants to see me. Are we still on for tonight?"

With the tip of her tongue between her two front teeth, she smiled softly and nodded.

"Great. I will pick you up at 7:00."

"I'll be waiting."

I turned and walked down the corridor towards Jackson's office. Although it was 'his' office, Jackson controlled most of the second floor. Originally given a small corner room, the Captain slowly and strategically acquired more, filling them with cabinets full of information and dossiers that made the CIA look like surveillance amateurs. Most of the files were expired or closed cases that would normally be tossed into some locked cellar. Other cabinets contained information about cracked cases in other States, even other countries. Jackson found these useful for studying all the latest crime techniques. But more importantly, he insisted, they were good for learning about the mistakes.

Jackson had been battling with Forensics for many months about space. The truth was that both departments struggled for room in the budget-strapped halls of the aging headquarters building. It was a constant tug of war whereby Jackson and his detectives, although muddied, always finished standing up. Both departments bickered like old spinsters about who was more vital to the Department's mission. Forensics maintained the integrity of the evidence and Internal Affairs ensured the integrity of the cops. One couldn't exist without the other, although neither dared admit it.

Jackson didn't fit the classic image of Police Captain and was known to be a little eccentric or a little strange, depending on whom you talked to. He was no doubt a dramatic figure, almost never seen in uniform. His outfit of choice included plain wool pants, a brown tweed jacket and slip-on loafers without socks. He had an intense gaze, which, combined with bushy white eyebrows, made him appear more the absent-minded scholar than top police brass. But Jackson was no starry-eyed idealist. He didn't reach Captain because he was a master sleuth or remarkable street cop. Nor did he rise up the departmental ladder because his uncle was a City Counselor. Jackson possessed a rare blend of intelligence and common sense. His mind was razor sharp and he had an almost supernatural sense for detail in even the most baffling cases. An intellectual at heart, Jackson probably could have gone to Harvard or Dartmouth. He used ten-cent words in a department of five-cent cops. But being a swamp Yankee from Cornish, Maine, he was a rare species in a force that was dominated by second and third-generation Boston Irish.

When he was coming up the ranks, Jackson was constantly derided for his down-East accent and the flat "R"s that were too often mistaken for a white-shoe country club twang. But he was no aristocrat. His father harvested blueberries, his mother taught Sunday school, and he and his four brothers grew up in a hardscrabble life of bleak winters and mosquito-infested summers. So it was no surprise that when he was offered a small scholarship to Boston University, Jackson leapt like a Maine black bear. And it was still no surprise that when he set his mind to a career in law enforcement, he would be the best.

"Captain."

Jackson lifted his head up from a pile of papers on his desk.

"Detective Brae, good morning." He paused and squinted. "You look exhausted."

"It's nothing. I drank too much coffee yesterday."

"Well, you'd better drink some more," he sighed.

"What've you got? Cops squashing speeding tickets for relatives? The Mounties stealing horse feed?"

Jackson looked back to his documents, holding them close to his face. When he was preoccupied, he spoke slowly and accentuated each word with a pause in between.

"More dire than that I am afraid. What do you know about fire, Brae?"

Jackson's conversations were always cryptic and like a Greek philosopher, he began with a simple question, an idea, and gradually worked up to a larger vision. He spoke carefully and selected each word as if making a chess move. When absorbed in thought, he looked up to the ceiling like he was conferring with the Lord himself. And though he may have had his quirks, Jackson's delicacy and dignified manner made him seem a modern Sherlock Holmes.

"It warms. It provides light. And it burns."

Jackson furled his eyebrows and put the papers down. He slapped his hands on the desktop and looked up to me.

"It's also lucrative, I'm afraid."

"Insurance?"

"An age-old crime. Arson. A crime that's always nipped at the heels of departments across the country, but never approaching epidemic levels like other social crimes."

Jackson ran his fingers through his grey, thinning hair and looked up with a sigh.

"Usually bored kids or pyromaniacs," I suggested.

"Perhaps. You know what's unique about fire? It's the only crime whose impact depends on how quickly it is discovered and contained."

Jackson rose from the desk and walked towards me. He navigated the stacks of paper and boxes of documents on the floor like he was crossing a mine field.

"Close the door, please."

I backed away and tapped the door shut. Jackson approached within two feet of me and stopped. Looking into my eyes, he lowered his voice and spoke.

"There's been a spate of building fires recently, most of which are taking place in Roxbury and Dorchester, along the northern half of Blue Hill Ave."

"That area has become pretty run-down...lots of abandoned buildings," I added.

"True, but that doesn't account for the number of incidents. What is more unsettling is the intensity and thoroughness of the fires. Every building so far has been completely unsalvageable."

"What are you suggesting?" I interrupted.

"I'm not suggesting anything yet. This past weekend there were two three-alarms in Grove Hall. One on Warren Street, the other on Brunswick."

"That area looks like the fall of Berlin."

"These people aren't Nazi's, Brae. They're Americans. Both buildings were in heavy disrepair, true. But they were completely engulfed in under an hour. What's worse is it took twenty minutes for the fire department to arrive at Warren Street. Nearly as long for them to arrive at the other."

"Any victims?"

"No, thankfully. Brunswick Street was abandoned, just a few squatters. The owner had been moving to have them evicted but the issue was tied up in Housing court. The Warren Street building was the same, derelict."

"Might be coincidence."

"Perhaps," Jackson said, puckering his lips. "I need you to review the incidents. You know a lot of people on the street. Put your feelers out. Take this..." Jackson tossed a folder, which I caught awkwardly. "It has reports of all the major fires in the past three months. Read through it. Let me know if you smell a rat."

"What about the Arson Unit?"

"They've submitted reports. All the recent incidents were deemed 'accidental.' I need a third opinion on this."

"I think it was arson," I snickered.

"Slow down now. I am not saying our guys are involved. The housing stock in the poorer neighborhoods is old and decrepit. Anyone would expect a higher rate of fire. But that doesn't account for the slow response times. Besides, we've gotten calls from some of the politicians in that area. They say people are scared. They say the city doesn't care what happens in Black Roxbury."

Jackson smiled, patted me on the back and led me towards the door. His vagueness about assignments always left me with a pit in my stomach. I had never been completely comfortable working in Internal Affairs. Cops investigating other cops seemed somehow contrary to the order of the universe. When a recent mandate extended our authority to other municipal divisions, including the fire department, we came to be viewed as a fifth column among all the city's protective services agencies. We were the bad guys. So it was particularly frustrating not to know whether I was on a case, if there actually was a case, or if I was being asked to do grunt work.

As he closed the door, I put out my hand to stop it.

"So is this a case?"

"You tell me, Brae."

"What if everything checks out?"

Jackson smiled. "There are always cops invalidating speeding tickets for friends and relatives."

Although only two miles from downtown, Roxbury was worlds away from what the average suburbanite, college student or summer tourist imagined as Boston. Once a separate town, it was transformed from a cattle-grazing escape for weary city dwellers to a densely populated streetcar suburb in only a few decades. A short trip by trolley and less than ten minutes by car, Roxbury was the natural release valve for Boston's ever-expanding immigrant population. In the late nineteenth century, hordes of Irish fled the wrecking-ball progress of the Federal Hill slums and settled in shanties outside of Dudley Square. Beginning in the twenties, German and Russian Jews began pouring into Roxbury and settling along the respectable boulevards of Grove Hall, a section of large Victorian homes that overlooked the symbolic heart of the Roxbury/Dorchester area, Franklin Park. Like the Irish and Italians before them, they soon climbed the economic ladder out of poverty and settled in better neighborhoods.

You could almost measure the path of immigrant progress by drawing a straight line, starting at the wharfs along Boston Harbor and continuing into the South End, then along the entire stretch of Blue Hill Avenue through Roxbury, Dorchester, Mattapan and beyond to the suburbs.

When I was a child, in the mid-nineteen-thirties, Eastern European Jews, either newly arrived or fleeing the confines of the congested North and South Ends of Boston, moved into Grove Hall and set up butcheries, delicatessens, haberdasheries, and every other conceivable shop. In time, they turned Roxbury and Dorchester into a miniature version of the old-world villages they had left behind.

I was probably the only Irish guy who had eaten bagels and lox or who knew that a Minyan, a quorum of ten men, was required to form a Jewish congregation. My entire childhood was spent two blocks from Franklin Park in the heart of Jewish Roxbury in a sprawling brick building that was the Home For Stray Boys. The institution was a city unto itself, massive and cavernous, stretching an entire block in length and nearly half as wide. It was said that the building could be seen from an airplane, protruding castle-like from the neighborhood of tightly packed multi-family homes that surrounded it. Yet no one I knew had ever flown, so it was never confirmed. Outside the Home, a high wall encircled the premises and gave it the impression of a medieval fortress. Inside, corridors stretched as far as the eye could see, disappearing into darkness like the Roman catacombs. Every door led to a room, which had a door that led to another room. The entire place was a maze of mystery to the young eyes of so many lonely waifs.

The neighborhood around the institution was so crowded with brick apartment buildings and triple-deckers that some streets grew dark before sunset. In winter, I looked out my third-floor window to see a bed of snow across every flat-topped roof. I gazed for hours, lulled into a daydream by the hiss of steam radiators, and marveled at the vast jungle of streets and alleyways. Except for the smoke of chimneys, nothing moved and the world seemed frozen by a gray drabness that permeated every porch, window, doorway and dormer.

In summer the area teemed with life as packs of Jewish kids ran to the streets for games of stickball, basketball and tag. Sons and daughters of immigrants, they clung to their turf with unusual ferocity, forming little groups and street gangs. For the most part, they left the children of the institution alone, seeing the building as more of a curiosity than a threat. But with the dull days of summer, interaction between our world and theirs was inevitable. With a two-handed hoist from a roommate, I would peer over the wall. Neighborhood kids gathered on the other side and we chatted back and forth. They would invite me to join them and taunt me when I declined. Once I hurled a rock over the wall and listened to the shouts and cries as they scurried for cover. I laughed. One holiday they threw candy over the wall to us. I cried.

When I was sixteen the isolation of the institution became unbearable. One night I broke the lock on a utility door with a hammer and chisel I had stolen from the woodworking shop. Like an escaping P.O.W. I fled into the darkness, and ran until I collapsed. The next morning I awoke in a cluster of damp bushes beside a litter-strewn vacant lot. Marty Mirsky, a friend I had cultivated across the wall over the course of many summers, stood above me grinning, his hand extended to help me up. He took me to his house and explained to his Yiddish-speaking parents that I had defected from the Home, was seeking asylum, and would work for my dinner. After only two nights, however, they told me in broken English that, although they respected my decision, I could stay no longer. I reluctantly returned and was punished with a loss of yard time for two months. The institution authorities never did discover the missing tools and broken lock.

I never forgot the Mirskys' hospitality. When I finished high school, Marty and I stayed in touch for a few years until I left for boot camp. We exchanged letters right up through my time in Korea. He ended each one with "Old Hoss," an epithet he had been given years before because of his big teeth and funny horse-like laugh.

When I returned from the war, shortly before I entered the police academy, I drove down Elm Hill Avenue in search of that cold yet colorful place of my past. But the world had changed and so had Roxbury. The tidy three-family homes and stone buildings that once housed thousands of immigrant families were unrecognizable. The quiet streets along Seaver Street and Blue Hill Avenue were littered with trash and sewage. Many of the old shops were gone and the store signs changed. Some were simply boarded up, vacant shacks with peeling façades and crumbling foundations.

The first thing I noticed upon my return was that there wasn't a white face in sight. I felt suddenly abandoned, as if some part of my past, my history, had been stolen. In the years since I had left, Roxbury had turned into a Black ghetto. I pulled over to the apartment building where the Mirskys once lived. I approached the first person I saw, a kindly Black man, elderly but still spry, who looked as surprised to see me as I was him.

"They all gone—the Jews gone up and left."

In one sentence he recounted the saga of ethnic transition that was taking place across the country. After the War, with the prosperity of the fifties, the social order of the old cities churned. People flocked to newly built suburbs like stampeding cattle, crushing everything in their path. What remained was urban decay. The only souls left to fill the void were poor whites, mostly elderly, and even poorer Blacks. As I drove through the area, I sadly spotted small hints of the past; an elderly Jewish couple strolling nervously, a shriveled Irish widow pushing a grocery cart, a few distrustful shop owners peering from behind iron grates. The Roxbury of my memories was no more. I was alone.

Later, when I joined the force, I spent a lot of time in the area and became accustomed to the changes. Whenever I had an assignment that brought me through those familiar streets and lanes, I commenced my investigation at the institution. In some strange way, that old brick building was the center of my universe and all roads to anywhere began at its front gate.

By the time I made detective, the institution had been defunct for over a decade. It was vacant, closed in the mid-50's as the area changed and the responsibility of caring for the city's orphans shifted to newer public facilities. The last I had heard was that ownership was transferred to the Department of Public Health, with a role that had yet to be determined. The building became just another dilapidated structure in a neighborhood of leaky roofs, sagging porches, littered yards and broken windows. Yet I returned faithfully, as someone would come back to be with a dying parent. Whenever I stopped at the front gate, I still heard the shrieks of laughter from the children playing in the yard, however faint they had become. As I looked up to my room, that small corner window on the third floor, I saw a young boy starring back through the frosted panes.

After my meeting with Jackson, I headed to Roxbury to inspect the fire scenes. I drove along the northern edge of Franklin Park and turned left on to Humboldt Avenue, a wide boulevard of corner shops and brick buildings that ran through the middle of the neighborhood like a main artery. After a few blocks I turned again, down a quiet lane of large Victorian homes, still grand despite their disrepair. As I rumbled quietly along, I glanced between the yards to see the brick façade of the Home rising in the distance. At the next block I took a left and there, as timeless and immovable as a pyramid, stood the building. I flicked my cigarette out the window and pulled to the front gate. Above the entrance door hung a large sign, faded and almost unreadable: Roxbury Home For Stray Boys. I was home.

I felt my heart beating and with my eyes fixed to the building, I stared hypnotically, imagining everything but thinking of nothing. Whenever I neared this place, I was both repulsed by and drawn to it, caught by a bittersweet magnetism I could neither resist nor yield to. Although I had suffered there, the Home was my only past, a singular parent that clothed, fed and sheltered me. In the shadow of its towering brick walls, I could do nothing but cower, a repentant half-man, half-child, calmed by reverence and consumed by a sour longing. No other force on earth, either human or material, held that power over me.

After a few minutes, I punched the gas and sped off. Just a few blocks away, at 550 Warren Street, stood the site of a recent fire. As I pulled up, I saw a large brick building, three stories high, with bow-front windows and an arched front entrance. It was an empty shell, soot-scarred and desolate, every window covered in fresh plywood according to insurance requirements. The littered remnants of what was once inside lay scattered across the front yard and filled the air with the smell of damp ash. Inside I heard the creak of weakened floor joists as the breeze blew against the exterior walls. I pulled the Valiant into an alleyway between it and the next apartment building. I stood on the sidewalk and looked around. The nearest firehouse was less than a half-mile away on Washington Street. Heading north on Warren Street, still under a mile, was the Dudley Street fire house. Both were within minutes of the building, yet it had burned completely. If this had been arson, I thought, they must have used either explosives or flame throwers.

I got in the Valiant, backed out and drove to the end of Warren Street, through the busy intersection at Blue Hill Avenue. In the glare of the noonday sun, I saw the sign for Sam's Hats and Menswear, a small storefront wedged between a liquor mart and hair salon, along an endless stretch of nickel-and-dime stores that began at Grove Hall and ended at Dudley Square, two miles north. Steel grates hung down halfway from shop windows like tired eyes, welcoming customers while discouraging thieves. I pulled over and parked.

No one knew Sam's last name, but it didn't matter since everyone called him 'Sam the hat man.' At one time, his shop bustled with activity, as avenue shoppers stopped in to browse, try on the latest fashions or just chat. Sam was now one of the last holdouts, a relic from another era. He had purchased his store just before the War and had sold everything from ladies church hats to sombreros. In my youth, he was a reliable source for lollypops and penny candy. On hot summer afternoons, he stood on the sidewalk and dispensed treats like he was feeding chickens. The neighborhood kids that gathered by the front door became so disruptive that they were often shooed away by adjacent store owners for fear of losing business.

By the time I joined the force, I hadn't seen Sam since childhood. Then one winter afternoon we were reacquainted when a call came into headquarters that a runaway named Jocelyn had been found dead in the alleyway behind his store block. The young girl, barely seventeen, had been bound and gagged, her throat slit to the spinal column. Sam discovered the body when he went to open up the shop that morning. Although I was happy to see him, he went about his business with a callous indifference. He pointed out the location where he discovered the body, between a dumpster and small cement wall, and walked into the store like any other workday. My partner at the time, a nervous rookie, was sure Sam's behavior was an indication of involvement, but I knew better.

Sam was a son of old Roxbury and grew up when street gangs were the social order and toughness was earned but not flaunted. The day after Pearl Harbor, although already married and in his early thirties, he handed the shop keys to his wife and cousin and enlisted in the Army. He saw action in Normandy, walked across Belgium, swam across the Rhine and, if you believed him, was the soldier who cut the lock on the front gate of Dachau. Sam had seen humanity at its worst, so nothing fazed him. The appearance of a dead hooker at his back doorstep was just a continuation of the horrors he saw in Europe.

Sam didn't stay in business because he enjoyed sitting behind the register for eight hours waiting for the one or two customers that might stumble in out of curiosity. He didn't keep the lights on and the shelves stocked out of nostalgia for a bygone era. The truth was Sam probably hadn't sold a hat in twenty years. Any cop who knew the area also knew Sam was a part-time bookie and small-time loan shark. He was one of a handful of elderly Jewish businessmen who ran small shops, traded information, operated numbers schemes and perhaps bought and sold a few stolen goods. But since he was a reliable ally in a neighborhood that was becoming increasingly tight-lipped about the violence and street crime that dominated, Sam was left alone. The local precinct Captain kept him on a short leash but allowed him to operate his little side-business as long as no one got hurt or went bankrupt.

As I sat in the car, smoking a cigarette, I wondered if Sam was even still alive. I hadn't seen him in five years and the old-timers died at the rate of flies. In the years after I got promoted to detective, I was shuffled around the city like a fugitive and was rarely assigned to the area. It was no surprise since the street crime and drug problems of Roxbury's ghetto didn't score high on the list of departmental priorities. Most murders were cold cases and the increase in theft and burglaries was whispered to be 'unavoidable' by a white police force that was largely resentful of this growing black slum.

When I opened the shop door, a bell rang and a cloud of smoke stung my eyes. I squinted. As my eyes adjusted to the dimly lit room, I saw the figure of a man hunched behind an old cash register, a cigar clenched between his teeth and a newspaper in hand. He ran a pen along the broadsheet, studying the day's race numbers like a Bible scholar. Before I could catch his attention, he said,

"Detective, nice to see you. It's been ages."

"It couldn't be that long Sammy, you're still alive," I shot back.

"Well, as my mother used to say, a man shouldn't die until he's paid all his debts."

"You'll live to a hundred and fifty, in that case."

"I couldn't do that, my wife wouldn't have it," Sammy said, taking a short puff.

"So how're things?" I asked.

"Dame it! 'Miles to Go' hit a trifecta in the fifth race. I should've known."

I tried once more to get his attention, "So how's business?"

"Business is business," he said, bobbing his head side to side. He still hadn't looked up to me, our eyes hadn't met. Sam obsessed on the race scores like they were the only thing in the world that mattered. He took another drag from the cigar, coughed and then blew smoke through his hands. Another few seconds passed before either of us said anything. I started to feel offended by such an icy reception from an old acquaintance.

Finally, the smoke parted and Sam looked up, "What can I do for you today Detective?" I saw the fleshy yellow of two old and tired eyes. His lids drooped from the exhaustion of a lifetime and his cheeks were marked with crevices. I was sure it was Sam, but the years had transformed him.

"I was hoping to ask you a few questions."

"Fire away Detective—not literally of course," Sam chuckled, "I'm always good for answering to a higher authority."

"What do you know about that brick apartment building on Warren Street, the one that went up in flames last weekend?" Sammy took another puff and glanced up to the ceiling like he was trying to coax memories from a failing mind. He leveled his head and looked at me.

"Didn't hear a word about it. Was it in the news?"

"How 'bout the building on Brunswick?" I continued.

"Nope. I barley know what's going on in my store. Didn't read anything in the papers."

"It wasn't in the news."

"That means it didn't happen, right?"

"I just came from a building on Warren Street. Totally gutted. The one on Brunswick Street went up in flames two weeks ago." I added.

"Acts of God, I presume." Sam said under his breath. "You fellers are a little late, don't ya think?"

"I don't know. You tell me."

"Roxbury has been burning for a decade. Fancy you start investigating now," he said with a hint of sarcasm.

"I was in Korea a decade ago, Sammy. But I am here now."

Sam looked up again and shrugged his shoulders. "I'm sorry. I have no information for you Detective."

The silence resumed and I grew impatient. Nothing frustrated me more than someone who was elusive. I paced in front of the counter, looking around like a window shopper. Boxes of hats were stacked along shelves that started at the floor and ended at the ceiling. Display mannequins, yellowed by age, were dressed in styles that had been out-of-fashion for years. In one corner lay a pile of fabrics and a collection of paint cans. The store was frozen in time. The stacks of random things made it look more like a consignment shop than haberdashery. Even the counter at the register was so cluttered that Sam looked trapped between collapsing piles of debris.

"You're losing your grasp on the neighborhood."

The front door opened, the bell jingled and a beam of sunlight broke through the musty air and nearly blinded us.

An elderly black man walked in, the wooden floor boards creaking with each step. When Sam and I looked over, he nodded and smiled.

"I lost my grasp on this neighborhood a long time ago," Sam grumbled, nodding to the customer.

"Did you know both buildings caught fire within thirty minutes of each other?" I asked, prodding for information.

"I've seen greater coincidences," Sam quipped.

"And they burned completely."

Sam looked up as if he was going to respond, but then looked past me to the man, who was reaching for a hat in the front window.

"May I help you, sir?" he shouted.

"I am looking for a felt fedora," the man replied softly.

"Check the second shelf, in those boxes," Sam said, pointing. "But don't knock anything over!"

"So you were saying Brae?"

"I need to know who owns the buildings." I said.

"I have trouble keeping track of what I own." Sam drew another puff of his cigar. Again he stopped mid-sentence, looking over to the customer, "Hey, if that doesn't fit, don't force it on. You'll ruin the hat. Get another size."

I knew Sam was irritated by a subtle twitch in his left eyebrow. I imagined that he wished everyone would leave the store and let him read in peace. I stepped away from the counter and reached in my jacket for a business card, "Just let me know if you hear anything."

"I can't hear much at my age, Detective."

I smiled and placed the card beside the register. "Then let me know if you see anything."

As I turned to leave Sam muttered, "I wouldn't waste your time Brae. This neighborhood has been suffering arson since the blacks started moving in." Knowing that the customer was within hearing distance, I felt an awkward embarrassment at Sam's comment. When I stopped and turned around, Sam dropped his paper to the counter and looked at me with a blank gaze.

"You say it was arson?" I asked.

"I don't imagine it was lightening." Sam grinned, gritting his teeth on the moist end of the cigar.

"Then give me a call if you have any weather reports."

"No harm, no foul, as my mother used to say," Sam whispered under his breath. I stood looking down on him, staring into his glossy eyes with a look that was fierce but not threatening. In his own subtle way, he was trying to tell me something. The tension between us grew. A sudden floor creak startled me and I turned to see the customer trying to even out a blue felt hat in the mirror. Sam and I looked over together and the man grinned uncomfortably.

"I thought you hadn't heard about the fires?" I asked, gritting my teeth to contain my irritation. Sam had the look of a child that was distressed yet too tired to cry. He had already said enough, perhaps too much, and now he had to answer for it. As I watched his sagging eyes, I felt a sudden pity for him. At one time, he had been razor sharp and navigated the subtleties of conversation like a sailing master would his ship. But Sam was tired and the years had softened him. Now he made the mistake of trying to be deceptive by being cute. He had to explain himself, there was no other way.

"What I meant was…eh…I would've heard if someone were killed in a fire."

"Don't bullshit me Sam." The front door slammed shut and I knew instinctively that the customer had fled.

Sam became defensive. "Look, it ain't my job to keep tabs on what happens around here. This neighborhood is gonzo. I am just trying to make a few more bucks before the wife and I move to Pompano Beach."

I grabbed the counter with my hands and leaned over, with inches of his face. With a stern smile, I looked into his bloodshot eyes. He tried to look away, to seem distracted. When he reached for his newspaper, I tore it from his hand and tossed it to the ground. My years in Korea had taught me that when a prisoner under interrogation starts to crumble, you have to keep the pressure on. There was a narrow window before which he will regain his resolve. Holding Sam's wrist firmly, I whispered,

"I need to know if you know anything."

Our eyes locked in a battle of wills. Neither blinked and neither breathed. The only sound was a muffled hum from traffic along Blue Hill Ave. The only movement was the ash from his cigar, which burned and fell to the floor. I waited for a reply.

Finally, Sam stuttered, "Maybe you should start with your own people." Then he started coughing uncontrollably, deep guttural thrusts from the pit of his lungs. Between spasms, he spoke in broken and distorted sentences, "That's... all... I have. I need...a glass...of water. Good...day...Detective!" Before I said a word, he slid off the chair, spun around and vanished through the curtain that led to the back storage room. Sam was gone.

CHAPTER TWO

~

I drove around in circles trying to find Ruth's apartment. Beacon Hill was a 19th Century maze of brownstone row-houses, nestled along a gently sloping hill in the heart of downtown Boston. As the oldest district in the city, its roads were built upon former cow trails and foot paths. The streets were hardly wide enough for a horse buggy. Any attempt to navigate them in my 1960 Valiant was like trying to squeeze an aircraft carrier down the Charles River. Roads began at wide intersections and ended at alleyways. Some defied even the most contemporary maps by terminating at a front door of a house then continuing on from the back, as if the house had been dropped from the sky. The layout of the neighborhood was so haphazard that it wouldn't be unusual to land on a one-way, dead-end street. I avoided Beacon Hill like I would a minefield.

With some luck I found Chestnut Street, a narrow lane lined with ancient brick row houses, pristinely maintained with black shudders and flowerboxes. Through the tall windows of each home could be seen laced curtains, chandeliers and bookshelves that stretched to the ceiling, indications of affluence both inherited and newly acquired. I scanned the numbers on the doorways, looking for ten, when Ruth's image appeared in my window. She stood on the sidewalk, holding her purse and smiling under the light of the street lamp. As she waved, I slowed to a stop, got out and opened the passenger door for her.

"You found it?"

"Wasn't hard. I just drove around for thirty minutes until I landed on Chestnut Street. The law of averages."

"You don't know Beacon Hill well?"

"It's not that I don't know it, but I find it suffocating."

As she slid in, I breathed her fresh perfume and hairspray and was suddenly uplifted. I felt like a hormonal teenager, as jittery as an adolescent on a first date. The tingling optimism I experienced in the presence of a woman was proof enough that, however hardened I had become by war and work, my soul was still alive. I put the car in drive and rolled along Chestnut Street, silent and focused on the road ahead.

"Beacon Hill is gorgeous, don't ya think?"

"Lovely," I mused.

A passing streetlamp broke the darkness and I caught a flashing glimpse of Ruth's face. Her teeth glistened like snow crystals and her face was unblemished. With her girlish spunk and soft features, she appeared years younger than she was.

"So where to?"

"I am going to surprise you."

"I love surprises!"

At the bottom of the hill, I turned right on to Charles Street and headed for the North End, another mess of tiny streets and alleyways, although far less handsome than Beacon Hill. Nevertheless, I felt at home in the North End, a blue-collar Italian enclave of small shop owners, city workers, dock hands, and the odd criminal. Unlike Beacon Hill, the North End was a place where you could kick back, eat like a horse, and speak your mind. The Italians controlled the neighborhood but welcomed outsiders as long as they brought money, a big appetite and no pretensions. There was probably more criminal activity in this twenty block neighborhood than the rest of the city and suburbs combined. But since the late 50's the department had given up on trying to prosecute every loan shark, bookie and sidewalk gangster. Whenever one was convicted, five others sprouted from the street corner to take his place. Besides, the recent gang wars between the Irish in Charlestown and the Italians of the North End had given the cops a respite, since the criminals were murdering each other by the car load. In a strange way, the police force had become a neutral third-party. As long as no innocent civilians got caught in the cross-fire, we allowed the feuding to continue.

"The North End?" Ruth asked, "Is it safe?"

"Don't worry. I have a gun," I laughed.

We pulled down Hanover Street and I squeezed into a parking spot. As we walked along the sidewalk, under the streetlamps, a light mist filled the air and mixed with the aroma of roasted garlic and stewing vegetables. Clusters of old men in wool sweaters and scali caps lingered on the corners, chatting in peasant Italian and chewing fat cigars. Young kids, out past their bedtimes, roamed the streets like packs of wild dogs. Middle-aged women with hair rollers hung out third-floor windows, exchanging gossip and watching the passers-by. The North End was a world unto itself, part American neighborhood and part Italian village, teeming with people and glowing from the endless neon shop signs.

We turned down a narrow side street and walked half a block to Joe Tecci's Restaurant, a small eatery that had been around since the twenties, but seemed to change locations every few years. When I had first eaten here, after returning from Korea, it was on Thatcher Street. Then it moved to Prince Street. In fact, the restaurant moved so frequently that many assumed it was Joe's way of keeping his customers sharp and committed. But I knew he was just evading the taxman.

I reached awkwardly for the front door, holding it open so Ruth could enter. She smiled and stepped in. In the smoky dimness of the front lobby patrons leaned against the walls, collected in small groups, holding half-empty wine glasses and chatting noisily while waiting to be seated. I took Ruth's arm and nodded that we should leave and find another restaurant when someone shouted my name through the crowd.

"Mr. Brae. Over here please."

Between the swarm of people, standing like a bear in a tuxedo, stood Carmen, the owner's son. He waved me towards him with an excited smile. The Tecci family was famously kind to cops and the rules of first-come-first-serve didn't apply to anyone with a badge. I took Ruth's hand and led her through the crowd. Carmen escorted us to a corner table beside the window and pulled out the chair for Ruth to sit. Surprised by his chivalry, she smiled and curtsied.

"It's always good to see you Mr. Brae. I'll send my father over if he's not too busy."

"Busy? We know your dad doesn't lift a finger," I joked.

"Just on payday," Carmen said smiling as he handed us menus.

As I glanced over the entrées, Ruth looked around curiously, her eyes darting back and forth as if looking for someone she knew. I was silent. We were as close together as we had ever been, forced into a sudden intimacy by the small table. The conversation became stilted, a disjointed interchange of meaningless remarks, trivial observations about the color of the drapes, the pattern of the tin ceiling tiles. I filled in the spaces with a forced cough or by rearranging the silverware. I wanted a cigarette but I wasn't sure if Ruth smoked. I stared at the menu for several minutes, unable to focus on the text and hoping Ruth would say something, anything. When I finally looked up, we each blurted out a sentence.

"Do you like Veal?" I said

"Do you come here a lot?" she said.

Our eyes met and we both burst into laughter. Ruth ran her fingers through her hair and tilted her head back.

"What was the question," she giggled.

"Do you like Veal?"

"I think so."

"You've got to try the veal."

"Do you live around here?"

"Huh?"

"Do you live around here?" she asked again.

"Mission Hill."

"Is that far?"

"Couple miles."

The waiter squeezed his way through the tables and stood before us. A pudgy man with no hair and a black mustache, he fumbled for his pen in between wiping sweat from his forehead. When he got his notepad out, he looked to us with a smiling frustration. I looked at Ruth and she shrugged her shoulders. I ordered a glass of wine for her, a ginger ale for me, two plates of Veal Parmesan and a salad. The waiter scribbled down the order and vanished back into the crowd.

"This place sure is popular?" she said with a sigh.

"That means it's good."

Ruth put her elbows on the table and rubbed her hands together, fidgeting as if uneasy.

"So, how goes work?"

"Busy."

"Anything interesting?"

"Well, you know I can't really talk about it," I said, lowering my eyes.

"No worries, I'm not listening," she said with a wink. I smiled and leaned closer to her. If anything interested Ruth it was my work since she had studied forensics. Yet each day she was surrounded by investigative secrecy that she couldn't be involved in.

"I'm investigating some fires in Roxbury."

"Some fires or a lot?"

"More than usual. Twenty-six this past summer, to be exact."

Her eyes widened and she quickly looked side to side before whispering, "That's an epidemic. Are there any suspects?"

"Um, no. What I mean is…there's no evidence that a crime has been committed. This city's old. Fires are common."

Just then another waiter, a young man, leaned over the table and rested two steaming plates of food. The pudgy waiter approached with our drinks and a basket of bread. I was so startled by their sudden appearance that I jumped back from the table and lay my hands on my lap. As we ate, Ruth seemed more interested in the conversation than the veal.

"So twenty-six fires in a few months isn't suspicious?"

"Hard to say. What is suspicious is that last weekend two brick apartment building went up in flames within minutes of each other. And only minutes from two fire stations."

"I guess coincidences do happen," she said between bites.

"You sound like Sam the hat man."

"Sorry?"

"Nothing. I'm just babbling. Long day."

"Why don't you have some wine?"

"I'll stick with ginger ale, thanks. Wine will put me to sleep."

"Am I putting you to sleep?" she said with a sour smile, leaning back sensuously. She held the wine glass between her thumb and forefinger, delicately, as if holding a sewing needle. Her flirtation caught me off guard and I looked away shyly. My brain raced from the day's work and I found it difficult to focus. I felt a subtle disconnect, as if we each were speaking at a different tempo, that made it impossible to finish a sentence or clarify a thought. It was an awkwardness I attributed to the distracting bustle around us, though I feared it was me. Finally, I put my fork down, took a deep breath and looked directly at Ruth.

"No, don't be silly. You're keeping me awake."

"I'm only kidding. I'm interested in your work. Are you working with the Fire Department on the investigation?"

"No. Absolutely not. It's not an investigation…"

"…because a man from the Arson Squad came in to Forensics today. He requested an evidence docket."

"Did you give it to him?" I said anxiously.

"Of course."

"That's against departmental policy."

"He had an override from the Police Chief."

"Lovell?"

"The one and only."

"Does Jackson know?" I asked, trying not to raise my voice.

"No. He had the override. We do it all the time. What's wrong?"

"Nothing. I'm sorry. Just a little uptight. Lot on my mind. How's the veal?"

When we finished the meal, I paid the bill and helped Ruth on with her coat. I took her hand and we gently made our way through the crowd. As we came to the front lobby, Carmen stood grinning, his arms wide open and waiting to give me a bear hug. When I saw it was unavoidable, I leaned into him like I would a brother. He squeezed my ribs until they cracked and I worried for a moment I might lose my dinner.

"Come back any night Mr. Brae. Bring your lovely friend," he said, bowing to Ruth.

We pushed through the people waiting in the hallway and burst into the night air. The temperature had dropped a few degrees, apparent from the steam of the breath of people strolling along the sidewalks. As we walked along Hanover Street towards the car, I thought I heard the sound of sirens in the near distance. I stopped abruptly on the curb, held a finger up and tilted my head to one side, listening intently and searching the cracks between buildings for lights. But there were none. What I imagined was the deep rumble of a fire engine turned out to be a passing bus.

"What's wrong?" Ruth said, her arms crossed and shivering.

"Ssh, did you hear that?" I heard the sirens again, but this time they sounded more like a high-pitched wheeze. I looked across the street to a churchyard and saw a pack of playful kids filing out a door, blowing kazoos and swaggering like a midget marching band. My heart sank.

"Jody, you jumped a mile."

"Looks like church just got out," I said with awkward sarcasm.

"More like a church youth group. When's the last time you went to church?" Ruth said with a playful frown. She was right. I clasped her hand in mine and we continued along the sidewalk, her heels clicking on the cement like a horse trot. I hoped the incident didn't make her think I was nuts.

When we got back to the Valiant, I opened the door for Ruth and we were off. As we drove along Hanover Street, the restaurant windows were clouded by a steamy condensation from the warm cheer inside. Ruth sat with her hands between her legs, slightly cold but not uncomfortable, and gazed out the window, as charmed by the Old World romance as any West Coast girl would be. Since this was as close as I had ever been to Venice or Florence, I let her dream.

"It's like being on the Mediterranean," she said.

"But without the palm trees."

"We don't have anything like this where I am from."

"You have palm trees."

"True. But nothing so European. I feel like I'm in Italy."

"It used to be Irish."

"How do you know?"

"'Cuz I am Irish."

"Where your parents from Ireland?"

"Nope."

"Grandparents?"

"Nope."

"How do you know that you're Irish?"

"Because I have a tattoo of a Shamrock on my back," I said jokingly.

As we rolled up to the intersection at Scollay Square, Ruth smirked and mockingly punched my shoulder.

"Actually, I got it right there," I said pointing to a small shop front: Wiley's Tattoo Parlor. I wasn't lying. I did have a tattoo of a shamrock, green yet faded, on my right shoulder blade. One drunken night, over a decade ago, I was out with a group of rookies, fresh out of the academy. What began as a few cocktails after work turned into a night of legless revelry, consecrated by alcohol and memorialized in ink. As Ruth and I passed the shop, I cringed at the memory of the needle, its electric sting tearing into my skin. The grizzled tattooist, a navy Veteran from WWI, chuckled each time I jumped.

"It's such a beautiful night. Can we go for a walk?" Ruth asked.

"I know the perfect place."

I drove through the South End past Boston City Hospital and turned left on West Broadway Street. In less than five minutes we were cruising down the long strand that hugged the beaches of South Boston. The road ended at Castle Island, a 19th century fortress with more than its share of tales and mysteries. It was now a national park, a shell of its former self, and protruded into the outer harbor like a barge of brick walls and stone archways.

Castle Island was my sanctuary and was as remote as anyone could get in a city of endless hustle and bustle. Other than a few couples strolling the shoreline and groups of local pensioners gossiping about the state of the nation, it was open and desolate. Whenever I awoke in a cold sweat, tormented by those dreams, I jumped in my car and drove here to escape the tormenting sleeplessness.

Although I had lived in Boston my entire life, I only discovered Castle Island a couple of years back when called to investigate the brutal stabbing of a merchant marine. Even his half-naked body, bloodless and bobbing in the surf, wasn't enough to tarnish the calm beauty of this place. Murder was temporary, the ocean was eternal.

We got out of the car and walked along the boardwalk. The cool, salty air made Ruth pull her sweater over her shoulders. We walked in silence, the black surf spreading across the sand, the squawk of two sleepless seagulls echoing somewhere beyond. In the darkness I spotted faint lights, as tiny as pin needles, a passing ship lingering at the horizon. All was peaceful.

"This place is wonderful," Ruth reflected. "Do you come here often?"

"Only when I need to."

We passed a few guys I recognized from the area. They nodded and I nodded back.

"Let's walk along the beach," I suggested.

"Maybe we'll find a message in a bottle?" Ruth said, kicking off her shoes as we stepped on to the sand.

I put my arm around her shoulder and nestled her closely into my chest as we walked quietly. With the sweet scent of her perfume and the sway of her hips against mine, I felt a dreamy contentedness that I hadn't known for a long time.

When I got home, it was just after midnight. I chugged along the street, searching for a parking spot but it was lined from corner to corner with cars. I pounded my hands on the steering wheel in anger. In my earlier years on the force, I would take out my parking frustrations by writing citations until the ticket book was empty. Instead of humbly parking on the next street, I would spend half the night inventing frivolous offenses; expired plates, worn out tires, parked too far from the curb. I took a vigilante's delight in pissing off every resident and visitor on the street.

These days, however, I didn't have the energy to fight back. I drove past my house, turned on to the next street and squeezed into the first spot I found. The streets were dead quiet and the homes were dark except for a few lights scattered randomly among the houses, one in a front parlor, another in a second-floor bedroom, another in a kitchen. I got to my house and stood at the front steps, fumbling for the keys, when I felt headlights creeping down the street too slowly. I had a knack for sensing when something was not right or out of place, a skill I had developed in Korea while sitting for hours in a foxhole under the moonlight, occasionally climbing out to piss or work out a leg cramp. That was when a soldier was most vulnerable. Some gook, who sat watching your position for days without blinking, would get you in his crosshairs and end it. As a result, I had developed an alertness that made me tingle.

I stepped off the stairs and stood in the alleyway besides the front porch, safe from the illumination of the street lamps. With my back to the wall and head turned towards the street, I watched as a dark car rolled by. A driver and passenger, both wearing dark hats, glanced unmistakably towards my house as they passed. My heart beat strongly and I instinctively reached behind for my 38. In a second they were gone, vanishing into the night like phantoms.

I climbed the front stairs, unlocked the door and walked up the narrow staircase to my apartment. Immediately, I peered through the blinds to the street below but saw only shadows. I sat on the couch, breathing heavily, overcome by paranoia and uncertainty. After having been startled by a procession of kazoo-blowing children, I decided to give the world the benefit of the doubt. The car probably had been searching for a parking spot, just as I had. I undressed, washed my face and lay in bed, praying for sleep. In the distance I heard the sirens of fire engines and imagined a midnight blaze somewhere in the city beyond. In the morning there would be another incident for the investigation list, another ruined building and, perhaps, the charred remains of someone's wife, husband, mother. I shut my eyes reluctantly and dreamt of the shoreline and of Ruth.

CHAPTER THREE

I didn't see Ruth for another week. I was in court testifying in a case that I had worked on the past spring that involved a mounted policeman who had been accepting bribes to ignore the illegal dumping of refuse by the shops and restaurants in Back Bay. The officer was an ex-Marine, over sixty and lived alone in a rat-infested apartment in the South End. He had always been considered odd, but the fact that a search warrant led to the discovery of a virtual zoo of exotic and domestic pets only confirmed he was either shell-shocked or insane. There was hardly a straight face in the courtroom when the details of the cop's bribery scheme were revealed. Each morning as the officer trotted through the alleyways, tasked with enforcing the strict disposal regulations, someone from the restaurant would stuff a bag of cash, small bills, into the horse's rectum. When his shift was over, he simply brought the horse back to the barracks, overfed him and picked through the droppings. It was brilliant, if not bizarre.

In the time since I had last met with Jackson there had been two building fires, one on Blue Hill Avenue in Roxbury and the other in the South End, near Boston City Hospital. Neither incident made more than a few sentences in the middle section of the daily papers. Things were heating up and I was sure Jackson would be looking for answers. Since he had taken a few days off to hunt deer in northern Maine with his brothers, I had time to pull together a preliminary report. The two fires from weeks before checked out fine. Each had been reported within a reasonable time-frame and the response efforts from both firehouses were well-documented.

The Arson Squad had completed its investigation—routine for any property fire with over five thousand dollars in damage—and determined both incidents were the result of "unintentional incendiary." Neither report referenced the other incident as if two buildings, only blocks apart, burning to the ground with minutes of each other was mere coincidence.

Since Jackson would need all the details, from the number and size of apartments down to the estimated temperature of the fire, I needed to pull the official building records. The City Records Department was a musty basement archives located in an annex behind headquarters. It was as welcoming as a cold sore and as organized as a kindergarten library. But it contained all sorts of historical information on property—residential, commercial, abandoned, public spaces, and city-owned. As a result it provided the definitive verification for any disputes, legal or otherwise, that had to do with building history and ownership.

As I descended the basement stairwell into the documents request office, I was met by a room filled with anxious customers—contractors, realtors, private investigators and property owners. The agency was a human circus that bustled from the moment it opened to the second the front door was locked at closing time. Patrons waited for their number to be called like they were in a third-world vaccination clinic. Some leaned against the wall, tapping their feet with impatience, while most stared at the linoleum floor in defeat. Like many city departments, the long lines and endless waiting could break the orthodoxy of the most ardent socialist.

I stood in the waiting room for less than a minute when I heard someone whisper from behind the counter. I look over the heads and hats of the crowd to see Maggie, smiling and waving frantically like she had a secret to tell. One advantage to being a cop was not having to wait, although I was self-conscious about special treatment, especially since I didn't wear a uniform.

"Hi sweety."

"Hey Maggie. I need to look up a couple of deeds."

She took me by the elbow and ushered me through the side door into the records facility. As the door slammed behind, I felt the stares of resentful onlookers. We walked down a narrow hallway and into a large room cluttered with filing cabinets that reached to the ceiling. The aisles between had barely enough room for one person and I was tempted to ask Maggie to pull the records.

"Where are the houses located?" She whispered.

"Actually, they're apartment buildings…mostly."

"Ok. All multiple occupancy dwellings are in the last aisle. It's organized first by district, then by street name. In alphabetical order, of course."

"You're a doll."

"Good luck. Don't take anything without singing the withdrawal ledger."

Maggie left the room and I went to work, scanning the towering cabinets like I was reading the names on a granite war monument. Allston, Brighton, Charlestown, Dorchester, Roxbury. When I pulled open the drawer I almost choked from the dust of so many ancient documents. I gently thumbed through the folder until I came to Warren Street, number 548-550. The records were neatly packed in an old manila folder that smelled like a basement after flooding. As I pulled it delicately from the pile, I saw coffee stains and faded pencil scribbling along the edges. I freed it from the pressure of the other folders and held it in my hand when the seam suddenly ripped, sending dozens of documents across the floor. I cringed. I glanced down the aisle and was relieved to see that a female clerk was too busy re-filing to notice the blunder.

I picked up the papers and scanned them for information. There were assessments going back to 1898; permits for improvement projects; a copy of the original deed, which, with its flowery writing and raised official stamp looked like a Civil War-era savings bond. I flipped through every document ever kept on the property but couldn't find the current deed. It was suspicious but not unusual. Deeds were sometimes stored in the Assessment Division, especially if there was a recent property transaction. I forced the folder back into place and looked for the records on the 66 Brunswick Street property. Again, the documents seemed intact but were missing the current deed.

I slipped out the records door, gave Maggie a wink and headed across the parking lot to headquarters. With Jackson due back from his hunting trip today, I could stop to see him and Ruth in one shot.

As I climbed the stairs, the figure of Ruth appeared over the last step like an unfolding vista. She sat obliquely, her hair pulled down over her cheeks as she typed. I paused for a split second to admire her before she sensed my presence. I held the handrail nervously, unsure of what to do or say. Thirty-three years on this planet, interacting daily with the opposite sex, and they never ceased to both fascinate and terrify me.

"Ah hem." I broke in with a fake cough. She didn't flinch, just continued typing.

"Ruth!"

Startled, she spun around in her chair.

"Hello stranger," she, frowning like a young girl. The phone rang and she picked it up, talking into the receiver while looking over at me. I stood with my hands by my side, waiting for her to hang up.

"You look as darling as ever," I said.

"Haven't I aged a bit?"

"Did you have fun last week?"

"That was two weeks ago?" she smirked.

"Nine days," I snapped back.

"I had a wonderful time."

"When can we do it again?" I asked.

"I don't know if I like you enough to go out with you again."

My heart sank. I felt like a million eyes were watching me as I was publicly rejected by the woman I had been thinking about for months. The tone of her voice was playful, but I couldn't be sure. The phone rang a second time but before she picked up, she looked at me.

"Let me see. Hmm…how about any time you'd like?"

Then she reached for the phone and winked at me.

"Friday night? 7:00?" I said, mouthing the words like I was talking with a deaf person. As she spoke to the caller, she nodded. Overjoyed, I turned and walked down the hallway to Jackson's office with a little skip in my step. I knocked a couple of times, but there was no response. That didn't mean Jackson was not in his office. Whenever he was immersed in case notes or reflecting on an investigation, he retreated to the catalog of his mind, blocking out the world like a contemplative monk. Some of the detectives assumed his hearing was in decline but I knew his senses were perfect. Even when Jackson wasn't listening, he heard you. Even when he wasn't looking, he knew your every move. He was a natural observer of people and situations and had a camera-like perception.

When I cracked open the door, Jackson was leaning over, nestled in a cabinet drawer and fumbling through folders and documents. I was afraid I had startled him, but he didn't flinch. I coughed to get his attention, when, without turning his neck to look over to me, he muttered, "Brae, good to see you." As usual, I was dumbfounded by Jackson's otherworldly awareness.

"How was your trip Captain?"

He stood up and pushed the drawer shut with the tips of his fingers.

"Could've been longer, Brae."

"Did you kill anything?" I wondered.

"Just my appetite."

"Sorry, sir?"

"Two days into the trip my brother Farnham cooked some trout he caught in the Kennebunk. I was sick the rest of the trip."

"Sorry to hear that…"

Jackson said no more about the incident. He stopped mid-sentence, as if to say the small talk was over. He dropped the folders he was holding on the desk and walked over to me. His every move was deliberate and steady, as if he had thought it through hours before. I knew something troubled him by the way his eyes twitched.

"Shut the door, please," he said softly.

Without looking behind, I reached back and pushed the door shut. Jackson offered me a chair and I sat uneasily. The seconds it took him to walk around the desk and sit down seemed an eternity. Something about his seriousness made me nervous. Had it been any earlier in my career as detective, I might have been worrying about my job.

Jackson believed that everything knowable about a case, whether it was murder, arson or a stolen pack of chewing gum, could be determined by context. In his mind, there was no perfect crime. And if there was any foul play in this situation, it would be apparent, as long as the research was thorough.

"I got a call this morning about the spate of fires in Roxbury."

Leaning back into the chair, as if to seem relaxed, I nodded my head to each word. I was prepared to give Jackson the most thorough update on the investigation. In the time he was away, I had researched the facts and taken meticulous notes; when the fires were reported, who reported them, who the witnesses were, etc.

"This thing is taking on a life of its own. There was another inferno on Blue Hill Ave. while I was gone. Some sort of rooming house."

"I heard about it." I said, lying like an amateur.

"It wasn't reported in the police briefs." With his two hands flat against the desk, he leaned over, looked at me fiercely from beneath two bushy white eyebrows, "so don't bullshit me." For a moment I was as embarrassed as I was stunned, until Jackson cracked a smile and winked. I breathed easy and stayed silent.

"I have a bad feeling. Hardly any press coverage. More fires in one summer than we've had in five years. And then a large inferno that doesn't make it into the weekly briefs."

"Pardon me, Captain, but how did you hear about it?"

"Let's just say I have my spies," he said with a forced grin.

"How is it the press isn't picking these incidents up?" I said, thinking aloud more than directly asking Jackson. Jackson sprung up from his chair and walked around the desk to me, "You're asking the right questions, detective."

There was a sudden knock at the door and I shook in the chair. As I turned, I saw Ruth peek her head through the crack of the door. When she saw me, she smiled. I tried to smile back but all I could make was a nervous grin.

"Captain, detective Harrigan is here to see you."

"I'll be out in a moment, dear." The door shut and the room was silent as Jackson stood before me, his arms crossed, staring and thinking. Finally he sighed and spoke.

"Listen detective, I am placing you on this assignment permanently, for the time being."

"Isn't that a contradiction?"

Jackson's eyebrows flickered, as if his mind was troubled by the sudden transition from seriousness to humor. Most detectives might fear insubordination, but I knew that Jackson always had time for irony.

"Temporary permanence?"

I nodded.

"Fine grammatical observation, Brae. An oxymoron."

I chuckled slightly.

"But I can do that. I'm your captain," he said, reaching over and patting me on the back. Jackson paced the room, his loafers clapping against the old oak floors.

"Are there any suspects?" I continued.

"...slow down detective. I am not saying its arson or foul play. Some things don't add up. And we don't need to wait until there is a death..."

"…or a murder?" I added.

"The good news is I am giving you a partner. Detective Harrigan has just transferred up from Providence. He grew up in the area and knows the streets. He's got four years in the Army and six in homicide, so you should get along. Wait here a moment."

Jackson walked out of the office, leaving me in the chair to brood. If he had given me a second to respond, I would have protested like a child who is told to clean his room on a sunny day. If he refused to hear me out, I would have gotten on my knees and begged for professional independence. Up until that moment, I had the best job in the department.

Since the department reorganized two years ago I had jurisdictional freedom that all cops and many detectives envied. If the police department was the world, then Internal Affairs was a sovereign nation, an island nation to boot. I worked under Jackson and answered to no one but him. He, in turn, answered only to the police chief, Darren Lovell. If Lovell answered to anyone, it was God himself.

It wasn't unusual that I ended up in the position I did. When I had joined the force, I never quite fit in as a street cop. My experience in Korea, with a bronze star and rank of Captain, gave me a unique set of skills that the higher-ups quickly capitalized on. I knew how to work the streets and understood how the enemy, which was now criminals, thought and acted. I understood their motives because I understood survival. Having no wife and no family, I was available to work investigations that kept me out on the streets for days at a time, tailing suspects and frequently working undercover. Like a method actor, I became the characters I played, sometimes living out the role long after the investigation was complete and the suspects were jailed. I woke up some nights unsure of who I was. I drank heavily, sometimes in the morning. One winter night during a snow storm, two patrolmen discovered me passed out behind the driver's seat, my face pressed against the horn and blind drunk on a side street in Roxbury. When they shook me to consciousness and asked my name, I mumbled Kenneth Strickland, an assumed identity from an investigation the year before. Those years on the streets were a blurred montage of dark alleyways, backyard chases, shakedowns and hangovers. The opportunity to join Internal Affairs came as a relief, a comfortable semi-retirement that I could nourish for the next twenty years. What was reputed to be a grueling selection process was complete in under a week. I must have been their ideal candidate; a loner, unemotional, non-political and committed to justice. I had no moral qualms about investigating fellow cops and anyone who was dirty was fair game. But what excited me the most was I could work alone.

"Brae, meet Harrigan."

I felt my jaw drop. In the doorway stood a six-foot two black man, broad shouldered and smiling nervously. For a split second I thought it might have been a joke—a belated birthday gag. Perhaps someone had pulled the custodian from the basement to act the part. But Jackson stood beside the man, hands on his hips, as dignified as if he were introducing his own son. As the seconds passed, his expression changed from cordial to scornful. This was no joke. Before I had time to frown, I walked over and reached my hand out.

"My pleasure," I mumbled and Jackson nodded sternly.

"Likewise, Detective," Harrigan replied with an anxious stutter. As we shook, my hand was swallowed up by his large black mitts. I squeezed harder but his hand was unmovable, as firm as marble. He was at least three inches taller than me and I had to tilt my head back to see his eyes. Anyone would be intimidated by his size, but his soft expression conveyed a gentle kindness that was as soothing as it was disarming. Harrigan was a gentle giant.

The irony of Boston was that its enlightened worldliness was coupled with a fierce and deep-seated bigotry. When school segregation had been declared unconstitutional a decade before, there was little celebration among the city's white working-class. It was a city of hardscrabble ethnics, still reeling from the pre-War nightmare of industrial blight; the Irish dockhands and longshoremen, Italian bakers and bookies, Polish shopkeepers and Jewish gangsters. In the provincial landscape of the city's ethnic map, there was little room for hordes of Black workers fleeing the sharecropper South. They might be tolerated as railway hands and day-laborers, but never as citizens.

The sight of a black cop in Boston was like witnessing a mongoose on Newbury Street, not impossible but strangely out-of-place. To be sure, there had been a few black officers throughout the years, mostly the assimilated sons of Jamaican immigrants who had arrived in the 1920's. I had worked with a black detective named Horace, who retired from the force years back. But even he was so light-skinned that he was more often than not mistaken for Southern Italian or Portuguese.

"You've both been briefed on the situation. Detective Brae, will you could be kind enough to take Detective Harrigan and show him around?"

I nodded to Jackson and looked at Harrigan. Next thing I knew we were walking down the hallway silently like strangers who happened to be going in the same direction. When I reached the lobby, Harrigan was already trailing ten feet behind.

"See you Friday?" Ruth waved as I passed.

I nodded, smiled and headed down the stairwell. I waited, holding the exit door open, until Harrigan came down. We crossed the parking lot to the Valiant without saying a word. I unlocked the passenger door and glanced at him from the corner of my eyes. He quickly looked away. As we pulled out of the lot the awkwardness became unbearable—I had to act.

"So why the transfer?"

"Oh yes, you see, my mother is in Boston. She's getting on in years. I spent the past few years in Rhode Island and thought it was time to come home."

"So, you from around here?"

"I grew up in Roxbury, graduated Roxbury Memorial High School in '53."

"You serious?" I said, turning to look at him, "I finished in '48."

Harrigan's exotic foreignness vanished and he was suddenly familiar, a son of Roxbury. As the tension eased, I even regretted acting so coldly towards him. If anyone had tried to make a good first impression, it was Harrigan. He wore a conservative dark suit, perfectly pressed, with a navy blue tie. He sat with the posture of emperor, his hands humbly folded on his lap. He even breathed easily and had a quiet dignity that was stern without being unfriendly. As we drove, he gazed out the window and spoke only in response to my questions and casual remarks.

We drove down Tremont Street and circled the Boston Common. A crowd of young men and woman, dressed like paupers and chanting angrily, marched across the grass holding makeshift signs. I didn't have to watch a second longer to know it was another student protest against our increasing involvement in Vietnam. A couple of mounted patrolmen stood on the sidelines, ensuring things didn't get out of hand. I was thankful I didn't have to deal with civil unrest. Being a detective, the lines between good and evil were generally clear. In politics, however, things were more complicated. Knowing many of these students were the same folks involved in the Civil Rights movement made me uneasy in the presence of Harrigan. If our conversation veered towards politics, I would stay as neutral as Switzerland.

"So, you been back long?"

"Well, two weeks now," Harrigan said.

"Where are you living?"

"I got an apartment in Roxbury, near my mother's house."

"I'm in Roxbury too. Mission Hill. We are beginning to sound like the same guy," I joked.

"Except I'm more handsome," Harrigan replied, staring ahead with a smile creeping across his face. I felt the warm tingle of companionship and drove easier knowing my partner had a sense of humor. I could read a person like a street sign, summing up their character and motives with one look in their eyes. As a soldier and as a cop, I often didn't have the luxury of getting to know someone and so I learned to assess a person's psychology through the most subtle observations—their posture, their accent, the way they held a coffee cup, the movement of their eyes. Even as a child at the Home, people entered and left my life with such dizzying frequency that I had to rely on gut instinct. As a survival technique, I learned to judge quickly whether they were a dependable ally or not, whether their loyalty was fleeting or firm. With that quick comeback, that ironic jab, Harrigan had passed the first test.

"How 'bout we get some coffee?"

"You read my mind," Harrigan replied.

I pulled down Newbury Street and searched for a spot. Back Bay, with its endless boutiques and tourist shops was as neutral as you could get in a city of tribal fiefdoms. It was a good place to start with a partnership so unconventional. I inched the Valiant between two cars, my hubcaps scraping against the curb like nails on a chalkboard. The autumn breeze blew between the buildings like a wind tunnel and I had to hold my overcoat together as we crossed the street to Creccio's Coffee. When we entered, the place was empty so we sat by the window.

"What'll you have?"

"Small coffee, cream and sugar, please." he said politely.

I ordered a black coffee for me and a regular for Harrigan, conscious of the irony that he preferred his white while I liked mine black. When I returned to the table, Harrigan had already hung his jacket on a nearby coat rack and sat facing the window with his hands on his lap. I took the seat opposite him, placed the cups down and leaned over the table on my arms. The fatigue I felt from long days and fretful nights made my body sore, my bones ache.

"So you spent most of your life in Roxbury?"

"Some of it. I was actually born in St. Kitts, in the West Indies."

"You're used to good weather?" I said.

"You could say that. When I was six, after my father died, my mother brought me to Boston. We lived in Cambridge for a year, then moved to Roxbury. And you?"

I looked at Harrigan and turned away, failing to respond. I stared out lazily, through the sun-streaked windows to the busy street and sidewalk, weighed down by an exhaustion even coffee couldn't cure. While Harrigan spoke I fell into a daydream, a sudden and unintentional retreat from the present. The people and places in my life, the expectations and uncertainties, flashed across my mind like a comet of pure anxiety and left me spellbound and not quite right. I thought of Ruth, her slight figure leaning over the typewriter, her golden hair drizzling over her cheeks. I saw the smoking ruins of the building fires. I imagined Jackson trudging through the brush in Northern Maine, a shotgun slung over his shoulder. I even thought of Mark Mirsky, in military fatigues, although we never saw each other in Korea. When the spell had run its course, I was restored to the moment, no more refreshed or renewed.

"Detective, you ok?"

"Oh, yeah, sorry. Didn't get much sleep last night. A little foggy."

"I was curious where you are from." Harrigan said.

"Right. I spent most of my life in Roxbury, off Seaver Street. I moved to Mission Hill when I joined the force."

"Are your folks still in Roxbury...? Harrigan wondered.

"...hey look at that..." Staring out the window, I watched as a meter maid stood beside the Valiant, scribbling in her ticket book. I got up from the table, flew out the door and ran over to the car. I flashed my badge, gave her a long stare and walked away. I burst back into the coffee shop and said "Those ladies think they own the town."

"I see," Harrigan said uncomfortably.

"So, sorry, you said you were born in Saint something?" I asked.

"St. Kitts. It's an island in the Caribbean."

"St. Kitts, right. I took geography with Mr. Armstrong." I added.

"Ah, Mr. Armstrong. The man with the inescapable lisp and hunched back. Strange fellow," Harrigan remarked. He stirred his coffee pensively, round and round, the metal spoon scraping the side of the mug. But Harrigan was loosening up. He leaned back in the chair and let his shoulders down.

"Where did you get an Irish name?"

"Harrigan? Lots of Irish names and Irish named places in St. Kitts." Harrigan paused. "As a child, my best friend was Emmet Mulloy," he remarked softly.

"That's odd," I said, turning to him with sudden interest.

"Centuries ago, a group of Irish colonized parts of the Island. A couple of drinks, a little dancing with the locals and two hundred years later and you have black guys running around with Irish names."

"You'll get along fine in this department. Just tell them you're black Irish," I said. Harrigan looked up from his coffee, our eyes met, and we burst into laughter.

I didn't see Ruth or Harrigan for another two days and Friday was fast approaching. I had managed to stop by almost every building that had burned since the past June, when the epidemic began. There was a vacant warehouse on Norfolk Avenue; a former hotel on Dudley Street; an old granary, long abandoned, on Albany Street. Three apartment buildings burned to the ground within a mile of each other one hot July night. Ironically, even a defunct fire station, the old E13, which was decommissioned years ago, had burned to the ground. I couldn't drive for five blocks in Roxbury or Dorchester without being within sight of some crumbling ash heap of brick and stone. My calls to the Arson Squad went unreturned. The only information I could get was by formal request and every incident had been cleared of foul-play. If the cops or fire department weren't somehow involved, then my role in the investigation was nil. As Internal Affairs, civilian crimes were beyond my jurisdiction. If I caught someone holding a match to a wooden front porch, the most I could do was restrain him and call headquarters.

By the end of the week I was frustrated. I drove through the streets with no destination, stayed up late, chain smoked and ate very little. The dreams had reappeared with frightening clarity and a persistence that wouldn't let up. I probably slept six hours the whole week. On Friday I found myself longing for the site of either Harrigan or Ruth. I met Harrigan only three days before, but he was my partner. I had known Ruth only a few weeks but she was my girlfriend, whether she knew it or not. I had so few close friends that they became the most important people in my life by default. I even found myself thinking of Ruth obsessively, imagining her face, her smile, the way she walked and those offhanded comments that peeped from her lips with unexpected delight. The anticipation was agonizing but our next date was the one thing that made the days bearable and the nights not never-ending. It was the dangling carrot that impelled me forward, the single goal towards which I strove: Friday night.

After work I headed home to take a shower and change. The days were getting shorter and the nights colder. I dusted off my brown wool pants and threw on an overcoat. I grabbed a wad of cash from the top drawer of the dresser and stuffed it in my pocket. On the coffee table, I reached for my keys, wallet and .38 revolver. I was ready for a night out.

I walked alone, smoking a cigarette and searching the side streets for the Valiant. The world was dead quiet. Although only 6:00 PM, it was dark and the streetlamps flickered to life, one after another, in an eerie succession that seemed to follow me along the sidewalk. Each time I reached the next light pole the lamp above would hum and then flash to life. At the end of the block, the last one lit up and there beneath it sat the Valiant, shining like a mirage. I hopped in, fired up the engine and sped down the hill towards Huntington Ave.

When I got to Beacon Hill, I glanced down at my watch and saw I was fifteen minutes early. I drove pointlessly, trying to pass time, turning up and down nameless narrow streets like a cabby seeking a fare. I circled the Boston Common, admiring the rows of lampposts glowing in the crisp evening air. It started to rain and I turned the wipers on. There would be no walks along the beach tonight, I thought. The city was strangely subdued, as if everyone was at a party I hadn't been invited to. A few cars cruised up and down Beacon Street. A young couple, probably students, ducked into the shadows of the gated entrance to the Public Gardens. A husband and wife walked hand-in-hand along the sidewalk wearing wool coats and long smiles. I felt like I was watching the world from a million miles away.

The rain increased and soon the windshield was being pelted with droplets. The gray haziness of the downpour was disorienting and I flipped the wipers on full blast. A car horn blared and I swerved back into my lane just in time. I rolled through puddles and potholes, heading towards Ruth's apartment, the eagerness I felt all week melting into a dull skepticism. Little voices whispered through the silence of my thoughts, discouraging demons that said it was all for naught. When Ruth discovered the real me, she would run back to California. For a moment I had the urge to spin around and race home through the storm.

Maybe Jackson had been right when he called me a recluse. Isolation always felt more natural than companionship. As a child, I cringed when the dinner bell rang through the hallways, preferring to stare dreamily out my corner window rather than sit among hundreds of restless children. I had seen too much horror, felt too much pain to believe in humanity, never mind the Almighty. What others termed cynicism, I called realism. In Korea I had witnessed a man's head blown into the air from a land mine explosion. Like a chicken at harvesting, he stumbled a few yards when suddenly his head came crashing down on the stump of his neck. Poor Randy Pullman had been clobbered by his own skull. As enemy fire spat through the brush, I laughed until tears streamed down my face. I wouldn't have been any more surprised to see a clown run across the battlefield. Since that day the violence I experienced on the city streets was like a schoolyard brawl. At times I thought that part of my own head had been lost along with Pullman's.

Beep! Headlights flashed into my eyes as the car swerved to avoid hitting me head on. I had drifted into oncoming traffic on Charles Street and was almost killed. Without knowing where I was, I turned sharp right, drove up a small street for a few blocks and pulled over. My heart raced and I was out of breath. I looked into the rearview mirror to see sweat glistening at my hairline. I sat still for a minute, clutching a cigarette with trembling fingers. When I looked at my watch, it was 7:15—I was now fifteen minutes late. Ruth would be waiting under her stoop in the cold. I slammed the car into drive and raced up the street. When I pulled up to the house, she stood on the sidewalk under the streetlamp holding a black umbrella with both hands. Slightly embarrassed, I hopped out and opened the passenger door. Water flowed down the gutter and Ruth had to jump to avoid getting wet. As she got in, I smelled her perfume, the same brand as before, the scent I would forever associate with her. I closed the door and we were off.

"Did you get lost?" she asked light-heartedly.

"I'm sorry. I lost my way."

"And you a city-boy?" she smirked.

"Are you hungry?"

"I'm always hungry."

"How about Chinese? You ever have Chinese?"

"That sounds maaaaarvelous…" Ruth sang, "…when I was a girl, we used to go to a place called Yang's in La Jolla."

"In China?"

"In San Diego, silly. Haven't you ever left Boston?"

"I went to Korea once, does that count?"

Chinatown was alive like a carnival. The neon signs that hung over the shops and restaurants flashed in wild colors, some in English and some Chinese. As I pulled down Oxford Street, people hurried along the sidewalk, some holding umbrellas, others waiting beneath the awnings. The rain descended wildly, spattering against store fronts and pooling at every street corner.

I found a spot in front of Dragon Soup, a two-story restaurant I frequented as a rookie. In my early career, the Dragon was my second home and I spent countless nights there raising hell and getting blind-drunk. The first floor was a haven for cops while the second was known as a criminal hang-out. Either way, everyone respected its neutrality like they would a battlefield Christmas truce.

When I opened the entrance door for Ruth, a burst of smoky warmth gushed out. The restaurant was crowded with smiling faces, seated at booths and huddled around square tables with starched tablecloths. To the left was a long oaken bar, lined with people sipping exotics drinks and chewing on appetizers. Waiters in white smocks scurried like mechanical manservants, taking orders, bowing and carrying trays full of drinks. Before my eyes adjusted to the dimness, someone shouted my name.

"Hey Brae! You lost?"

I recognized the voice of Daniel McQuillan like the notes of a favorite song. I turned to see him nestled among a group of cops at a corner table. Mac pushed through the crowd and walked towards us with a Mai Tai in one hand and cigarette in the other.

"This is like old times, eh?" Mac said excitedly.

"I wouldn't remember, Mac, we were always too drunk."

"Some things haven't changed then."

As I looked into his bloodshot eyes, I saw Mac had a heavy buzz and it was only eight o'clock. At six-foot three and close to three-hundred pounds, his stumbling hulk put anyone near him at risk. Mac had been a star athlete at Lynn Classical high school before his career was cut short by a knee injury at the hands of the great Harry Agganis. The blow was so devastating that he hobbled twenty years later. When drunk, he acted out the great maneuvers and plays of his athletic glory days. And as disappointed as he had been, he felt it an honor to have been maimed by the 'Golden Greek.'

Aside from Mark Mirsky, Dan McQuillan was the closest thing to a best friend I had ever known. We met on the first day of the academy when he begged to borrow a pair of socks. The connection was instant. We had both been to Korea, although Mac was hundreds of miles from where I was stationed. When his football career was cut short, his father marched him down to the nearest recruiting station and forced him to enlist. Despite the disability, Mac graduated with the help of a sympathetic drill sergeant and ended up as a radio operator miles from the front, a job that suited his boisterous personality.

Mac and I spent our rookie years together as partners and later worked closely as detectives. Our drunken nights out, after work parties and weekend jaunts to Cape Cod suddenly ended, however, when I joined Internal Affairs. Mac was fiercely defensive of the force and didn't believe cops should investigate cops. Nevertheless, we had a bond that, although at times strained, remained unbreakable.

"I recognize this lovely young lady?"

"Ruth, this is detective Dan McQuillan," I said.

"My supreme pleasure..." Mac said with a slight, exaggerated bow.

"Ruth works in Forensics," I added.

"Oh, the details," Mac said.

Ruth smiled.

"Bullistics or fingerprinting?" He wondered.

"Actually, I studied forensic psychology."

"I can't even spell that," Mac joked.

"It's not as glamorous as it sounds," Ruth said, mildly annoyed. There was a sudden lull in conversation.

"Well, enjoy your meal. Stop by the table for a drink."

"Maybe after we eat, Mac."

As we walked away, Mac grabbed my shoulder, "Oh, and partner..."

"Yeh?"

He moved close to me and softly asked, "I hear Jackson has you running through burning buildings?"

"Jackson has me doing a lot of things."

McQuillan leaned closer and whispered in my ear, "Watch yourself. Not everyone's on your side."

"What do…"

"Not now," he said with restrained force, looking over his shoulder. "Just be careful," he mouthed as he pulled away. He winked and returned to his table of cronies.

I nodded and followed Ruth to a booth at the rear of the restaurant. As we sat, I felt strangely uneasy. Mac was always direct, it was his nature, but had never been so mysterious. Whenever we ran into each other we talked shop, exchanged gossip and made false plans to get together for a baseball game or golf. I knew he was still uncomfortable with my role on the force, as much as I tried to explain that Internal Affairs was there to protect good cops. It was no surprise that Mac knew about my recent assignment. He had friends in every division, department and office. Yet something in his voice was not right, as if he was trying to communicate to me beyond words and actions. I was left painfully curious.

"I'm starved." I mumbled, distracted but trying to forget the incident.

"Then let's eat. Tonight is on me," she smiled.

When I looked at Ruth straight on, I almost blushed at how lovely she looked. Her smooth skin shone beneath the soft lighting. She was feminine but self-assured, a woman in the true sense. Nothing about her suggested the clinging sentimentality of so many women I had met before. She gave to you just what you gave to her, nothing more and nothing less, like perfectly matched tennis opponents.

When the waiter came over, I ordered Shanghai noodles and ginger soup. I looked over to Ruth.

"What will you drink?"

"Anything, as long as it's strong and sweet," she said.

"A Mai Tai and soda water for me." The waiter's face was stoic. He gave us a quick smile, nodded and walked away.

"Are those friends of yours?"

"Mac is a good friend. I'm not sure about the others." I said, glancing over across the tables and trying to see without being seen.

"I've never seen them in Forensics."

"Mac is in Homicide, mostly in the field. You won't find those guys hanging around an office."

"Do I hang around an office?" Ruth said with a smirk.

"No you sit at a desk, isn't that where I met you?"

"But I technically work in Forensics."

As I predicted, Ruth was unhappy with her work. Expecting to work with evidence was far different than answering phones and shuffling paperwork. For a woman with a passion for law enforcement, she had her foot in the door but was at the wrong end of the hallway.

"I didn't realize you were in forensic psychology?" I wondered.

"I studied nursing but changed my major. I was always interested in crime, in the dark side of society…"

"Is crime dark?"

"It's certainly not holy!" Ruth laughed.

In minutes the food arrived on a large ceramic plate. With the steam rising, we dug in eagerly.

Ruth turned to the waiter, "Another one of these," she said, tapping on the rim of the glass.

"So how's the investigation going?" she asked.

"Not bad. I've sort of hit a brick wall. This wouldn't be the first time Jackson's had me investigating coincidences. No evidence of a crime, just a hunch."

"Maybe he thinks you're intuitive? Much of what is true is not always visible."

"And not every cry in the dark is a monster."

As we ate, I heard the officers in the corner table getting loud. The clinging of glasses, the roar of laughter, the back-slapping and revelry—wherever cops went they dominated like unruly pirates. I missed the camaraderie but not the rowdiness. I looked over my shoulder, but didn't recognize anyone except McQuillan, who sat in the center of the group like a king before his court. When I turned back to Ruth, her head was propped on her hands and she looked at me sensuously. Her eyelids hung low beneath a wisp of blonde hair and she smiled without moving. I sipped my soda like a prude.

"Why don't you drink?" Ruth blurted out.

"Huh? I am?" I said, holding up the soda water.

Ruth leaned back into the chair, crossing her arms cutely and with her eyes fixed to mine.

"This is the second time we've been out. Each time you've had water."

"Is this the forensic psychologists coming out?"

With each sip of the Mai Tai, Ruth became less reserved and more playful. The tensions of the day melted away as the sweet tickle of alcohol flooded her veins. She began to speak louder and she moved her hands clumsily with each sentence. The glossiness of her eyes reflected her mascara and by the time we finished eating she was beyond tipsy.

"So why the water?"

"Let's just say that I once had a love affair with booze and now we're divorced."

"Gosh, Jody, everything with you is a metaphor."

"Meta who?"

We both laughed and Ruth slapped her hand on the table. While we waited for the bill, she slugged the remainder of her drink. I took a quick look over my shoulder to McQuillan and the others. My eyes landed on a man who sat with his back against the wall and arms crossed. He was tall and broad-shouldered, with close-cropped hair the color of brass. He had a tense expression, almost angry, like he wanted to leave but couldn't. I had seen the face before but couldn't quite place it.

"I don't know who is drunk, you or me." Ruth said, wiggling up to the table.

"Sorry?"

"I was telling you about the homeless man that panhandles on Charles Street..."

"...the one who wears a fur coat and speaks with a Dutch accent, right. Sorry, I have a lot on my mind?"

As Ruth put her jacket on, I turned again to see McQuillan staring back at me. When our eyes met, he raised his drink and grinned. By now he was spread across the chair like a drowsy bear, a glass in one hand and cigarette between his teeth. A cop was ridiculing the waiter, pulling his eyes apart and bowing like a Chinaman. The rest of the officers exploded in laughter, knocking glasses over and holding their guts. But Mac sat motionless, staring across to me with a mysterious smirk—something between irony and wonder—that left me uneasy. I nodded a second time but couldn't break his concentration.

"Are we leaving?"

Startled, I turned to Ruth and smiled awkwardly. She reached over the table and wiped her finger across my forehead.

"You're sweating. Are you ok?"

"I'm fine. Just need some fresh air."

I took Ruth's hand and we headed for the door. The two Mai Tai's had kicked in and she bobbed behind me like a loose buoy, bumping into chairs and brushing against the shoulders of patrons. When we reached the doorway, I turned to give Mac and the others a salute goodbye. I took Ruth by the waist and dashed out.

"See you around Jody. Pleasure to meet you, Miss." Mac yelled as the door shut behind us. Once outside, I breathed the cool air and felt renewed. The rain had ceased and the entire street was immersed in a misty white fog.

"So, I should get you home."

"Is it past my bedtime?" she said between hiccups.

Ruth wobbled along the sidewalk, swerving every few steps as if the earth buckled beneath her. Her heels clicked against the cement unsteadily and I held her arm in case she tripped. When we got to the car, I leaned her gently against the hood. As I opened the door, she tripped on the curb and fell into my arms. Without a word, she pushed her head into my chest, looked up and put her lips to mine. We stood locked in a kiss in plain view of passers-by and all the patrons at window seats in the restaurants that lined the narrow street. The world faded into the backdrop and for those few seconds we were alone. The warmth of her body was like standing over a fireplace after coming in from the cold. When we finally let go, Ruth slid down my chest and into the car seat as if the event was choreographed. I shut the door, looked around with a bashful pride and skipped to the driver's door.

I sped down Essex Street towards Beacon Hill, intoxicated by a female comfort I hadn't had in years. As we passed the Boston Common Ruth reached into her purse, took out a cigarette and looked to me.

"Mind if I light up?"

I nodded ok and she rolled down the window. Watching Ruth smoke was like seeing a nun drink—shocking, unthinkable but excitingly rebellious. There was something sexy in the way she took quick, powerful drags and blew the smoke out her nose and mouth.

I pulled up to Ruth's apartment building and put the car in park, hoping for a goodbye kiss that would seal the night.

"Oh, damn it!" she blurted out. I realized that I had never heard her swear before.

"What's wrong?"

"I left my keys at the restaurant. They were in my bag. I think I put them on the table."

"Let's go get 'em."

"Wait, what time is it?" she asked.

"11:35."

"We won't make it."

"Huh?"

"I am renting a room here and the house matron locks the doors at midnight."

"How old are you?" I asked sarcastically.

"I know, I know, it sounds crazy. I got the place through a Mormon mission network."

"You're a Mormon?"

"Sort of. I was raised in the church. My father thinks I'm still active. Anyway, it's cheap but the rules are strict."

"I'll say."

Ruth pushed the hair out of her face and turned to me. "I don't mean to be forward. Can I stay at your place?"

Before she finished the sentence, I slammed the Valiant into drive and headed to Mission Hill. Fate must have been on my side because the entire way, down Beacon Street, along Huntington Avenue, there wasn't a single red light. The waters of traffic parted as if by an act of God. In less than ten minutes we were on my street and miraculously there was a spot in front of the house. I helped Ruth up the stairs, guiding her by the waist as she dug her heels into each step. The stairwell was as dark as a cave and when we reached the third floor I groped for the doorknob. I fumbled with the keys and opened the door to an apartment that was darker still. I was reluctant to turn on the lights, my place being as sparse as a prison cell. Ceiling paint peeled in large sheets and the light switches were disgorged from their old plaster casings. The walls were barren and the few pieces of furniture I possessed—an old couch, a few wobbly end tables, and a rusting coat rack—would qualify as antiques by age but not condition. I couldn't recall the last time I cleaned the apartment, but I was sure it had been weeks. Nevertheless it was my home and I would act like I wasn't ashamed, even if I was.

I helped Ruth off with her coat and she fell to the couch. I put the kettle on the stove and lit the burner.

"Would you like some tea?"

Ruth sighed. The rain clouds had given way to a clear and star-filled sky. When I opened the shade, moonlight shone through the kitchen window and gave the musty room a sort of Bohemian charm. I walked over to the couch and reached for Ruth's coat to hang it up when suddenly she stood up, grabbed my shoulders with both hands and kissed me. We embraced, neither daring to let go, until the kettle started to whistle. Just when I thought she was pulling away, Ruth took one of my hands and placed it under her shirt to her breasts. I felt their soft warmth and pulled her closer. The shriek of the kettle added a sense of urgency, like the warning sirens before an air raid. We began to undress each other frantically, unbuttoning, unzipping, stretching and tugging. Ruth's blouse came off and her skirt floated to the floor. She moaned. I rubbed my hands along the sides of her body, admiring each curve and pressing my palms into every contour. I gasped. As we wrestled our way into the bedroom, I reached towards the stove and hit the switch for the burner. The kettle went silent.

Hours later I awoke on my back, staring at the ceiling. The moonlight shone through the torn shade of the bedroom window and cast a gentle purple light across the room. The half-open window let in just enough air to be refreshing without making the room cold. In the distance I heard automobiles and an occasional honking horn. I turned my head to see Ruth cuddled beside, her head propped up on one elbow and staring at me. Her mascara was smudged and a mop of disheveled hair hung over her eyes, revealing a raw and sensual beauty. When she yawned I smelled sour alcohol, when she moved her neck I detected faint perfume. I didn't stir, only watched. It was so perfect that I feared any movement might upset the moment. I lay silently and breathed.

"You sleep so restlessly," she whispered.

"A lot on my mind, I guess."

"What are you thinking about?" she asked, rubbing her hand over my shoulder.

"Just things."

Without warning, the phone rang. The metallic bell sent a shiver up my back. Startled, I sat up and looked around the room. It rang a second time.

"Who could that be?"

"I never get calls this late. What time is it?"

As I jumped out of bed, Ruth pulled the sheets over her body and curled up with a nervous modesty. She seemed suddenly embarrassed, as if she woke up next to a stranger.

"Probably a wrong number."

I rushed to the kitchen, fumbled for the phone on the counter and picked it up.

"Hello!?" I shouted.

"Detective?"

"Who the hell is this?"

"Detective Brae, it's Harrigan."

"How did you get my number? What time is it?"

"It's 2:15 A.M. You gave me your number today—remember?" Harrigan explained. "Sorry to bother you. There's a building on fire at the end of my street."

Through the phone I heard the dull drone of sirens in the distance, muffled by the apartment windows but clear nonetheless. Harrigan spoke with an anxious politeness, trying to convey urgency without panic. His words were quick, breathless, insistent.

"Detective, this is bad. I think you should come down here."

"Where?"

"Blue Hill Ave—at the corner of Intervale Street."

"I'll be there in ten. Wait for me on the opposite corner."

"Please hurry," Harrigan said and hung up.

I slammed the receiver and ran to the bedroom. I dressed so furiously that I almost forgot Ruth was in the bed.

"What's wrong?" she asked.

"Not sure. That was my new partner. He says there's a building fire near his apartment."

"Is the fire department on-scene?"

"Yes. But I need to check it out."

Clinging to the sheet, Ruth curled over and sat at the edge of the bed. "Can I go?"

"Please stay here—I'll be back in an hour."

"Like hell. I'm going," she insisted.

Struggling with the buttons on my shirt, I looked down to Ruth. She was propped sweetly on the bed, wrapped in the sheet with her legs together and arms crossed. Her eyes were wide and her teeth clenched in a pose that was determined yet feminine. Since she worked for the department, I couldn't tell her it was business, that it didn't concern her. She was so eager that, even if I refused to take her, she would be behind me the whole way. I reached to the floor for her skirt and tossed it on her lap. She smiled and started to dress. Minutes later, we scurried down the stairwell and hopped into the Valiant like Bonnie and Clyde.

We sped to the fire in silence. Ruth put her hand on my knee and looked ahead like a trusting co-pilot. I knew the back streets and lanes of Roxbury and Dorchester like the scars on my body. The tires screeched against the asphalt as I blew red lights and raced around corners. The steering wheel bounced with the potholes and contours of the city streets. When we drove over a road bump, the Valiant went momentarily air-bound and Ruth dug her nails into my thigh. We were almost there.

We reached the fire in less than five minutes. The cops had blocked off the intersection so I pulled over and parked a half block away. Like an eager journalist, Ruth leapt out before the car had come to a complete stop. I ran to her side, took her hand and together we rushed down Blue Hill Avenue towards the building. As we neared the scene, a rookie cop, directing traffic around the fire trucks, waved and called to us.

"Sorry, we're asking residents not to..."

Before he finished the sentence, I reached into my jacket and flashed a badge in his face. Stunned by both my rank and boldness, he held his hands up and backed away as if I had drawn a pistol. Ruth and I walked another few steps when suddenly I heard my name called. I looked to see Harrigan on the opposite corner, standing beside a mailbox in a dark trench coat. He motioned to us discreetly and we walked across towards him.

"This is bad Detective," Harrigan said, his voice cracking.

"Let's take a look. Stop calling me Detective. You're a detective, too."

The fire trucks were parked haphazardly along Blue Hill Avenue, their lights flashing and sirens wailing through the night. When an ambulance arrived, it was forced on to the sidewalk to get by. As we got closer, we passed four or five exhausted firemen, crouched on the curb and covered in black soot from their helmets to their boots. A medic in a crisp white uniform held a canteen to the mouth of one, who drank faster than he could swallow.

We slowed to a stop and stood before a scene of chaos and devastation as a three-story brick apartment building lay smoking and besieged by fire. Flames lashed from every window, sparks flew from the roof as firefighters doused it with streams of hose water from every angle. The sizzle of the water caused glowing embers to shoot from the windows, crackling in the night air like a fireworks display. We watched from the corner, captivated by the yellow, white and red glow like a summer campfire. The wind changed without warning and a gust of scorching air blew in our faces, repelling us, causing us to back away. Ruth held a handkerchief to her mouth. Harrigan fended off the smoke with his hands. I squinted and looked away, but only for a few seconds. The heat was followed by a wall of smoke that flooded the street, obscuring the building and fire trucks, making it as hard to see as to breathe. I heard cries of panic as a second rush of smoke shot from the building into the street. Ruth and Harrigan had vanished and the street was gone, consumed by a thick cloud of grey mist that stung my eyes. I dropped to the sidewalk and held a hand to my mouth. As the smoke thinned, the building came in and out of view like a ghastly vision. Through the darkness I saw five or six black children, half-naked and shivering in the cold. Their white undergarments were soaked, either from hose water or sweat and their skin glistened in the light of the flames as they huddled together like dogs, wide-eyed and terror-stricken.

I was overcome by a rage I hadn't known since Korea, a lamentable fury that made me shake and convulse. I called to the children, but was hit by another burst of smoke that sent me to the ground, choking and blinded. I was disoriented, dizzy, when I felt the hand of Ruth, soft and unmistakable, take my arm and guide me up. I heard Harrigan's voice somewhere in the near distance.

"Detective, let's move away."

We backed away together, along the sidewalk, yearning to escape but somehow unable to take our eyes off the inferno.

I watched the children on the sidewalk, their frightened faces staring into the nothingness as their entire world burned to the ground. I broke from Ruth's grasp and ran to them, but the thick, oily smoke knocked me back like a tidal wave.

"Jody, we got to move away or we'll asphyxiate," Ruth cried.

As Harrigan took my shoulder to pull me away, I spotted the white uniform of a fire captain, leaning against a fence and smoking a cigarette like it was lunch break. I shoved Harrigan's arm aside and ran at him. As I approached, I whipped out my badge and held it to his face.

"What the hell's going on here? These kids need to get to a shelter?" I shouted.

He flicked the cigarette into the gutter and crossed his arms with a smug indifference.

"Let us do our job? Go catch a thief. Move along," he growled.

Before I could respond, he frowned and turned his back to me.

"I don't take orders from jakes!" I yelled, leaning towards him with my fists clenched.

The moment the words came out, I had crossed a line. Ruth and Harrigan stood at either side of me in disapproving silence. Harrigan tugged on my coat arm; Ruth was pale with apprehension. Before the captain turned, two firefighters rushed at me, helmets dangling from their heads, equipment swinging from their belts.

"Is there a problem?" one shouted.

"Mind repeating what you just said?" the captain asked without looking at me.

"I said I don't take orders from jakes!"

Smack! I heard the sound before I felt the punch. A sharp pain shot through the side of my head in front of my ear. I hit the pavement and smashed my hip on the curb. The noise of the sirens, the rumble of the fire engines and the whoosh of hoses faded into the background. All I heard was a constant buzz, like a phone left off the hook. When I tried to get up, I fell back into a chain-linked fence. The vague image of Harrigan came towards me and pulled me up by the waist. I reached into my belt but my gun was gone. Dazed and dizzy, I scanned the sidewalk. There at the edge of the curb lay my pistol, shining in the light of the fire like a crime-scene photo.

"He's got a gun!"

As I lurched towards the gun, two cops came out of nowhere and tackled me into the fence. I swung and kicked but they had me restrained. Ruth screamed. Harrigan pleaded for calm. As the officers forced me to the ground, my elbow caught the fencepost and tore my jacket. I peered up through the large bodies on top of me to see Harrigan moving frantically, holding his badge out and screaming for them to let me go. I was suddenly freed. The officers lifted me up and I leaned against the fence, breathless, panting and scraped up. One cop pressed the gun into my hand.

"Sorry Detective—we had no idea."

"That asshole did," I gasped, pointing to the captain, who leaned against the fence with a subtle grin.

I pried myself from the fence, dusted off and tucked the gun back in my belt. With my legs apart and arms out, I started towards the two firefighters, who stood nervously beside the captain, holding their helmets like shields. As I aimed towards them, their bodies swayed and contorted like reflections in water and I began to feel nauseated. The punch had impaired my vision, but not my resolve. Yet before I could get to them, I felt two arms under my ribcage as Harrigan took me from behind and dragged me away. With my heels scraping across the ground, I struggled for a minute before giving up.

"Detective, we need to go."

"Jody, please, let's get out of here." Ruth cried, a tear rolling down one cheek.

I've done it this time, I thought. Every firehouse in the district would know a detective, off-duty no less, was snooping around a fire scene and started trouble with a captain. Worse would be if anyone found out I was with Internal Affairs. The police and fire departments had a tenuous relationship at best. They had collided on more than one occasion on issues ranging from union contracts to jurisdiction and oversight. The cops got paid more but were less respected. The firemen were paid dirt but were lionized by all sectors of society, from admiring schoolchildren to the elderly. The fire department despised Internal Affairs because it held a range of discretionary enforcement powers over them as well as the police. Tasked with investigating corruption and internal mishandlings, we were viewed as a fifth column, betrayers of both forces.

Even if the incident was overlooked, it wasn't going to make my job any easier by making enemies with firemen. In the narrow world of Boston public-sector culture, it would only take one phone call to find out who I was and what I was doing there at 2:30 in the morning.

Ruth, Harrigan and I crossed Blue Hill Avenue and walked up Intervale Street as the smoke and sirens faded in the distance. Tired and aimless, we sat quietly on the stoop of Harrigan's apartment building. I rotated my neck, trying to relieve a pain that throbbed near the top of my spinal column.

Getting clocked in the head without warning could cause the same whiplash as hitting a tree going thirty. A swollen cheek would heal but a neck injury might haunt me forever. Even so, it could have been a lot worse and I turned to thank Harrigan for his help.

"I shouldn't have called you," he replied softly, his hands clasped and staring down between his shoes.

"Of course you should have," I said.

Ruth sat on the last step, her elbow resting on one knee as she stared out to the street blankly. I couldn't tell whether she was disappointed or just drained from the excitement.

"It's strange, Detective," Harrigan said, "I just passed that building thirty minutes earlier."

"Fires can be quick," I suggested, wiping blood from my lip.

"It's just unusual."

I looked at him and said, "More unusual than you walking around at 2:00 in the morning?" Harrigan tapped his foot and grimaced as I waited for a response. There was none.

"Can we just go," Ruth moaned.

CHAPTER FOUR

~

Jackson called me into the office Monday morning. The swelling on my face had only gotten worse and I knew I'd have a hard time convincing him I walked into a lampshade. Jackson was anything but naïve. At the same time, it would be tough to admit I showed up to a building fire, insulted a captain and got clobbered. So I decided that, if questioned, I would lie. If someone had told him I was at the scene, I would deny it straight-faced.

As I walked up the stairs, I saw Ruth's chair but not her. I peered over the counter to see if her jacket or purse lay nearby. But her workspace was empty. When we had left Harrigan's Friday night, I drove her home and waited for her to walk inside safely before pulling away. I didn't call over the weekend because I didn't have her number. If I knew it wouldn't violate house rules, I would have brought flowers by to apologize for my recklessness. The hours since I last saw Ruth left me with a hollowness borne of remorse.

I stood at the counter for a couple of minutes, hoping she might pop through the door behind the desk. When it was clear she wasn't around, I walked down the hallway to Jackson's office. I knocked twice and stepped inside.

"Detective, what the hell are you doing getting into fist-fights with firemen in the middle of the night?"

I was stunned. I had expected at least a 'good morning'. The time I had spent icing my face was a waste. The false stories I had rehearsed were useless. My eyes slowly dropped until I was staring at the floor like a shamed child.

Jackson came over to me with heavy feet and stood with a sternness that demanded attention.

"I got a call from Harrigan. He told me an apartment building was burning. I had to check it out," I murmured.

"So you attack a firefighter? A Captain?" Jackson shouted.

"What?" I gasped. My face went blank.

"I got a call from Chief Knowles this morning. He heard you showed up on-scene drunk last night and attacked Captain Prendergast."

Jackson lingered before me, inspecting the side of my face as if reading a map. He shook his head side to side, spun around and paced the office.

"Look Jody, this isn't any way to start an investigation that is jurisdictionally questionable to start with…"

"But I …"

"…Let me finish. And don't interrupt."

Jackson lowered his voice. "Please, close that," he asked, nodding to the door. I tapped it shut and turned around to listen.

"We need to be very sensitive about this." His voice sank to a whisper. "I don't care that you were there, or with the Forensics intern for that matter," he said with a wink. "But there was something the Chief said…"

"Sir?"

"I mentioned you were on assignment."

"I'm a Detective. I'm always on duty," I said.

"Knowles said he would appreciate it if any investigations began after the fire was out." Jackson was working up to a crescendo, blinking wildly and rubbing his chin.

"But it was sloppy work. They left children shivering on the sidewalk…"

Jackson held his hand out, stopping me mid-sentence. He leaned into my shoulder, inches from my ear, so close I smelled the morning coffee on his breath.

"But Brae, I didn't tell him you were there to investigate."

Jackson backed away, a wry smile creeping across his chin. We were each silent. The only sound was a jackhammer grinding cement at a worksite outside. Jackson tilted his head, sighed and then chuckled. He walked to the desk and left me there to wonder. I wasn't convinced that what Captain Knowles said had any meaning. He simply may have assumed I was there to investigate something or someone. I had to put my trust in Jackson. His ability to detect inconsistencies in speech, awkwardness of manner, had broken cases before. Regardless, the investigation was in the backdrop of my concerns since I was worried more about being censured for insulting a fire captain. Any interference by a detective during a four-alarm blaze could be viewed as obstruction.

"I was only observing…I didn't attack anyone. I had a few words with a Captain and one of his henchmen attacked me from behind. I swear."

Jackson fended off my protest with extended arms. Before I said another word, he pointed at me and said, "This is officially an internal review. You and Harrigan are on the case. I will need reports bi-weekly."

Jackson walked behind his desk and sat down. He pulled some documents from a folder and started to read. I stood in the center of the room, waiting for him to finish, waiting to be dismissed. When he peered up from reading and stared with one eyebrow raised, I knew our business was done. I let out a dry cough and turned to exit the room. As I walked towards the door, my feet dragged with the weight of frustration. Jackson needed to know I didn't attack a fire Captain. Someone was lying. With a hand on the doorknob and one foot in the hallway, I turned and blurted,

"Sir, I just want you to know I didn't attack the captain—in case there's an inquiry."

He looked across the room and smiled.

"Don't be ridiculous Brae. I don't trust Knowles as far as I can throw him. His corpulence is exceeded only by his ego."

"Sorry Captain?"

"First, you don't drink—you're far too serious about life. You couldn't have been drunk. Second, your knuckles are unscathed so you didn't hit anyone. And finally, the bruise on the side of your face begins at your ear. Someone surprised you."

"Thanks, Captain."

As I walked through the parking lot to my car, I debated whether I should stop by Ruth's apartment to see if she was alright. The minute I put the key in the lock, someone called my name and I looked to see Harrigan strutting across the parking lot, one hand in his coat pocket and the other holding down his tie. If Harrigan was anything, it was a gentleman—quiet and reserved but exquisitely dressed, much like a foreign dignitary.

"Detective!"

"Stop calling me Detective," I barked. "You're a Detective too. We're peers. You don't hear doctors calling each other 'Doctor' in the emergency room."

"Does that mean we're on a first name basis?"

"Maybe. Get in the car."

Harrigan hopped in and I sped out of the lot, down Tremont Street and past the Boston Common. When I rolled the window down and lit a cigarette, he slid towards the door as if repulsed. I blew smoke through my nostrils and he waved his hands around in disgust. All the while he didn't say a word. He probably detested smoking and couldn't understand such a nasty habit. Maybe he thought it ironic that a Detective investigating fires was a chain-smoker. The ashtray overflowed with butts and the floor was littered with half-used matchbooks like the remnants of a July Fourth bonfire. If he only knew about the can of gasoline in the trunk, Harrigan would have opted for a cab. Or maybe he would have kept his opinions to himself and trusted me.

Harrigan was polite beyond measure and his subtle lilt, much like an Englishman who has lived abroad half his life, made him sound like an island prince. Even when he didn't speak, which was much of the time, his manner and body language suggested a gracious refinement. Harrigan was dignified without being snobbish, a remarkable feat in a city of class-conscious social climbers and old-moneyed elites.

Yet something about Harrigan made me uneasy. He was too soft, too good-natured and I couldn't ignore that he had been out walking the night of the last building fire. I wasn't suspicious. But if Harrigan and I were going to work together there could be no mystery, no private lives either during or after work hours. I had to trust him completely, without reservation, like a fellow soldier or childhood friend.

"What's the agenda for today?" Harrigan asked, breaking the silence.

"To find some witnesses."

At the first red light, I flicked my cigarette, rolled up the window and brought the car to an abrupt halt. Knowing I had twenty seconds before the light changed, I turned and looked straight at him, "And we'll start with you!"

Harrigan's eyes popped open.

"What were you doing walking past Intervale Street at two in the morning?"

I expected a long pause, a regretful silence.

"I'm sorry, that is my business. I wasn't on duty."

Harrigan's tone had gone from light-hearted to defensive. His politeness was fading. When the light changed, a cab blew its horn and I punched the gas. I drove erratically, stopping and starting, weaving and turning, hoping to shake the truth out of him. When I realized a driving tantrum wasn't going to get him to talk, I pulled into a parking lot. I slammed the car into park and flung my hands from the steering wheel in exasperation.

"Listen Harrigan, if we're going work together then everything we do is each other's business. I don't care if you were out screwing a prostitute or selling vacuum cleaners door-to-door. My old neighborhood is burning to the ground and it's not by accident."

"Our old neighborhood, Detective," Harrigan interrupted.

I sat quiet, staring out the window as traffic rolled along Tremont Street. I was overcome by a strange agitation. I wasn't sure if it was Ruth, the investigation, Harrigan or the weather. My breathing was shallow and I felt a chill, like the early symptoms of the flu. I looked across the street and saw a sign, Metropolitan Theater, hung in vertical letters from a building like the jib sail on a schooner. I recalled going there with the Home as a child, a ticket donation by a wealthy brewery owner.

In the reflection of the glass I saw Harrigan, arms crossed and jaw clenched, fuming with passive indignation. He tapped his fingers on his knee, a subtle indication of the anger he contained so civilly within. I slammed the shifter into drive, the transmission clicked and the Valiant jumped forward. Harrigan and I ignored each other like a bickering couple after a shopping tiff, eyes averted, silent and both red in the face.

I sped down Columbus Avenue towards Roxbury, hoping the old neighborhood would loosen up Harrigan and get him to talk. It wasn't that I didn't trust him. But in this line of work a hazy skepticism, broaching suspicion, hung over every person, place or thing. A detective experienced so much betrayal, so much violent unraveling of reason and human empathy, that he was bound to question whether there was a God. Just because someone was a colleague, a department brother, a lifelong friend, or even a doting parent, didn't mean they weren't capable, under certain circumstances, of the most heinous actions. There were shades of darkness in even the most well-lit corners of the human soul.

I bit my tongue and let things cool down. With my window open to the wind, I wandered through city streets, turning on a whim, sometimes ending up where I began. I stopped at green lights and raced through red lights, cruised under rusting bridges and swerved around potholes. With the aimless monotony of motion, I tried to both calm and wear Harrigan down. I had studied torture in boot camp and understood that dull and repetitive actions would break a man's defiance.

We drove for almost an hour before Harrigan even sniffled, coughed or blinked. He was as still as a cadaver, except for his eyes, which darted back and forth to watch an approaching truck or group of school children skipping along the sidewalk.

Finally I pulled to the side of the road and stopped. I leaned back in the seat so Harrigan could see clearly the faded sign that hung above rusting double doors: Home for Stray Boys.

"This is where it all began for me, in this piss-smelling brick hell-hole. I keep no secrets…"

"…I was at a meeting in the building next door to the fire," Harrigan said softly, looking past me, through the wrought-iron gate and to the institution in the distance.

"Meeting? What kind of meeting?"

Again there was silence, the only sounds the rustle of leaves across the vacant courtyard and the impatient rumble of the engine. I held my breath. With his head tilted down, staring at the glove compartment, Harrigan sighed wistfully, as if preparing to confess.

"Nation of Islam."

I almost jumped through the roof.

"You're a fuckin' Black Muslim?" I screamed, smashing my fists against steering wheel, causing the horn to get stuck. The shrill ran up my back and vibrated through the seat. An elderly couple on the next corner looked over with hands cupped over their ears. Harrigan sat in bitter frustration as I tried to free the horn with my fingernails. The blare was grating and, I couldn't ignore, an ironic accompaniment to the outrage I felt. I slammed the car into drive and sped off as if fleeing a burglary, only the alarm followed us. Once I turned the first corner, the horn became miraculously unstuck. Harrigan murmured, then mumbled, then spoke.

"I don't know what I am Detective. I find their message soothing. I don't take everything they believe to heart. But there're a lot of problems with this country and they have some answers."

It was too early to discuss politics or theology. From the department's point of view, the Nation of Islam was a terrorist organization, a gang of gun-toting dissidents who did their dirty work under the guise of religion. To the underclass, however, it offered an alternative to the Bible-drunk complacency of Black Christian churches. They seemed to have solutions to timeless dilemmas. In Boston, they hadn't caused as much trouble as in other Northern cities, like Chicago or New York. To some, Nation members seemed like humble churchgoers when compared to the militant antics of the Black Panthers or radical student groups. Either way, if anyone on the force heard my partner was a member we would be shunned by colleagues and investigated by the department.

"Where are we heading?" Harrigan wondered.

"Listen, Harrigan," I said, ignoring the question, "For now let's pretend you never said what you just said."

Harrigan nodded and rolled down the window, clearing the air of tension and refreshing the mood of the morning.

"So, where are we heading?" he repeated. With nothing more said about the incident, we sat uneasily under a gentlemen's agreement that neither settled nor soured the situation. But it would come up again, I was sure.

"Blue Hill Avenue."

"Huh?"

"Blue Hill Avenue & Intervale. The fire. Let's see if we can find any witnesses. Any idea what happened to those kids?"

"What kids detective?"

"Nevermind."

We drove down Blue Hill Avenue and pulled over slowly near the corner of Intervale Street, trying not to draw attention. The Valiant was about as plain and non-descript as you could find, but any white person, clean shaven and neatly dressed, was awkwardly out-of-place in this area. Residents were so suspicious of outsiders, cops especially, that any sudden or strange behavior could send an entire city block running for cover.

We got out and walked along the sidewalk until we came to the building. The smell of fresh ash filled the air as if the fire had been extinguished only moments ago. But there was a peaceful silence, a graveyard serenity, which reminded me of a torched village I had stumbled upon in Korea. I recalled how the odor of death hung in the air like a thick fog, although there were no bodies. All that remained were collapsed huts, still smoldering, and household items that somehow had survived the flames—a miniature bronze bull, hand-painted tea set, can of salted radish, a framed portrait of President Syngman Rhee. Thousands of those artifacts littered the dirt road like an Appalachian flea market. Fire had a strange way of consuming the significant and leaving behind the trivial.

Harrigan walked down Intervale Street, along the side of the building and pulled at a charred basement door. When he was frustrated enough, he picked up a plank of wood, debris from the blaze, wedged it in the doorframe and yanked, sending a cloud of ashen dust into his eyes. I laughed. On the third attempt there was a loud crack as the door broke loose at the hinges and came crashing to the ground. Harrigan sprung back, his arms flailing as if spooked. Then he turned and gave me a quick, stern glance before peeking into the doorway. He looked right, then left, and then slipped into the darkness.

I leaned against a signal light on the corner, thumbed a cigarette from a pack and struck a match. I looked up at the burned brick shell, imagining how many tons of wood and concrete had vaporized. Pieces of debris blew across the sidewalk, no different from the dead, autumn leaves that littered the gutter, alleys and doorways along Blue Hill Avenue. The windows were covered in fresh plywood, adding a strange sense of newness to a building that was no less dilapidated before the fire. I walked over to the front door, put my ear to the crack and heard the wind whistling through the hollow rooms and hallways. I peered through a hole, probably from a pickax, and stared into the blackness at the tragic yet peaceful tranquility of the aftermath.

"Sir!"

I looked up to see a thin middle-aged black man, dressed in a long overcoat and wearing a newsboy's cap. When our eyes met, I recognized him instantly as the man who had wandered into Sam's shop. I had a gift for remembering the smallest details of every situation, a talent that suited my work but made it hard to forget the bad stuff. I was constantly recording and filing away in my brain every face, conversation and chance meeting I had. We stood facing each other, an arm's length apart. He was smaller than I recalled, almost shriveled, with a tired face that would have seemed sullen if it weren't for his dark, contented eyes. He smiled almost reactively, as if he had seen too much suffering to be a cynic. I had the sudden urge to ask if he was a veteran.

"Can I help you?"

"You investigating the fire?" he asked humbly.

"Maybe. You know anything about it?"

"Maybe." he said, still smiling.

I stepped closer and the steam from our breaths collided in the crisp air. I stood a good four inches taller and looked down upon him with a professional seriousness. His snappy response had caught me off guard and, had he been twenty years younger, I would have knocked his cap off. But as I stood over him I saw he quivered with each word, like a frail grandfather, helpless and harmless. I was overcome by a squeamish pity that almost made me lose my balance. If I could have leaned over and hugged the man without regret, I might have.

"What can you tell me, sir?"

"What do you already know?" he said, his jaw struggling to form each word.

"I know you were in Sam's store a few weeks ago."

"And I know Sam was in that building last night?"

I was caught off-guard, stunned, and so astounded that I stumbled to reply. I requested he repeat what he said and he did. Either it was true or he believed it to be true, but I sensed no insincerity. It wasn't often a witness wandered on to a scene and volunteered information. He was either a bored pensioner seeking excitement or perhaps that rarest of species, a concerned citizen hoping to further justice.

Skeptical but not unconvinced, I looked down to a patch of dried leaves and twirled them around with one foot, acting coolly indifferent without appearing uninterested. Witnesses were fickle creatures and any sudden eagerness could make them exaggerate their story or recant entirely. Besides, most people willing to help cops always wanted something in return. Maybe he had a grandson with a pending case or daughter who needed a speeding ticket fixed. Investigations always attracted favor-seekers.

"Is that so? How'd you know it was Sam?"

"Ain't too many white folks walking around this area at that hour."

"How about elderly Black folks?" I asked, raising an eyebrow.

"Do I look elderly, officer?" he said with a chuckle.

"Only when you lie."

"That's the truth. I was on my porch that night," he said, extending his bony arm to point out a three-family house on the opposite corner, "I'm out there every night having a smoke. C'aint sleep at my age."

"You saw Sam enter the building?"

"No. I watched him leave." Squinting in the sun, I looked in his eyes intently, following each word and listening for contradictions. "I saw Sam come out that there side door. Clear as day—the streetlamp is just there…" he said, nodding up to a light post. He continued, "A few hours later I saw smoke coming out the roof. I was just going to call the fire department when I heard sirens."

We stood facing each other in silence. I knew he was finished when his attention wavered and he was distracted by ordinary daytime activity, a passing bus, mischievous schoolboys by a storefront, police sirens in the distance.

"Would you be willing to give a statement, at headquarters?"

"You know where to find me."

I reached and patted the old man on the shoulder, grinning in thanks. He tipped his cap, made a slight bow and continued down Blue Hill Avenue.

I watched the old man hobble along the sidewalk with the humility of Gandhi. He turned at the next corner and was gone. On occasion, the humanity of people inspired me. In a neighborhood where it was better to keep your mouth shut, he had nothing to gain and everything to lose by providing information. The contradiction baffled me and all I could do was stand and shake my head. Maybe he was tired of crime and reached a point in his life where he wouldn't be intimidated by anything or anyone. Or perhaps he was somehow atoning for the mistakes and missteps of his own reckless youth. Age could do strange things to a person. Whatever his motives or intention, I had a lead on the case.

I walked around the right side of the building, which abutted a tree-covered vacant lot, and scanned the ground for clues that might appear with the same unexpected suddenness of the old man. At the rear of the building I sat on a low brick wall, beneath an ancient elm that was blackened with soot but had survived the blaze. I leaned against the tree trunk, shut my eyes and listened to the sounds of children playing in a nearby schoolyard.

I heard a smash and sprung to my feet. I ran to the front just in time to see Harrigan bust through the front door from the inside, a black Frankenstein, kicking up splinters and spitting dust. He walked over to me, dusting off his jacket and rubbing ash and debris from his eyes. I was going to say something sarcastic, but Harrigan was too shaken.

"Find anything?"

"Just a lot of ash," he said, trying to suppress an irritating cough.

"And you detective?"

"We'll have to see…"

When we got to the car, Harrigan paused.

"Oh, I did find this near the side door…"

Harrigan reached into his coat pocket and showed me a small stuffed baby doll. The blonde cotton hair was singed but still intact. The body was a deep ash gray, stained but not burned, and it reeked of smoke. I held the doll in one hand and wiped the film of dust from its face. As I looked into its plastic, lifeless eyes, the images of the shivering children flooded my mind. Then I imagined a young girl, terrified, trembling, screaming in the darkness and clutching her mother with one hand while holding the doll tightly with the other. They choked uncontrollably as smoke filled the hallway and smothered them slowly. The girl must have held the doll until the last second, when someone discovered the side door and they burst into the night.

"We'll have to get this doll back to her mother."

"Yes we will Detective," Harrigan said, "Yes we will."

CHAPTER FIVE

~

I hadn't heard from Ruth in over a week. Each night I lay spread across the bed, sheets thrown in every direction and gazing alternately at the ceiling, window and bureau in a restless semi-stupor, imagining her. She was beside me, half-drunk, her warm body sunken into the mattress and hair in a bushy mess but smiling nonetheless. The lingering vapors of French perfume sweetened the staleness of my bedroom. From the corner, the hiss of a steam radiator lulled me into an erotic trance as my eyes swept the length of her body, back and forth, endlessly.

The next morning I woke up late. I peeked over at the alarm clock which sat motionless, unwound and stuck at 11:12 from the night before or possibly days before. The glare of sunlight, slithering through cracks in my window shade, suggested it was well into mid-morning. I fired up the kettle, ran through the shower and put on yesterday's clothes. As I sipped my tea, I thumbed through the notebook of case notes I had scribbled down the previous day. I still hadn't been able to find out who owned the Warren and Brunswick Street buildings. I called over to Maggie in Records who said they were either missing, stolen or taken out without signing the withdrawal ledger. "It happens all the time," she whined like any disgruntled municipal employee, "Maybe if there was more money in the budget, they could hire more help and get a better system…" As frustrated as I was, I couldn't argue with her. The registry was so underfunded and disorganized that documents could vanish for months before miraculously reappearing. If they didn't, historical property information would have to be recreated from recent deeds, legal filings, building permits, etc.

I rushed to headquarters for a late-morning meeting with Jackson to go over the case. But first I stopped at the basement cafeteria to buy a muffin before breakfast ended. The second I walked in I saw Harrigan sitting at a table in the corner, his back to me and leaning over a tray of food. I had the urge to sneak up and surprise him, maybe with a flick on the back of his neck or a startling growl. As I got closer, however, I saw a somber face, tilted downward and staring at an omelet while he fidgeted with a plastic fork. Harrigan was troubled, edgy, his brow furrowed as if arguing with a voice in his mind. I slid on to the cold bench opposite him and folded my arms.

"Mind if I join you?"

"You already have," he said, looking up quickly, forcing a smile.

Harrigan remained silent. I looked around the cafeteria at the rows of empty tables littered with remains of the morning rush. Kitchen staff wheeled carts of trays, plates, utensils and smatterings of half-eaten breakfast items. A couple of cops, just off third-shift, pleaded for butter, as a black waiter dismantled the buffet table. Breakfast was over, no exceptions. I sighed and looked at Harrigan.

"Listen, about the other day…"

He looked up. "About what detective?"

I cringed whenever he called me 'detective,' unable to tell if he was being deferential or too polite.

"About your situation. Your affiliation."

"That's alright," he murmured. "I owe you an explanation."

"No." I said, holding my hand out. "What you do on your own time is your business. Let's just try not to advertise it. Agreed?"

"Agreed. It wouldn't win me any friends…"

"…I've got my own problems with credibility. That confrontation with the fire captain…"

"His men shouldn't have assaulted you," Harrigan said, shaking his head.

"Part of that's my fault. I shouldn't have approached the captain. I just didn't like the way they were handling things. Those children should have been escorted to headquarters or a shelter…"

Harrigan frowned. "Who? Which children?"

"On the sidewalk—the kids from the apartment building?"

He tilted his head to one side, replaying that night in his mind like a movie reel. "I didn't see any kids. Are you sure?"

"You must have been blinded by smoke. A group of black children were on the sidewalk…"

Harrigan interrupted, "It doesn't matter. Did you hear the new today?"

I shook my head.

"Another building fire, last night near City Hospital," Harrigan said.

"Did it make the papers?"

"Nope. I heard it from a neighbor who works nights at City Hospital. A three-alarm. She said flames were visible from the 2nd floor."

"Anyone hurt?"

"Don't think so. It was an abandoned factory building. Some firemen came to the hospital with smoke inhalation."

The conversation seemed to lighten up Harrigan so that he even nibbled a few bites from the cold omelet. Maybe he mistook by words for an apology, which it wasn't, although I was happy to let him think so. He looked up, pointing the fork at me and chewing ferociously.

"Listen, Detective, I may have a lead of sorts."

"Let's hear it. Anything's better than nothing."

"Well, it concerns my affiliation with…"

"The Nation…" I interrupted.

"Unfortunately."

"Let's hear it Harrigan. We could always say you were undercover."

Harrigan smirked.

"I went to the Mosque to drop off donations last night. The supply room was closed but there were some men hanging around. We got to talkin'…"

"Would have loved to been a fly on that wall."

"We got to chatting. One of the men, a boy actually, asked what I knew about the fire next door."

"Next door?"

"Yes, on Intervale Street. The Mosque is behind the building that burned on Blue Hill Ave."

"Right."

"I said it was good no one was injured."

"And?"

"He kept pressing me, almost taunting me, like someone with a secret to share. He said he works for a company called Drake…"

"Drake & Stanton?" I said and Harrigan. "A disaster clean-up outfit. They specialize in toxic spills, fire damage, etc."

"Correct," Harrigan said, grinning nervously. "He goes into a lot of the fire-damaged buildings, to board-up the doors and windows."

"That's what they do. They've had a hefty contract with the city for years," I said, lowering my voice.

"Anyway, I remarked that old buildings are tinderboxes. He chuckled. They think all islanders are naïve."

"And?" I asked anxiously, wanting Harrigan to get to the point.

"He said it was no accident."

"That's no surprise. Where's the evidence?" I asked.

"This guy was real cocky, the Malcom X type. I played into his ego. I told him I had seen the reports and that the fire was accidental."

"Well?"

Harrigan slugged down a half-glass of orange juice as I bit my lip waiting for him to finish. Everything he said was a complete sentence, every idea carefully constructed. What he said in ten words I could have said in one. I was ready to explode from suspense when he leaned across the bench and whispered,

"Said he'd prove me wrong. He wants to meet."

"When?" I shouted, unable to contain myself. A kitchen worker in a soiled smock came up to the table.

"Can I take your tray? We're cleaning up before lunch."

Harrigan smiled politely and handed him the tray with both hands. We stood up and exited the cafeteria, lingering in the hallway and speaking in tones that were soft without appearing secretive. A police lieutenant passed by holding a briefcase against his white uniform shirt. I nodded and he nodded back with a formal coldness. When the officer was safely down the hallway Harrigan resumed.

"Tonight, after dark. He's going to meet me at the apartment building."

"We'll be there."

"No, Detective…I mean, Jody. You can't. This guy knows something. I can't let him know we're cops. I will get further with these people than you."

I couldn't argue with Harrigan. He was right. He had the advantage of familiarity with Nation members and my presence, no matter how discreet or well-hidden, would arouse suspicion and put us both at risk. The Nation of Islam had a network that extended into every street, alley and back hallway throughout the black slums of Roxbury and Dorchester. If anyone knew anything about the fire epidemic, or had the ability to find out, it was them.

"I understand." I said.

"Let's meet Sunday night at my apartment," Harrigan suggested.

"I want you to squeeze this guy," I said, patting Harrigan on the back and then turning to walk away.

"Like a lemon, Detective."

As I breached the top of the stairwell, the faintest wisp of blonde hair came into my view from behind the counter of the lobby. With each step a little more came into view until finally, with one last step, I saw Ruth's face. I waited for a moment, balanced on the top stair, admiring the way she typed, intently, furiously, as if drafting a treaty for world peace. Her bangs poured over a set of chestnut-colored glasses, slightly too large, that I had never seen her wear before. She wore a pony-tail, pulled back tightly, that gave the impression of a stern librarian. As I watched her, I felt guilty in a way that was exciting but not devious. I had imagined her all week, a respite from dreams that left me agonizingly sleepless, and now her vision was made flesh. I took a deep breath and walked to the front desk.

"Hi, Ruth."

"Hello," she said with a quick glance, as if distracted.

"Is Jackson around?"

"Should be, check his office."

There was a short pause as Ruth shook an uncooperative pen, trying to coax it back to life so she could make notes. I stood a moment too long, hoping she would look up, smile, frown or do anything to give me an excuse to stay. All the while my moment of opportunity lingered like a train held up for a single late passenger. I struggled to say the next word, paralyzed by stage-fright, dumbstruck by hesitation, too scared to stay and too stubborn to leave. I coughed a little, and then tapped my fingers against the counter. The desk phone rang and Ruth picked it up. As if by cue, I realized it was time to walk away. I mumbled 'thanks' and headed towards Jackson's office.

"You're all the same," Ruth snickered, covering the receiver with her hand. I stopped and turned around.

"What?"

"You are all the same. Either you don't have the balls to say you're interested or you don't have the balls to admit you're not!"

A female clerk in the back office peeked through the door-way. I smiled at her uncomfortably and looked down to Ruth. When she slammed the phone down, I wasn't sure if the call was completed or cut-short. She sat with arms crossed, bit-ing the side of her lip and shaking her head. Her glasses had come loose from the outburst and rested on her nose at an angle. We stood for ten seconds, eyes locked tensely and wait-ing for the other to speak. Without even thinking of what to say, I blurted out,

"I'd like to take you to dinner again."

"Tomorrow at 8:00," she said, her expression still bitter, her mouth puckered. "Pick me up. Don't be late."

I stood before the door of Jackson's office, staring at cracks in the wood grain that were so brown they were al-most black, layers of lacquer that bespoke the building's age like the rings of a tree trunk. On the other side, I heard the faint sound of violins. After a crescendo, there was a pause and I knocked, three times quickly. I tilted my ear to the door, but there was no reply. The music continued and I waited patiently, reluctant to disturb Jackson but afraid to miss our meeting. Again the chorus of strings peaked and again there was a space of silence. I knocked once more.

"Enter."

I turned the brass knob and gently pushed the door, its tarnished hinges creaking every inch. I stuck my head in and saw Jackson at the window, hands clutched behind his back and facing into the morning sunlight. Beside a bookshelf, a mahogany console turntable spun Classical music. The mel-odies filled the room, giving it the solemnity of a church ser-vice. I withdrew apologetically and started to close the door when suddenly he spoke.

"Brae, come in."

As usual, Jackson astonished me with a perception that was almost supernatural.

"Just checking in, Captain."

He turned away from the window, majestically, as if he had been conferring with the Lord himself. His pupils were dilated from the brightness and he stood with the hypnotic calm of someone exiting a state of meditation.

"Come in, sit down. Do you like Strauss?"

"I've never met him."

"Of course you didn't. He died in '49, which would put you at…"

"Eighteen, sir."

"Ah, the onset of adulthood." He crossed the room and turned down the volume. The moment the music ceased, the trance was ended. Jackson stood with arms crossed, leaning against the desk and ready to talk business. Although shorter than most of his detectives, he had this ability of appearing to stare down at you, an illusion created by his unusually large head, fierce stare and eyeglasses that dangled from the tip of his nose. Although deceptive, it more than compensated for his slight physique and soft manner.

"What can I do for you, Detective?"

"I wanted to bring you up to date on the investigation."

"Proceed," he said, standing motionless with his mouth slightly agape.

"Well, first of all, I can't get my hands on the deeds to the Warren and Brunswick Street buildings."

"Of course you can't Brae, they're in my top drawer." I felt the rush of blood to my face as I blushed. I stuttered a bit, fumbling to respond. Jackson loved to stay one step ahead, always knowing a little more about an investigation than his detectives. He was the consummate mentor, helping with every step of the problem but never giving away the answer. To an outside observer, his case meddling may have seemed like micromanagement. But Jackson never took direct credit for any convictions, regardless of how much he had assisted. His intentions in crime-solving were pure and his motives were selfless.

"Ok?" I said, "I also called Records for the fire at Blue Hill Ave. and Intervale. That too was gone--either missing or stolen."

"It was merely borrowed Brae, don't be so cynical. That, too, is here in my top drawer. Maggie is a wonderful spy. It always helps to have friends in low places," he said with a smirk.

That sneaky bitch, I thought to myself. Maggie had been as straight-faced as a poker champ yet the whole time she was doing Jackson's bidding. I felt betrayed although I had no right to.

"What's important about property records?" Jackson wondered.

"To see who owns the buildings?"

"Good. But you could go to city hall for that information,"

"I need to see the official record. I need the deed to verify the ownership."

Jackson nodded in semi-agreement.

"The City Records Department is as secure as a fruit stand. Don't trust a single piece of paper in there. The real documents are at the Registry of Deeds, under lock and key.

You need official approval and photo identification just to view them."

"Then I know what my next step is."

"I pulled these folders from Records so I could keep tabs on anyone who was looking for them. Maggie is watching for any suspicious inquiries."

"You think there's a conspiracy?" I asked bluntly.

"Hardly. Conspiracies are for Hollywood. I do, however, know that the three properties in question were until recently owned by an 'A. Cohen.' The ownership was transferred on all within the past year."

"Never heard of him. Any leads?"

"No. I traced his address to a P.O. Box in Fall River. Better yet, the attorney who did the transfer died in August. A heart attack, I think."

Jackson walked closer and looked into my eyes. He lowered his voice and said, "See if you can find any information on a James Loomis. His office was on Blue Hill Ave, in Mattapan." He walked over to the desk, opened a drawer and pulled out a stack of manila folders, stuffed with papers and wrapped with rubber bands. With an underhanded swing, he tossed them to me. As I dove for the catch, the weight of the folders made me almost lose my balance. Our business was concluded. Jackson walked to the other side of the office, turned the volume up, and the music of Strauss filled the room. As I waltzed to the door, Jackson shouted,

"Get to work Detective. This is starting to look like trouble."

It bothered me that I hadn't told Jackson about Harrigan's lead. I felt I was being disloyal by withholding information that might prove critical to the investigation. It was an

ethical dilemma that forced me to choose between my partner and my commander. Had I told Jackson about Harrigan's chance meeting at the Mosque, I would be revealing that he was a Black Muslim. As understanding as Jackson could be, he may have removed Harrigan from the case, if not altogether suspended him pending an ethics violation inquiry. We were too close to a lead to take that risk and so I chose to keep my mouth shut. But I also failed to tell Jackson about the elderly Black man at the Blue Hill Avenue scene. I had a witness statement, priceless evidence, although it was verbal. I was intimidated by Jackson's cleverness and didn't want to seem like a rookie by listening to an old retiree handing out clues on the sidewalk. Before I told Jackson anything, I needed hard evidence.

When I walked past Ruth's desk, she was gone. I got into the Valiant and drove through the gray city streets, the bustling afternoon of business and busyness. The windshield was my window to the world. I drove with no purpose and no destination, silently reflecting on my life and on the day, wondering what lay around the next corner. If I had accomplished anything today, I told myself, it was that I had made things right with Ruth. She had taken a risk, went out on a limb. She took initiative where I floundered and I admired her deeply for it. All the relationships I ever had, the many few, ended because I hesitated to take that next step. The moment I got close to a woman, I retreated into the hollows of my past, content to live in solitary bitterness.

I attributed this malaise to the war when, in fact, Korea was only a corner piece in the puzzle of my life. The deep restlessness I felt, that constant and edgy uncertainty about all things, had been sown years before within the corridors and brick walls of the Roxbury Home For Stray Boys. In a strange way Korea was the highpoint of my life. It wasn't the camaraderie of battle or the exhilaration of surviving near-death that made those memories so sweet. I loved war because, for the first time in my life, I knew terror not as an abstraction but as it really was—torn flesh, splintered bones, jeeps upturned, the scent of cordite, the wails of dying soldiers. Living through that hell made the disappointments of my youth seem insignificant. Somewhere between the Kum River and Kongju the burden of my own self-pity was lifted. Maybe that was why, during that period of my life, the nightmares had ceased entirely.

By the time I got home, it was dark. I reheated some beef stew and sat on the couch holding a chipped ceramic bowl and wooden spoon like a P.O.W. On the little television, Walter Cronkite reported on a military coup in Bolivia. The lights from the picture tube were mesmerizing, the sound of his voice a comforting monotone that soon sent me into a drowsy stupor. The lids of my eyes slowly closed as I fought the urge to sleep. Ring! Startled, I jumped up and, out of instinct, reached under the couch for my gun. Across the television screen were quivering lines of random black and white and the only sound was steady static. The network had ended its daily broadcast so it must have been well past midnight. When my foot hit the floor, I slid on the stack of folders Jackson had given me. I took another step and kicked the ceramic bowl, sending chunks of beef and soupy carrot bits across the rug. I groped along the wall until I found the receiver.

"Hello!?"

"Brae?" a voice called.

"Who's this?" I demanded, leaning over to peel off a stew-soiled sock.

"Brae, this is Lieutenant Hogan from headquarters. I'm at City hospital. You need to get down here immediately."

"Why? What time is it?"

"It's urgent. Just get down here."

Without another word, I hung up. I stood in the dark corner of the living room and rubbed my hand across my shirt to feel the dampness of perspiration. My face was cold and clammy and I was overcome by a feverous shiver. In an instant I recalled the images of the nightmare that had returned without warning. I smelled the rain as if still dreaming. With a shudder, I remembered running down an endless maze of dark, nameless streets, mumbling "more air, more air" in gasping repetition. But this time she hadn't appeared. The phone call had awoken me and I was spared the frustration of chasing a vision I couldn't reach. Whenever I had these episodes and she didn't appear or I was interrupted, I knew they would return again soon. Whereas on nights when I ran to her and came so close I could almost touch her face, they didn't return for weeks, sometimes months. Throughout the years, I had learned their patterns like the quirks and habits of a best friend.

I ran to the closet and threw on pants, a shirt and some clean socks. I grabbed my coat from the living room floor and was off, speeding through the night with no regard for traffic lights or street signs. I was in a state of manic urgency, rushing to City Hospital with blind determination as wild scenarios of tragedy formed in my head. When I drove up to the front gate, three police cruisers were parked at the entrance. I pulled into the fire lane, slammed into park and ran towards the door, my overcoat flailing in the wind like a cape. I came into the lobby and was blinded by the fluorescence of endless ceiling lights. Someone called my name and I squinted to see Jackson, flanked by two patrolmen, rushing towards me. Beneath his full-length trench coat, he wore a plaid robe and tank top as if he had been interrupted from pipe-smoking, cognac-sipping bliss. Under any other circumstances, I would have laughed aloud.

"Brae, this is bad. Real bad." Jackson's face was pasty white and he spoke with a quiet firmness that was more fearful than business-like.

"Captain?"

"It's Harrigan. He's been attacked."

"Attacked?"

One of the patrolmen stepped forward. "We got a call around midnight that a man had crawled into a gas station, nearly beaten to death. When the medics arrived they didn't even have a pulse."

Jackson continued, "Apparently it was cardiac arrest but they were able to revive him. He has severe contusions around his head, a possible cranial fracture; his shoulder is broken. We don't know the extent yet."

I reached for a lobby chair while the other cop handed me a cup of cold water.

"Brae," Jackson asked, "when was the last time you spoke with Harrigan?"

"This morning. We had breakfast."

"Did he give any indication he was in trouble?"

"No…I mean…he was supposed to meet someone tonight," I moaned.

My head throbbed like a New Year's Day hangover. As I tried to speak my tongue and mouth froze. Thoughts, words, sentences, images and faces flashed through my brain in a kaleidoscope of confusion. Jackson and the patrolmen assaulted me with questions as if I was under interrogation. The sounds from the hospital lobby—nurses rushing, orderlies pushing stretchers, the sirens of arriving ambulances—they all blended into a dizzying and indistinguishable mush. All I could do was cup my hands and hold them over my ears.

"Brae, Brae" the voices cried and I felt someone shake my shoulder.

"We need to get whoever did this!"

In an instant, the madness ceased and everything was quiet. I was suddenly calmed and looked up to Jackson eyes. He smiled and patted me on the back.

"Um, Harrigan met someone who had information on the Blue Hill Avenue fire. They were going to meet tonight." I said regretfully.

"Where?" Jackson demanded.

"At the building. This person had evidence it was arson."

"What evidence was that?"

"Harrigan wasn't sure. The guy had been in the building to patch up the doors and windows. He worked for Drake…"

"Drake and Stanton?" Jackson asked. "They don't do accident cleanup for the city anymore. They lost that contract three years ago."

I rubbed my eyes and shook my head back and forth.

"Where did he meet this person?" Jackson asked.

I was backed into a corner. I hadn't mentioned Harrigan's meeting to Jackson this morning. Now I had to tell him Harrigan met the informant at a Nation of Islam gathering. My partner was dying and I had to expose his personal life to a captain and two street cops. But if there was any hope of finding Harrigan's assailants, I had to come clean—I had no choice. My two greatest fears were that Harrigan would die and Jackson would lose his trust in me. I could handle one or the other, but not both. I took a breath, shrugged my shoulders and spoke.

"He met him at the Mosque in Grove Hall." The patrolmen raised their eyebrows and I felt their scorn. Jackson, however, didn't flinch. I continued, "He'd been doing some community work." The cops stepped back, looking to each other with disgust.

"I see," said Jackson. "I won't judge a man by what he does in his spare time. But the Nation isn't a Catholic bingo club, you know."

"I know, I know."

"When did you hear about this meeting?" Jackson asked.

"This morning."

Jackson paused and rubbed his chin, gazing at me with an austerity that made me cower. I averted my eyes, staring down at the white parquet floor and sipping water from an even whiter paper cup. Everything in the hospital was a sterile white and seemed only to emphasize by contrast the sordid business that brought me there. I waited for Jackson to respond as a child would expect a lashing. The tormenting silence, a tension that was gut-wrenching, was atonement enough for my misdeeds. Jackson struggled with the ethical implications of the information I withheld from him earlier that day. My only hope was he would decide that losing a partner was sufficient punishment, a hard lesson learned.

"I need you to give a statement at headquarters tomorrow morning."

"Yes Sir."

"Now go home and get some sleep. We need you rested Detective."

Jackson took my arm and helped me up, escorting me through the entrance door while the patrolmen lingered in the lobby. As we passed a crowd of nurses hurrying for a shift change, Jackson smiled and they smiled back. We walked to the hospital gate and stood in the shadow of a brick column. Looking furtively from side to side, Jackson leaned in and whispered, "You need to keep this incident confidential. Not a word. No one. Understand?"

I looked in the direction of his voice, searching for his eyes in the darkness and nodded. "Yes, Captain." I then turned away like a wounded dog, my shoulders slumped and hands in my coat pocket, and staggered across the pavement to the Valiant.

A few days later I received the second worst news I could possibly get. The first would have been that Harrigan died, which thankfully wasn't the case. The second was that Harrigan was in a coma and his recovery was uncertain. I hadn't felt so defeated since I lost my first man in Korea one snowy January night in 1952. Private Malachi Oveson requested to leave his post to repair some communication wire that was severed when a rogue mortar overturned a tree. I consented because I knew he played telephone chess with the next observation post, one of the many escapes from the boredom of midnight watch. He wasn't gone five minutes when the crack of gunfire, a single sniper shot, ended the game forever.

I came home Friday night to find a note under the door stating that Harrigan had stabilized and his doctors were allowing limited visitation. It was typewritten, a single sentence on a folded piece of notebook paper, marked with neither sender nor recipient. I guessed Jackson had left it since few others in the department knew about the incident. Everyone else thought he had broken his ankle. I had a cold dinner, leftover pork and rice, and headed to City Hospital, hoping to at last see Harrigan, knowing the moment our eyes met that everything would make sense. I would know instantly if it had been a setup or bad luck.

I pulled into the hospital parking lot and sat for a few minutes, smoking a cigarette and trying to calm my nerves. As I looked up to the main building, the countless windows and bland uniformity of the grey brick exterior reminded me of soviet factories buildings I had seen in counter-intelligence training books. It was hard to imagine that somewhere in there was Harrigan, strapped to a stiff bed, tubes and wires dangling from his body. The more I thought of him, the more I trembled. When I finished the third cigarette, I found myself subconsciously reaching for the ignition, wanting to back up and drive away.

Reluctantly, I walked into the front lobby and scribbled my name in the guest ledger on the front desk. As I turned to walk to the elevators a little squeak called from behind the counter.

"Sir, please print."

I looked to see a pudgy nurse, hardly as tall as the counter, looking up from behind black, thick-rimmed glasses and tapping her forefinger on the sign-in ledger.

"I can't read this chicken scratch."

I was suddenly self-conscious, anxious and blushing like a bumbling actor on his stage debut. Some might call it paranoia, but I was overcome by the strange feeling that I was being watched, monitored, observed, and assessed. Faces passed by in the lobby, crowds of people entering, leaving, laughing and crying. I felt feverish and slightly light-headed, which I attributed to the pork. As the desk attendant waited,

I reached for the pen and wrote on the next line, in clear block letters, "Martin Mirsky."

"Thank you, mister," she said with exaggerated politeness.

I nodded and darted to the elevator bank. The elevator was packed with visitors, doctors, janitors and nurses and ascended at a tortuous rate, stopping on each floor, creaking under the strain of overuse. When the doors opened to the fifth floor, I wriggled through the crowd and into the hallway. I passed a nurse's station and scanned the doors until I came to the last room of the corridor, C12. I held my breath and reached for the knob, having no idea what to expect. As I gently pushed open the door, the first thing I saw was the uniform of our police department, impeccably blue, accented with epaulettes, brass buttons, a baton and gleaming pistol. His figure stood like a recruitment poster at a college job fair. Beyond the officer I saw Harrigan, his long body slung across an undersized bed and a breathing tube taped to his mouth. He was perfectly still, the only indication of life being the slow, continuous movement of the cylinder in the oxygen chamber next to the bed. The side of his head was covered in white gauze, loosely wrapped and stained with purple patches of dried blood. My heart sank.

Before I went any further, I looked to the officer and he nodded stoically. I knelt beside the bed and looked into Harrigan's face. He was so content, so peaceful, and had the glowing perfection of a finely-dressed body at a wake. I wanted more than anything for him to open his eyes, tear off the apparatus and say 'Hello, Detective." My lower lip started to quiver and I felt a poignant sorrow I hadn't known since youth. I stood up and turned to the officer.

"How's he doing?"

"He's breathing. If he wasn't so young, he would've died at the scene."

"At the gas station." I mumbled, looking back at Harrigan.

"In the basement of that whorehouse on Blue Hill Ave. The one that burned down."

"Whorehouse?"

"That's right. We've been watching that place for months. It's a filthy brothel."

"Do you know why he was there?" I asked, prodding to see what the officer knew.

"Not my concern." the cop said bluntly.

"He had a lead on who torched it. Someone from his church."

"You mean the mosque? That's been closed since the fire. It was next door and was heavily damaged. We spoke with the minister this morning. No one has been there."

"But Harrigan was sure..."

"That building is unoccupied, Detective."

The officer spoke with an air of condescension, a subtle but unmistakable impudence that burned my blood. As I stood before him, he was at least two inches taller than me, thirty pounds heavier and probably ten years younger. Nevertheless, my honor would not be outmatched. I wouldn't be insulted by a street cop while my partner laid half-dead, comatose and struggling to heal. I stepped closer, within inches of the officer, so near I could smell the sour coffee on his breath. His face was round and featureless like a mongrel and his eyes were just slightly too far apart, the sure sign of a half-wit, an imbecile. He stared back like a fuming idiot, too wise to provoke a Detective yet too foolish to conceal his disrespect. The longer we stood, the more he questioned his own audacity; I could see it in his eyes, the way they flickered. When I made a sudden move, reaching into my jacket, the officer flinched like a startled jackrabbit. With a sardonic smile, I pulled out my wallet and handed him my card.

"Call me if his condition changes."

"I wouldn't count on it," he said.

"What's your name officer?" I demanded.

"Rollins."

"Well, Rollins, don't give me any lip. Just give me a call if our brother improves."

"He's no brother of mine."

Struggling to restrain myself, I pointed my finger at his nose. "Listen you shit, Harrigan got pummeled so you didn't have to!"

"He got beat by his own."

"What the fuck does that mean?"

"You hang around trash, you're gonna stink. Maybe his fellow Muslims should pick up the hospital bill?"

Rollins stood with the poise of a sentry, stiff and emotionless. I had underestimated him since he was clever enough to rile me without saying anything that might warrant an official grievance. I was with Internal Affairs and he was a common patrolman and there was no love lost between our divisions. Since I wasn't his superior, he could speak as freely as he wished, to a point. If our disagreement turned physical, however, he would have a tough time explaining to his captain how he got into a scrap with a detective in the hospital room of his injured partner. As the tension reached a climax, I thought of Harrigan and slowly backed away. A sinister smirk broke across Rollins' chin, one last final taunt that left me shivering with rage. For Harrigan's sake, I let Rollins think he triumphed, at least for now.

"If anything happens to Harrigan, good or bad, and I don't hear about it I am going to come looking for you." I said coolly. I took one last quick look at Harrigan and exited the room.

The next day I drove along Blue Hill Ave, trying to get my mind off Harrigan. I was haunted by the constant image of him walking into that trap, brazenly attacked in the darkness, bludgeoned and beaten and left to crawl along the sidewalk like a slug. Just the thought filled me with the same barbaric anger I had experienced in Korea, early in my tour, when two of my men were killed one night on patrol. I spat and fumed and fired my Thompson in the air until a lieutenant calmly talked me back to sanity. It was a hatred so powerful that if not directed at something or someone, it would have destroyed me from within.

I pulled in front of Sam's hat shop and parked. At this point he was a suspect, although he didn't know it. I couldn't barge into his store with wild accusations and vague witness testimony. Sam was too old and tired to be involved with arson, but his presence that night, whether real or imagined, might give me the leverage I needed to get some information.

When I opened the front door, the bell rang and the first thing I noticed was no cigar smoke. That meant one of two things; Sam was dead or his wife was working in the shop. Although Sam owned the store, his wife Agnes managed it and didn't tolerate his filthy habits. When I was a child, the sidewalk was littered with the half-smoked cigars she ripped from his fingers.

The sunlight broke the darkness and as expected I saw Agnes standing on a footstool, dusting hat boxes as she had thirty years before. She seemed not to have aged, a perpetually middle-aged babushka, five-foot nothing and stout as an ox. She had the forearms of Popeye and always wore variations of the same dress, a peasant robe of heavy cotton that kept her warm in the winter and cool in summer. She spoke with a thick Eastern European accent, in simple declarative sentences that lacked nuance but got the point across. But Agnes was as lovable as everyone's grandmother and when I was a child she walked along Blue Hill Avenue handing out lollipops to the little waifs that lingered on street corners. She became known as the "Lollypop Lady" who married the "Hat Man," a cute pairing reminiscent of a children's storybook.

"Hello Dear," I said. Agnes looked over with her thick rimmed glasses.

"Hello. Who's that?"

"You remember Jody Brae dear?" Sam announced from behind the counter, fixed to his chair.

"Oh yes, nice to see you hoooney."

"Sam, I was hoping to have a chat, if you don't mind?" I said discreetly, hoping Sam would take the hint and ask Agnes to leave the room.

"What do I have to mind about?" Sam asked while gnawing on an unlit cigar. "Agnes was just going to go out to buy some milk before we close up, right dear?"

"That I vaaas, righto!"

Agnes stepped down and took her coat. She grabbed a purse behind the counter, slung it over her shoulder and then put the coat on over the purse. Her careful concealment of the handbag was another indication the neighborhood had changed. She reached for a cane leaning against an old Singer sewing machine and started for the front door. She walked with a slight limp that was wobbly but not unsteady and she smiled politely as I held the door open wide. When the sunlight broke across her face, she looked suddenly much older. Deep wrinkles encircled her eyes; crevices crisscrossed her forehead like the lines of a person's palm. Sam's shop, with its dimly-lit mystique of the past, seemed to make anyone appear years younger.

For an instant I feared for Agnes' safety as she hobbled down the Avenue, defenseless and unsuspecting, in a neighborhood where daytime muggings were not uncommon. I held the door open a second too long, but decided that any wife of Sam's would be alright, his fading influence still enough to discourage the street hoods and sidewalk predators of Roxbury and Dorchester. Besides, no one would dare rob a white woman who had the audacity to walk the streets like it was still nineteen fifty-four.

I shut the door and walked across the shop to the counter. Sam reached for a lighter and lit the saliva-drenched cigar. There was a short pause as he took a few puffs, just enough to get the cigar started and satisfy his nicotine craving.

"What can I do for you Detective?"

"Sam, I need some information. No bullshit," I said with a subdued firmness that masked the boiling impatience I felt within. Sam hopped off the stool and held his arms out.

"I told you Brae—I don't know anything."

I moved towards the counter with a slow intensity, like an oil tanker approaching port. My jaw was clenched, my entire body tense with frustration.

"Sam, my partner is in City Hospital with a split skull! I need to know who's burning buildings."

"I'm sorry son, but you can't come into my shop and start giving me orders. I was giving orders when you were still in diapers!" Sam said, his eyelids flickering in the cloud of smoke that surrounded him. There was a light sheen on his forehead and I felt his nervous anxiety. As I moved closer, Sam started to back away, imperceptibly, like the hour-hand on a clock. But I sensed he was beginning to crumble. I reached down inside my coat and felt the cold steel of the .38, a gentle insinuation that would keep the pressure up, although I would never have harmed an old shopkeeper.

My face was only inches from his when I gritted my teeth and whispered, "I got a witness Sammy. You were seen leaving a building on Blue Hill Ave. the other night, minutes before it burned to the ground. Maybe we can make a deal. Just between us. Huh? Or do you want to be known as a cop killer?"

"I had nothing to do with that Shvartzer!" Sam cried, his milky eyes glaring through me as if hypnotized. I laughed, looked to the floor and shook my head. His cigar had slipped from his fingertips and lay smoldering on the floor beside my shoe. I stamped it with my heel, grinding it into the old floorboard in the same way I was grinding my will into his conscience.

"What did you call my partner?" I whispered, looking down on his trembling body, the smell of sweat apparent.

"I had nothing to do with that, I swear."

When I coughed slightly from the dry smoke, Sam startled like a fawn. Any trace of cool defiance, proud stubbornness, had now vanished. When Sam also coughed, I knew I had broken him. In Korea I had witnessed the same mimicry while interrogating prisoners or village collaborators. The moment a man's resolve was destroyed, he began to mirror the actions of his subjugators.

"Listen, Brae, I really don't know about the fires. I hear rumors. I can tell you they aren't accidents. But I have nothing to do with this business. I'm an old man. I just want to close shop and move to Pompano with Agnes."

"Then what in God's name were you doing on Blue Hill Ave. that night?" I shouted, slapping my hand against the counter so hard the store shelves rattled. Sam looked down in shame, fretting like a child, his eyes tear-filled although he was not crying.

"I was visiting a lady friend, I swear. Please," Sam looked up at me, "You can't tell Agnes." I looked at him in disgust, cringing at his immorality as if I cared.

"Oh, c'mon Sam. I need something to keep me quiet."

"What else can I say? I am telling you the truth."

"Who's 'A Cohen'?" Sam shook his head. "He used to own that building…and several others that have been, um, struck by lightning recently," I said with a sardonic frown.

"C'mon Brae, that's like me asking you if you know an 'A Sullivan' from South Boston."

"How 'bout a guy named Loomis from Mattapan?"

The name seemed to catch Sam's attention and I waited as he rubbed his chin, reviewing his mental catalogue of acquaintances and contacts. When he struggled to recall the name, I knew I had hit a homerun.

"Loomis, Loomis…yes! I knew a Loomis. A defense lawyer for wise guys. That was years ago. He used to hold court down at the G&G Deli."

"He won't be holding court any longer," I shot back. "He's dead. A heart attack a few months back."

Sam shrugged his shoulders and sighed.

"People come and people go," Sam reflected.

"Like whores and wives?"

Sam's face dropped and I turned to walk to the door. I reached halfway across the shop floor when his squealing voice rang out, "Brae, wait!"

I turned around and watched as Sam scurried around the counter and came towards me, nearly knocking over a mannequin in his excitement. I hadn't seen Sam on the shop floor in years; he was perpetually glued to the counter stool, huddled amidst the familiar clutter of his hat boxes, newspapers and cigars. I was amazed by how small he was, a frantic midget, rushing up to me with the submissive eagerness of a slobbering dog. I stood like a giant, waiting for the prize, my arms crossed and feet apart.

"You need to find 'Rags' Levinsky. He hangs around Gropen's Pool Hall." He leaned in and looked up cautiously, "There you will find your answers."

Then the door opened, bells jingled and we both turned to see Agnes coming in, an overfilled bag of groceries under one arm. I quickly walked over, held the door open, smiled and walked out.

CHAPTER SIX

Idrove through the night, blinded by snow flurries that pelted my windshield and accumulated around the side-view mirrors. The dull wiper blades, which I had planned to replace months ago, pushed and tossed wet clumps of snow from one side of the glass to the other, offering only flashing glimpses of the road ahead. Headlights came at me with such nerve-wracking randomness that at times I wasn't sure which side of the road I was on. Such was an early winter snowstorm in Boston.

By some miracle of either good fortune or gut instinct I reached Charles Street at the foot of Beacon Hill and turned right, up the steep slope of Mount Vernon Street, my rear tires spinning on the icy slush. I tapped the gas pedal lightly to avoid fishtailing into the parked cars that lined the curb like boxcars of a freight train. More than any other night, I could not keep Ruth waiting.

I turned right, then left, then right again, gazing up to snow-covered street signs in an effort to blunder my way to her apartment. I reached a dark corner and rolled down my window to clear off the flakes and get my bearings but the nearest street sign was obscured by snow. In a fit of frustration, I slammed the car into drive and skidded over a corner, the Valiant jumping across the curb with a thud but no scraping of metal. I rolled down a small side street, as blank and featureless as the street-filled no-man's land that haunted my dreams. The windows of all the brick townhouses were completely dark, the only light being the faint glow of the gas lamps along the sidewalk. In the distance I saw traffic along Beacon Street and knew I was in the right vicinity. Suddenly my wipers hurled a clump of snow to reveal the sign of Ruth's street. I had arrived. I turned sharp right on to Chestnut Street and idled across the slippery cobblestone, waiting for her figure to appear on the stoop. Beneath the ray of a single street lamp, Ruth stood like a shivering maiden, patiently huddled under a thick wool coat, her handbag close by her side.

I slid to a stop and started to get out, intending to open the door for her, when she darted to the passenger side and hopped in.

"I love the snow."

"As long as you don't have to shovel it," I said.

"Don't be such a square. This is beautiful."

"What would you like to do?"

"Anything in the world."

I pulled out of the narrow maze of Beacon Hill and on to Beacon Street, driving south past the Boston Common. The frog pond was frozen over and occupied by dozens of circling ice skaters, hat-covered and giddy under the heavy falling flakes. The scent of Ruth's perfume refreshed the cigarette staleness of the Valiant and made me feel more alive. As we drove, she was silent but happy, staring through the steamy window to the world of white and light outside. I reached for the radio, thumbed through the channels and settled for the Everly Brothers, Let It Be Me. When I turned to Ruth for approval, she smiled and swayed her head to the rhythm.

"I've never skated," she said dreamily.

"No?"

"I am from California, remember?"

Without a second thought, I pulled over and parked. We got out and scurried across Beacon Street, wiping snowflakes from our eyes. I took Ruth's hand and together we walked into Boston Common, through the wrought-iron gate and down the paved trail that led to the frog pond. Ruth slipped and almost fell backwards but I caught her in my arms. She laughed girlishly and we descended a small slope, kicking up fresh snow and trying not to slip. Beside the frog pond was a skate rental both—fifty cents for an hour. I got two pairs and we sat on a bench to put them on.

"How did you know my size?" Ruth asked.

"It's one size fits all."

"Then why are yours larger?" she frowned.

"One size for guys, one size for girls."

We hobbled over to the ice edge unsteadily, holding each other up as if our combined lack of balance somehow equaled stability. In seconds we were sliding awkwardly over choppy ice, dodging other skaters and trying to turn with the contour of the pond. Ruth held me closer than ever, moving her feet like mine although I was really dragging her. Young boys flew past us, laughing mischievously and leaving clouds of snow dust in their wake. An elderly couple in dark full-length coats hissed at their naughtiness and then chuckled. Under the soft light of the wintry park, everyone smiled and laughed and frolicked like the world was just made.

Finally, Ruth and I collapsed to a bench, out of breath and sore from the hard leather of the cheap ice skates. As I took off one skate, she nestled close to me and I could feel her warmth through the layers of clothing. When I took off the second skate, she turned to me. Instantly we kissed, as shameless as newlyweds. The large flakes fell across our faces, melting on my cheeks, clinging to her eyelids. For a moment I felt as if I had been reborn in another time.

"Where did you learn to skate?" she wondered, wiping the snow from her eyes.

"Franklin Park."

"Oh? Where's that?"

"In Dorchester."

"Did your parents take you there?"

"Sort of…" I said hesitantly. "Let's go get a cup of coffee?"

"I don't know anything about you." Ruth said with a yearning curiosity.

"What's there to know?"

"You never mention your parents, your family. For all I know, you were married before."

"No, no. I was never married."

I leaned into the bench and stared out to the skaters. I had never been reluctant to talk about Korea, but I always recoiled from the memories of my youth. Unlike many vets, I could talk about the war with complete candor, retelling stories of midnight firefights, earth-shaking bombing campaigns, villages of starving children and the mutilated gray corpses of civilian victims. I could throw it on thick, with all the animation of an action cartoon. But when it came to my childhood, there was a mental block, a shadowy pasteboard of memories, vague and colorless, that began nowhere and ended at nothingness. I could recall a young child, toothless and muddied, running across the ice of the schoolyard, a hard-packed snowball splattering off the back of his neck while a group of boys laughed in the distance. There were scenes of birthday parties, Thanksgiving dinners, Easter pageants and even a Christmas show in a makeshift theater in some cold basement storage room. Some events were clearer than others, like the time a German house matron, stuttering insults in broken English, smacked my wrist with a wood cane for playing hide-and-seek in the corridors. Yet each scene was strangely disconnected, incongruent, and had all the detail but none of the sentiment. It was like I hadn't even been there. I wondered how I could ever explain this to Ruth.

As if awoken from a daydream, I turned to her and said, "It's a long story. Let's get coffee." As I moved to get up, she took my hand and stared at me, her eyes as still as glass.

"I have time."

We walked quietly across the Boston Common, through the Public Gardens, and crossed Arlington Street to the Four Seasons Hotel. Adjacent to the reception area was a restaurant with a small coffee room overlooking the Public Gardens. The moment we entered Ruth was struck by the luxuriance of the lobby, with its gilded fresco ceiling, crystal chandeliers and second-Empire décor. Couples in expensive evening attire walked past the concierge desk like dignified aristocrats. Many assumed that you had to be a dinner or hotel guest to even enter the building, but the restaurant and coffee room were open to all, regardless of position or pedigree. I urged Ruth along as she gazed starry-eyed at the opulence within. We took a comfortable seat by the window and a maitre de came over immediately. I ordered two coffees and a pastry and we sat snugly as white flakes whipped against the window.

"I want to know more about you," Ruth said, breaking the silence with a reserved smile.

"Ok, like what?"

"Um, how 'bout your family? Do you have any brothers or sisters. Have you ever been married?"

"...I already told you I've never married."

"Do you have any siblings?"

"Uh, no." I said plainly.

The waiter returned with our coffees and placed them on the table. When he walked away, I realized I was cornered, unable to deny or deflect Ruth's curiosity. I decided that if she needed to know who I was, where I was from, then I would let her have it, unrepentantly. I couldn't determine for her what was significant and what was meaningless about me. I wasn't scared to let her into the dark obscurity of my past but I also wasn't prepared for her sympathy. Every transaction had a price, however, and if Ruth was going to get the whole of me then I would get something in return.

I leaned towards her and with a mischievous grin said, "Why don't we finish the coffee and talk about this at my place?"

She giggled with a false modesty and rolled her eyes as if carefully considering the proposition. Then she smiled, kicked one leg over the other and said, "What will I tell my Mormon house mistress?"

"You lost your house keys."

As we lay in bed, I listened to the steam blow in and out of the cast-iron radiator and stared at the ceiling, imagining what it would take to scrape the peeling paint and refinish it. Whenever I had mentioned repairs to the landlord, he pointed to his mouth and pretended not to understand. Once, when I sketched out the issue with a dull pencil, he pointed to his eyes and mumbled something in peasant Greek. Cataracts, I assumed. It was ironic that I had been practicing the same selective silence with Ruth.

"When do I get what I want?" she whispered.

"I thought you just did."

She frowned.

"Take me to meet your parents?"

"I can't."

"Why not?"

It was her turn. I sighed and let the words tumble from my mouth like a reluctant informant.

"I don't have any parents. I mean, I have—or had—parents. I never met them. I grew up in the Home For Stray Boys in Roxbury. It's closed now."

"I didn't know," she said softly.

"How would you? I didn't tell you."

"I am so sorry," she added.

"It's ok."

"Do you have any idea who your parents are?"

"None. I don't even know how I got there. I pulled the records when I got back from Korea in '54."

"You were in Korea?"

"I'll get to that, if you'd like. Anyway, by that time the institution had closed. The records were transferred to the archives at the Commission of Public Health. I eventually found my record. Under the parents entry was 'unknown' and 'remanded to H.F.S.B., March 19th, 1934."

"You must be able to get more information than that," she said hopefully.

"I never pushed the issue. I figured if I was meant to know anything then it would someday be revealed."

"Sometimes fate needs a little coaxing," she smiled, running her fingernails through my hair, tickling the back of my neck. It might have been uncomfortable had I not been so completely relaxed. My legs and arms were still, my muscles so calm they lost sensation. As I stared to the ceiling I felt Ruth's heavy eyes, mascara-laden and piercing, watching me from the side. If it weren't for the tranquility of the moment, I would have fretted from self-consciousness.

"Fate is just the present moment," I mumbled drowsily, as my lids slowly closed and the soft warmth of her body lulled me to sleep.

Suddenly I awoke. The room was dark and silent and the cotton sheets beneath were damp with perspiration. I was strangely disoriented and overcome by a trembling confusion. On my lips, I felt the words, "more air, more air," repeated with the rhythmic persistence of a drumbeat. I looked to see Ruth crouched at the foot of the bed, the sheet pulled over her half-naked body, her eyes wide in a look that was part fright and part shock. I fell back to the pillow and rubbed my forehead with yawning frustration.

"Jody, what's wrong?" she moaned.

"I'm sorry. A bad dream. Are you ok?"

"Of course. You scared me."

She crawled back to the front of the bed slowly and cuddled near but not against me, her warm sympathy tempered by fear. When she put her hand on my shoulder, I shuddered.

"Jody, you are shaking. What's wrong?" she whispered sadly.

With a glowing gloss of sweat over my body, I breathed heavily and tried to calm down. I was discovered. In the safety of my isolation, the years of solitary nights in a small apartment, I was able to hide from friends and colleagues the source of my constant fatigue. Most probably assumed the black rings under my eyes and the perpetual yawn were from long work-hours and late nights. But now I lay exposed, shaking in agony, with nowhere to hide and no one to lie to. I turned to Ruth like a broken warrior and spoke as freely as if I had been thinking aloud.

"I have these dreams, sometimes."

"What kind of dreams?" she asked softly.

"I am running in the rain." Ruth listened silently. "I spot a woman in the distance. I run to her but she vanishes."

"What does she look like?"

I shrugged my shoulders. "I can't tell. Whenever I get close her face is a blur."

"Does she say anything?"

"No. The only sound is the rain. Thick rain. But soft, like a summer shower." I turned to her. "I am saying 'more air, more air.'"

"Are you suffocating?"

I sighed and began to think, trying to recall the images and sensations.

"I don't know."

"Can you breathe? In the dreams, I mean."

"I think. All I know is that I am running. They wake me up. I've had the same dream all my life, since I can remember."

"Dreams have meaning. Maybe they mean something you haven't figured out yet. Was there a woman in your life?"

"None." I said and Ruth smiled.

"We need to find out what they mean. Otherwise, they might continue to disturb you."

"Are you a shrink?"

"No," she chuckled, shaking her head. "But I studied psychology in college. I know that reoccurring dreams are the mind's way of seeking answers to unresolved questions."

"I have plenty of those."

The phone rang early the next morning and when I swiped my arm across the bed I felt the barren emptiness that had been Ruth. She was gone, left for work, and all that remained was the lingering scent of her, faded yet still tempting. When the phone rang a second time, its metallic bell sent a tingle up my back. It was the same electrifying jolt I experienced in Korea when a .30 caliber machine gun rattled nearby. I rose from the bed, naked and half-awake, and ran to the kitchen.

"Hello!?"

When the voice at the other end finished his short courtesy call, I almost leapt through the ceiling. Harrigan had come out of the coma, was conscious and responsive to people. I threw on some pants and a shirt, grabbed my coat and flew out the door. I raced to City Hospital through the melting snow of the late-morning sun. The city was sedate, lumbering under the inconvenience of the first snowstorm. I passed idling plow trucks, whose exhausted drivers sipped coffee and waited to end their night-long shift. When I reached the gate of the hospital, I pulled into the parking lot next to the main building and sprinted inside.

When the elevator opened to the fifth floor, I could hear commotion at the end of the hallway. There before Harrigan's room stood a crowd of men, all smartly dressed and chatting excitedly. I knew it was a gang of city officials, cops, well-wishers, reporters and likely a politician or two. Cameras snapped and flashes flashed as they hovered around the doorway to room C12 as if waiting to meet a foreign dignitary.

As I approached the room someone in the crowd hollered for everyone to step aside. I could only imagine the vision of me, disheveled and wearing yesterday's clothes, hobbling towards them like a man late for his own wedding. The bodies parted and I entered the room with a baffled demure. Inside, I nodded to familiar cops and stood with an uneasy grin as all eyes focused on me. I hadn't yet looked at Harrigan but I felt his presence. I feared the moment our eyes met, the entire circus would be real. I received congratulations from total strangers and a hearty pat on the back that startled me. The room was abuzz with the reckless cheer of a locker room after a winning game.

I scanned the room timidly. At the foot of the bed stood the Chief of Police, Darren Lovell. Broad shouldered and stout, his thick white hair suggested a man in his early sixties. He had hands the size of catcher's mitts that were plainly visible since he always stood with arms crossed. Surrounding Lovell was a collection of his top brass, an administrative official, his public relations man and two personal body guards who stood like bulldogs by his side.

I had known—or should I say 'known of'—Lovell since my early days on the force. He had a reputation as a ruthless public official and tyrant, depending on who you talked with. He had risen from street cop to the most powerful man in the city, excepting the mayor. Drawn from the slums of the South End, his record was far from clean and he escaped more than a few scandals throughout his career in public life, usually at the mercy of some willing fall guy. Rumors had long circulated that as he rose up the ladder his first priority was to expunge any record of his prior misdeeds. So although he never served, Lovell practiced the military technique of destroying ordinance so the enemy doesn't get it when you flee. By the time he made chief, even the press was hard struck to uncover any dirt from his thirty plus years in law enforcement.

I cringed at the hypocrisy of it all, since Harrigan's assault wasn't mentioned in the news and the administration had instructed detectives to keep the incident quiet. With the unspoken tension between Internal Affairs and the rest of the department, I understood the confidentiality. Any violence against an officer of my unit was unofficially assumed to be targeted or retaliatory. Yet there was something sinister about the fanfare surrounding Harrigan's recovery.

Lovell reached out a hand and extended a kindly welcome, his smile lingering just long enough for photographers to snap a picture. Rumors were that he was aligning himself for the ultimate prize, one that would ornament his illustrious career like a feather in a silk hat, the Mayoralty. There had been no formal announcement, no press release, no midday speech before supporters. Lovell was far too cunning for convention. Although the primary was still ten months away, he would leave nothing to chance. Lovell spent his days making friends and obliterating enemies with backroom deals, binding handshakes, threats and maybe a few suitcases full of cash. To the press he was a darling and to the underlying power structure he was a danger. In other words, Lovell was the perfect criminal.

"Welcome Detective. I am sure you are beside yourself with joy," Lovell announced, taking my arm and escorting me to the bedside. Although still on a breathing machine,

Harrigan's eyes were wide open. When he slowly turned his neck to look at me, I smiled and patted his shoulder. Sighs of sympathy erupted from the onlookers and for a moment I felt myself getting choked up.

"He's got a way to go, but looks like he's gonna pull through. Just like a member of my force," Lovell boasted. "How's about a photo of the detectives?" he added, waving his hands to direct our positioning for the picture. "Now, a hearty handshake and big smiles," Lovell continued as the photographer readied the lens. When I took Harrigan's hand, it was as cold and limp as a cadaver. But there was also a pulse and the subtle, desperate squeeze that cried out for life.

As we shook before the cameras, the flashes lit up an already bright room and I began to see spots. Holding the pose, I scanned the audience dizzily, feeling cramped, a tinge claustrophobic, and wanting nothing more than to finish my business and leave. It was then I felt something in the palm of my hand, an object so small and insignificant that at first I assumed it was just a piece of gauze or medical tape that had come loose. If we hadn't been forced to hold our pose for the twenty seconds of picture-taking, I might have simply let go. But when a photographer paused to change film I glanced down to Harrigan and saw in his eyes an urgency that transcended verbal communication. In a fleeting moment, his brow quivered and his still eyes darted, shouting to me in complete silence. I had lived long enough—been in enough grave circumstances—to know that a second was the difference between hesitation and action. So when the pose was done, when the last reporter got his day's pay, I snatched the paper from Harrigan's hand and stuffed it in my coat pocket. No one saw a thing.

With the ceremony over, I was no longer needed. I chatted with a few officials, thanked some newsmen and slipped out of the room. Once in the corridor, I made my way, quickly but discreetly, out of the hospital, taking the stairwell instead of waiting for the elevator—exiting through a side door rather than the front entrance. I rolled out of the parking lot, looking over my shoulder, waiting to be followed, as paranoid as a fugitive. I reached for my cigarettes, tearing open the pack and finishing two before the first red light. When I was safely distant from the hospital, I turned down a side street and pulled to the side of the road. I pulled my collar up and sat for five minutes, breathing through my nose, staring ahead and waiting for the right moment. When I felt safe, I reached into my pocket and took out the paper Harrigan had passed me. It was folded so tightly, wrapped so meticulously, it could have fit in a pen cover. I opened it gently, one layer at a time, as if dissecting an artifact of ancient parchment. Words slowly began to appear. As the short sentences, scribbled in pencil in large block letters, took form, I shuddered;

THEY ARE INVOLVED. I HEARD EVERYTHING. DON'T TRUST ANYONE.

I read it over and over and over again, trying to make sense of a message that was as cryptic as it was terrifying. I recalled the blank look of desperation on Harrigan's swollen face and knew he was right. The world was turned upside down. Everything I had imagined to be true and honorable was now in question. I felt as isolated as a star and sat frozen to the car seat for an hour until the cold outside began to penetrate and I was forced to move.

I drove through the narrow streets of the South End, thinking and smoking, trying desperately to gather my thoughts and settle my nerves. Since the day Jackson had sent me to investigate the Warren and Brunswick Street fires,

I sensed a hidden motive behind a fire epidemic that was plaguing the city with remarkable impunity. The signs of misconduct circled around like mischievous sprites, taunting me with half-crimes and vague inconsistencies. And like the womanly vision that came to me in dreams, they lingered hazily in the distance, tempting me onward, inviting me near and then vanishing the moment I closed in. My heart grew heavy and my head throbbed. I needed to eat.

I sat at a corner table in the headquarters cafeteria, half-heartedly chewing meatloaf and mashed potatoes, sipping black coffee. Every few minutes someone passed and mumbled congratulations on Harrigan's improvement. What was until recently the biggest secret in the department was now spoken about openly, as if everyone was willing to acknowledge the recovery but not the assault. I took my tray and started to walk towards the door when I felt a light tap on my back, the unmistakable softness of a woman's touch.

"Hello, Jody."

I turned to see Ruth, smartly dressed in a tartan skirt and wool sweater. The instant I saw her face, I knew she was upset. I should have told her about Harrigan's assault.

"Hi, Ruth," I said. "Listen, about Harrigan…"

"No need to explain…'

"It was classified until the investigation…"

"I said there's no need to explain," she added curtly, a forced smile breaking across her chin. The intimacy we shared in so short a period of time implied an openness and honesty that had been violated. Although I stood in the middle of the cafeteria, I had the strange sensation of being against a wall.

"I'm just glad he's alright."

Ruth looked down to the floor, tilted her head and there was a strained pause.

"Ruth, I…"

"Listen, I have to get back to work. I'll talk with you later…"

She strutted off through the doors, her heals clicking across the linoleum and her arms swaying with an improvised confidence. I looked down to my tray of cold meatloaf and potatoes and was repulsed. I put the tray down on a table and headed through the doors after Ruth, following the echo of her heels and catching up to her on the second floor landing.

"Ruth, listen…" I said, putting my hand on her shoulder. She stopped and spun around.

"I would have told you—confidential or not. I just needed a few more days…"

Her eyes were glossy, filling with tears as she stood with one hand clutched to the railing. Without a thought, I moved closer and put my arm around her back, pulling her towards me so abruptly that she lost balance and almost tripped on a step. She chuckled slightly and held me.

"I know. I am sorry. I would've just worried anyway."

"It hasn't been easy," I whispered.

She pulled away, wiping her mascara, and looked up and down the stairs, concerned as was I that someone might see us.

"At least he's ok. Now you can say you've had your picture taken with that ass Lovell."

"What? How'd you know that? He was at the hospital this morning."

"He came in with his entourage a little while ago—to see Jackson."

I was stunned. Lovell rarely, if ever, spoke with Jackson and any correspondence between divisions was done through formal memos or phone conversations between secretaries. Direct communication and friendly conversation would only give credibility to Internal Affairs, a unit that even the chief was hostile towards. With my arm around Ruth, we walked up another flight of stairs to her office. I gave her a quick peck on the cheek and headed down the corridor to Jackson's office. I reached to knock and the second before my knuckles hit the door, I heard:

"Enter Brae."

Jackson amazed me as usual with his awareness, as if his entire world was made of glass. I entered and shut the door. He leaned against the desk in a tweed jacket, holding his glasses in one hand and reading from a binder with the other.

"I understand Harrigan has pulled through."

"Thank God, sir," I replied.

"He's a fine detective and a good man. We don't know who did this but we're going to find out."

"I agree."

Jackson put the binder on the desk and walked towards me.

"Listen Brae, I don't know what Harrigan was hoping to gain meeting an informer in a dark alleyway. Alone, nonetheless. Between you, me and the walls, that was sloppy detective work."

"He met the guy at Church…"

"At the Mosque. A Nation of Islam mosque."

"Right," I frowned. "The guy had a big mouth. Implied it was arson. When Harrigan challenged him, the man said he could prove it."

"Did you know the Mosque has been closed since the fire? Being next door, it sustained some serious damage."

"I was told, recently," I said, somewhat embarrassed.

"Then who could Harrigan have possibly met if the Mosque was closed? The food pantry has been locked. Structural engineers only cleared it this week. We spoke with the minister. He's insisted none of his members have been there since the fire."

"I don't know who Harrigan met. All I know is he thought he had a lead," I said with uncharacteristic bluntness. I was irritable, cranky and unsettled. Before I could restrain myself, I blurted out, "Frankly Captain, I don't see how we can blame the victim."

Jackson was silent for a moment, his lips puckered, his eyes askance, as if trying to decide whether the boldness of my statement rose to the level of insolence. Luckily he judged men less on behavior than intention. He lowered his tone and spoke, his raspy voice cracking in the dry air.

"We are not blaming anyone, Detective. But I have a rash of building fires, possibly arson, possibly connected. I don't need any of my men being led into traps of their own making!"

I looked to the floor, made uncomfortable by Jackson's outburst and humiliated by my own.

"I understand, sir. When Harrigan gets out, I'll consult with him and make a full report."

"Speaking of reports, do you have a case update for me?"

"Not yet."

"Where did you get with the records I gave you? Have we found our 'A Cohen?'"

"I haven't had time to look through them."

Jackson walked back and leaned against the desk, immersed in thought and chewing the side of his glasses. Something troubled him beyond the obvious. He fretted more than usual, paused when he should have spoken and spoke when he should have been silent. He behaved with an air of uncertainty that made him appear ten years older than he was. For a moment I pitied him like I would a helpless grandparent.

"Listen, Brae" he said. "You've been through a lot in the past two weeks. I want you to take a break."

"But Captain..."

"I am taking you off the case."

"But Sir I..."

"This isn't open to debate," he said firmly. "I'll need your case notes, any contacts you've made, witnesses, etc."

I fought to remain straight-faced, to retain the self-composure of a professional before a superior, an instinct that had been bred into me in Korea but never challenged until now. Jackson was doing the unthinkable. I bit my lip and nodded, trying to appear indifferent while a firestorm of anger and distrust burned within. For the first time since joining the force, I felt like a soldier without an army, a solitary warrior with neither friend nor foe. The man I had come to love and respect like an uncle was now, to me, a turncoat. Whether or not Jackson was put up to this did not matter, since he had abandoned me nonetheless. I silently thanked Harrigan for his loyalty, for the one gesture of trust that let me know I was not alone.

"Furthermore, why don't you take a few weeks off, to get some rest. You're due a vacation."

I stood firmly and nodded with a soldierly obedience, while inside I protested with bitter disgust. For the remainder of our short meeting, Jackson didn't look at me. He concluded with some trivial details about the case, and then lied about a phone call he needed to make at 2:00 P.M.

"Let's talk in three weeks, shall we?" he ended, reaching for a black phone on the desk.

I said goodbye and left the room, giving a mock salute and shutting the door as gently as possible. In the corridor I had the urge to punch out every office window but I chose rather to walk with the calm dignity a cop on-duty. I smiled at everyone who passed and even winked to a couple of young secretaries. As I exited headquarters and walked through the parking lot towards the Valiant, I had the strange sensation of escaping a POW camp wearing a stolen uniform.

I got into the car, lit a cigarette and drove aimlessly for over an hour until finally I came to Blue Hill Avenue, Roxbury, that unseen magnet of my existence which constantly drew me towards it. The harsh sunlight of the winter afternoon highlighted the filth and decay of the urban despair. I stared through abandoned brick buildings, faded storefronts and vacant lots where litter blew freely in the wind. I spotted a dead dog, matted and famished, lying on a street corner like an exotic taxidermic doormat. Yet as repulsed as I was by what the city had become, I felt inextricably wedded to its misery and mystery.

I drove on and on, up and down streets, tracing and chasing the memories of my childhood. The sun grew dim, rush-hour traffic increased and the streetlamps flickered to life, one by one, as evening descended. I reached for a cigarette, the last one, from a pack that was fresh and new only hours before. Night was the loneliest time in Roxbury and Dorchester and the sidewalks were empty. I thought back to my youth when Blue Hill Avenue churned day and night with pedestrians, bobbing in and out of the mom-and-pop shops, lingering on the street corners like the world was one big family. Fruit carts had once lined Crawford Street and children played along sidewalks that were extensions of their own front yards. I wondered how it all could have vanished.

By the time I pulled into a service station at the corner of Morton Street, it was after ten o'clock. I bought a pack of cigarettes and leaned against the car hood in dreamy self-reflection. It was a quiet evening, still and dark, with an arctic chill and a few rogue snowflakes. I looked at the Valiant, my old friend, with a warm sentimentality. She was as tired and scarred as I was, with scratched fenders, rusted wheel hubs, a faded green roof and stained chrome fenders. But she carried on, as faithful as a German Sheppard. The Valiant had been with me since I became a detective one cold November day in '60, the same day Kennedy was elected. I was so thrilled with the promotion I ran to the first automobile dealership I saw and bought the first car I test drove. Since then, she was as committed as a friend but as temperamental as a woman. On a winter morning, it would have been easier to wake a hibernating bear than to get the engine started. Guys at headquarters joked that I could have hired a full-time chauffeur with the money I spent on repairs.

The quiet was shattered by sirens, roaring in the distance and getting closer. Suddenly two fire engines from the Mattapan station roared through the intersection and down Blue Hill Avenue. I flicked the cigarette, hopped in the car and sped off. The fire must have been a multi-alarm since the Mattapan firehouse exceeded its jurisdiction by crossing

Morton Street. When they reached Seaver Street at Franklin Park, the trucks turned sharp left. After two blocks, they turned right at Elm Hill Avenue and stopped so abruptly I hit the brakes, slid on ice and crashed into the curb, narrowly missing a telephone pole.

Dazed by the impact, I jumped out and stumbled towards the scene. Fire trucks, police cruisers and ambulances were parked in every direction, their doors open and emergency lights spiraling. In the foreground stood a massive residential building, four stories high and a half block wide, burning from all corners. Flames burst from the windows, illuminating the structure like an oversized jack o'lantern. From the sidewalk, firefighters pounded the building with hose water, creating white clouds of steam that blended with the smoke. Terrified neighbors watched from across the street, pointing at the blaze and screaming. Others looked away in tears.

When the wind shifted, thick black smoke flooded the street and sidewalk. I held the arm of my coat across my mouth but fell into a coughing fit. I fought through the smoke and flying embers, trying to get close but the heat was scalding. I fell back to a chain-linked fence, spitting up black mucous and wiping my eyes. I clutched the fence pole and gazed upon the scene like a witness of the apocalypse. Across from the inferno were the families and residents of the apartment building, huddled like cattle on the sidewalk. Through the smoky wind I spotted three little black children, half-naked, shivering and bewildered. A savage rage welled up inside me.

"Hey Brae, get away from this scene. You're out of your jurisdiction," a voice yelled.

I turned to see Prendergast, the fire captain I argued with weeks before on Blue Hill Avenue. He stood on the safe side of the street with two firefighters and a cop. They started to cross, coming at me like a pack of wolves, their eyes fixated, their mouths snarling. I clutched the fence and stood my ground. When they were halfway across, they were startled by a sudden shriek and so stopped and looked up to the building. It was an ungodly cry that rose above all the chaos and commotion. I had heard the sounds of human anguish before. In Korea the squeals of dying men were like the cries of a newborn; jarring at first but something you got used to. Yet I had never experienced a sound like this. I looked to see two figures crouched in a top floor window, their bodies flaming as if they had stepped out of a pool of lava. Their torsos smoked, their limbs shook and flesh dripped from their ears and elbows. Time seemed to stop and all movement ceased as the world watched these two hideous figures buckling on the sill, arm in arm, as fire lashed their backs. It was ghastly.

A lieutenant signaled frantically for the ladder truck to reverse towards the building but it was too late. Without warning, the two blackened images leapt from the window, fell forty feet and hit the pavement with a thud. Paramedics rushed over and firefighters doused the steaming bodies with water. They were dead, as lifeless as dirt, with their limbs bent and contorted like charred rope. With my hand to my mouth, I uttered a silent prayer to a god that wasn't there. I felt squeamish, dizzy, even nauseated, like a winter flu that comes on strong. For no reason, I turned and sprinted down Elm Hill Avenue with all my strength, past the fire, past the cops and firemen, into the dark safety of the side streets. I ran until I could run no more, then ducked into an alleyway and puked uncontrollably, yellow stomach acids sizzling on the icy pavement. I held one hand against the brick wall for stability while I breathed deeply to calm the convulsions.

"Hey motherfucker!"

Hunched over, I glanced up to see three black figures walking towards me. Their body language suggested they weren't there to offer assistance. I stood erect in agony, spitting chunks of vomit and panting. As they approached, they spread out as if to surround me. I moved back a couple of feet and the ray from a nearby streetlamp illuminated my face just long enough for them to see me snicker. For the first time in months I experienced the orgasmic joy of impending violence. In some perverse way I was grateful to them for the reawakening. They were nearly on top of me when I sprung to the side and kicked one in the testicles. He dropped like a dead elephant. As the two others moved in, I reached into my belt, whipped out the .38 and stuck it in their faces with the lever cocked. They stopped instantly, holding out their hands pleadingly and backing away. I waved the pistol side to side, in a wide sweeping motion, laughing like a lunatic and lusting for the opportunity to put a bullet between someone's eyes.

"Get the fuck back into the hole you crawled out of!" I shouted. "Go! Now!"

Immediately, they turned around and fled down the alleyway into the shadows.

I dusted myself off and walked a few blocks to Blue Hill Avenue as the snow increased and flakes began to accumulate on my hair and shoulders. I walked faster and faster until I was in a full sprint, running with no destination, past closed storefronts and dark windows. I thought of returning to the Valiant, but feared I had broken an axel or damaged the rim on the curb. After seven or eight blocks, I was struck by a strange amnesia. I couldn't recall what I had been doing before the fire or how I had gotten there. I was so confused that running seemed the only relief, the only barrier between sanity and madness. When I reached Dudley Square, a police cruiser darted across the intersection and pulled alongside me.

"Jody? Are you ok? What's going on?"

The driver was young and had the nervous, wide-eyed look of a rookie. I walked over to the cruiser and looked in to see McQuillan peering across from the passenger's seat, a cigar in one hand and bag of potato chips in the other. As I leaned in to speak, I realized I was holding my gun, having run over a mile with it in my hand. I cringed at such carelessness and quickly tucked it into my belt.

"You out pigeon shooting, partner? What's up?"

My mouth was frozen from both the cold and a dementia brought on by days of distress. I struggled to speak, each word and half-sentence coming out in a gasping stutter. It was a strange sensation of not making sense but being fully aware at the same time. McQuillan jumped out of the passenger door and came around towards me.

"Hop in Jody. It's cold out here," he said, taking my elbow and ushering me into the back seat. I collapsed on the vinyl and leaned back into the headrest. They drove onwards, through the quiet, snow-covered streets, passing midnight plows and an occasional car. After a few minutes, McQuillan turned and offered me some chips.

"No thanks Mac."

"What the hell happened?"

"My car broke down."

"Where were you heading?"

"Not sure. There was a big fire on Elm Hill Ave. Did you get it on the radio. Must have been three alarms, at least."

McQuillan looked to the rookie, who looked back and shook his head.

"No action tonight. You sure?"

"Of course I'm sure," I said angrily. "I was just there."

"Everything cool partner?" McQuillan asked with a wink. "Wanna go have a chat somewhere?"

"No Mac, just get me home if you could," I groaned.

"Where's home?" the rookie interrupted, looking at me in the rear view.

It was the simplest question but for the life of me I couldn't answer. My mind was a barrel of confusion, with images and emotions swirling like fireworks. The more I tried to focus on a complete thought, the more elusive it became. I was able to envision my apartment, Demetrius the landlord, even the other houses on the street but I couldn't remember my own address. I rubbed my head in frustration, searching for sanity and praying desperately for the episode to pass. When I looked up I saw both McQuillan and the rookie peering at me, waiting for an answer.

"Take me to Chestnut Street—Beacon Hill."

I felt the car accelerate and knew we were on our way. I lit a cigarette and cracked the window enough to let the smoke out without letting the snow in. We cruised through the city in silence, the only sound an occasional voice crackling through the static of the police radio. When we pulled down Chestnut Street, I was half asleep. The car stopped and McQuillan turned to me.

"Jody, here's my number. If you have any trouble, you need to call me first. Any trouble. You understand?" McQuillan said with emphasis, staring me in the eye as if trying to speak without talking. He handed me a piece of paper and I thanked him with a groggy indifference. I opened the door and stepped out on to the snow-dusted street.

"Call me," McQuillan said as the cruiser drove away under the humming streetlamps. I nodded and waved goodbye. When the car had turned the corner, I stood for a moment in the middle of the street. Everything was dead silent. Snowflakes floated down like the quiet ash of a nuclear winter, creating an eerie charm that was both comforting and frightening. I limped towards the front steps of Ruth's building and tapped the door knocker. After a minute, I heard the soft patter of footsteps coming down the stairway. When the door opened, I was relieved to see Ruth's face. I nearly collapsed in her arms.

"My God, what's happened?"

She put her arm around me and helped me up the stairs. I didn't say a word, only clung to her helplessly. When she brought me into her small rented room, I fell to the couch.

"You need to get out of these clothes. How did you get here? You smell like smoke. What happened?"

The questions burst from her lips like gunfire, each more difficult to answer than the previous. I tilted my head back and allowed her to undress me. Under the strain of exhaustion, both mental and physical, I was surprisingly unaroused as she peeled the sweat-damp clothes from my body, one piece at a time. When she went for my belt, I held one hand out and reached for the .38 with the other. Upon seeing the shiny steel of the barrel, Ruth recoiled. I checked the safety latch and placed it on the coffee table. She continued to tend to me, her soft hands restoring sensation to my limbs as she pulled the shirt from my back, the socks off my feet. I looked into her eyes with a drowsy gratefulness. Had Ruth not opened the door, I would have collapsed on the pavement and froze to death. But tonight she was my angel and as my eyelids slowly closed, I felt safe.

The next morning I awoke on the couch, naked and covered in a wool blanket. My neck cracked, back ached and my throat was raw from vomiting. As I scanned the room, Ruth popped her head from the bathroom with a white towel around her head. She smiled.

"Thank God you're alright. I was worried sick," she said, rubbing the sides of her head with the towel.

"Ruth. I am sorry."

She walked over and knelt beside the couch.

"There's no reason to be sorry. What happened last night?"

"I was at the fire. My car broke down."

"What fire?"

"Elm Hill Ave. It's gotta be in the paper. It was huge."

Ruth reached behind the coffee table and handed me the morning paper. "I flipped through when I got up. I didn't read anything about a fire."

"Of course you didn't."

"Are you sure you didn't have a nightmare?"

"Ruth, I'm not crazy. I was there."

She leaned in closely and kissed me on the lips. "I believe you. You smelled like a charcoal grille last night. I'm just surprised it wasn't in the news."

"I'm not surprised."

"What?"

"Ruth, something isn't right. I was taken off the case yesterday…"

"Oh, I am so sorry…"

"Don't be. Jackson thinks I need time to relax. But it doesn't make sense. There's a rash of fires no one is reporting. My partner gets bludgeoned in a setup—that also doesn't make the paper. When I finally get a lead I'm taken off the case?"

"It could be coincidence?" Ruth suggested, leaning over for one last kiss. She stood up and headed back to the bathroom. "I washed your clothes. They are drying on the rack in the bedroom. You should relax today. Are you coming into headquarters?"

"Don't know. I didn't ask if I was on administrative leave or a free vacation."

"Well, get some rest. We're both lucky. The house matron is away for two weeks. She's gone to Salt Lake City to visit friends."

Ruth grabbed her coat and purse and walked out the door.

The moment the cab turned on to Elm Hill Avenue I could smell the ash. The cabbie pulled up beside the Valiant and I got out. Squinting in the morning sun, I held a hand over my forehead and gazed at the brick shell that only yesterday was an apartment building. I knew then I wasn't crazy. The building stood like a dead giant, scarred and beaten, with streaks of soot like black blood smattered across every opening and along the roof's edge. The windows had already been secured with plywood, the midnight work of Drake & Stanton or some other disaster cleanup company.

When I walked to the passenger side, I was relieved to see the Valiant had nothing more than a dented rim. The tires were fully inflated and there was no sign of axel damage. I hopped in and started the engine when I was overcome by a feeling of being observed. I looked in my rearview and noticed a car parked along the opposite side of the street, a dark late-fifties Chevy Impala with out-of-state plates, probably Rhode Island. In the front seat two large figures sat unnaturally still. Exhaust vapors indicated an idling engine and made their surveillance obvious. The sun was at my back and in their eyes, so I could have turned the table and observed them for hours. Sunlight was that often overlooked advantage. In Korea we would advance only when the sun was behind us and even the most daring commander wouldn't dare send out a patrol at high noon.

Without taking my eyes of them, I levered the car into drive and pulled on to Elm Hill Avenue. An elderly driver stopped and waved me on. There is still some civility left in the world, I thought to myself. I nodded in thanks and drove down the road, waiting for the Chevy to take the bait and follow. By the time I reached the next cross street, they had pulled out and lingered a few car lengths behind in an amateur's attempt at stealth. I reached for a cigarette and punched the gas pedal. I was going to teach them not to tail a Roxbury kid on his own turf.

Without warning, I cut the wheel right and sped down a tree-lined side street. I raced around a yellow school bus and came to a stop sign at Warren Street. When I looked in the rear view mirror, the Chevy was lumbering towards me. I looked to the road ahead, then glanced back to see them tailing me by only a few feet. I turned left on Townsend Street, in the thick of residential Roxbury, and cruised down a road of tidy single-family houses. With a few rights and lefts, I found myself in a maze of narrow one-way streets with only a foot of clearance on either side. I came out to Harold Street and cut the wheel left, flooring the gas and leaving a cloud of burning rubber. Morning commuters, sipping coffee and clutching newspapers, looked up from every corner and bus stop. As I sped past a convenience store, two retirees waved for me to slow down.

The Chevy rode my bumper relentlessly, accelerating when I accelerated and swerving when I swerved. At the next stop sign I slammed the brakes and they skidded to within inches of my trunk. I came out to Humboldt Avenue, a wide road with plenty of room to maneuver. I reached for a cigarette, fumbling to light it while holding the wheel, when suddenly the Chevy sped forward, pulled along my passenger side and veered towards me. I went for the brake but hit the gas instead. Before I could change course, the car swerved and barreled into my passenger side. Ohhh, I shouted aloud. The thud of metal against metal knocked the wind out of me. My cigarette flew out the window and burning ash fell across my lap. The steering wheel spun out-of-control and I quickly yanked to the right to avoid plowing into oncoming traffic.

The Chevy kept apace, swerving wildly into my passenger side, blowing out the window and sending shards of glass and metal to the pavement. Oncoming traffic pulled over to avoid the mayhem. I heard the cries of startled onlookers and even watched a man turn and run across a front lawn. I was adrenalin-drunk, my senses heightened to a degree where everything was slow-motion. I observed the minutest details, the slightest sounds and the faintest scents.

I held the wheel steady and looked over my shoulder for a half-second. The driver was a heavyset black man, in his late twenties, maybe early thirties. His shoulders were so broad they pressed against the side door. He wore dark sunglasses that covered his eyes but not his stare. When our eyes met I noticed beneath his left eye, spread across his cheek like a bleach stain, a huge birthmark. As if suddenly exposed, the driver turned and slowed the car to escape my observation. He swerved again and crashed into my back tire. I felt the rear of the Valiant fishtail from the impact, a jolt that made my ears ring. By now, however, I had learned his pattern and knew his behavior so when he turned towards me, I turned away. Like an enraged beast, he swerved again and again and again, each time missing by inches. It was like teasing a child.

As we raced to the next intersection, side-by-side, the driver hesitated, looking away for a split second to mumble something to his accomplice. In that instant, I cut the wheel hard right and floored the gas. The Valiant chirped then smashed into his rear passenger door like a sucker punch. I watched as their heads snapped back and forth in unison. Before they could react, I turned left and sped down a side street while the Chevy, trapped by its own momentum, continued straight ahead.

I drove another few minutes, blowing stop signs, speeding down one-ways and spinning around corners, sometimes coming out to where I had started. All the while I scanned yards and alleyways, searching adjacent streets for the roof of the Chevy like a shark fin in water. Finally I stopped, convinced that they were gone or lost, abandoning the chase for another day. I was out of breath and sweated despite the cold air that rushed in through the shattered window. I leaned into the vinyl seat, unbuttoned my jacket and turned on the radio. It was the Beatles, "I'll Get You." I chuckled at the irony and glanced out to the quiet multi-family homes along the street. And there in the distance, beyond the far corner, peering through a cluster of homes and apartment buildings, sat a large sign whose letters I could faintly distinguish: Roxbury Home For Stray Boys.

CHAPTER SEVEN

The next few days were a hazy sequence of sleep, tea, television and more sleep. I had succumbed to a deep desperation that most would call depression. I didn't call anyone and I hardly ate. When the phone finally rang, it was the landlord, Demetrius, asking for help removing a water heater from the basement. I spent the next six hours squatted beneath a low-hanging ceiling, disconnecting pipes and adjusting valves as Demetrius looked on from the bulkhead. When I finally came out I was covered in ancient dust and the bronze smudges of rotting pipes. As repulsive as it was, my spirits had been lifted and I was ready to rejoin the world.

The following day I got up early and covered the broken window of the Valiant using clear plastic and tape. I used a tire iron to pull out the dented fenders, just enough to prevent them rubbing into the tire. The passenger side was hopelessly mangled from bumper to bumper, with pieces of trim, twisted and bent, dangling like exposed tendons. She was badly bruised but not beaten. When I rolled into Boston City Hospital, she limped over the pavement like a wounded animal.

I drove to the rear of the lot and parked so the damaged side was hidden by the hospital wall. I entered the front lobby, crept up the stairwell and tiptoed down the hallway to Harrigan's room. Compared to the media zoo of the previous week, it was eerily placid. I tapped the door open and looked in to see the long figure of Harrigan, covered from head to neck in a starched white sheet. Tubes dangled from his arm and the ventilator made a sucking sound every few seconds. The bed was reclined rather than flat, suggesting a patient in recovery. I smiled. Propped up, he looked more alive than dead.

Harrigan must have sensed my presence because the moment I entered his eyes flickered and his head turned. I rushed to his side, knelt down and stared into his bloodshot eyes. As I clasped his hand, his dry lips began to move. Before he could get the first word out, I was pulled away by the shoulder, a forceful tug that caused me to stumble into the breathing machine. I jumped to my feet and turned to engage when I saw a shiny badge and blue uniform. It took every bit of strength to restrain myself from knocking him to the floor. I stood breathless, enraged and snorting like a boxer.

"You're not to speak with Harrigan. Orders from the Chief."

I was completely astounded.

"Now leave before I call for backup!"

There was a soft groan and I glanced back to see Harrigan shaking in frustration. Either he was trying to warn me of something or he was urging me to obey the officer. As I straightened out my jacket, the cop walked around and stood between me and Harrigan, holding one hand out and placing the other firmly on his nightstick. As I stood still, my arms to the side, the cop began to hiss and shout like he was having a seizure. I tried to calm him when another cop burst into the room and reached for my arm. It was Rollins, the officer that had insulted Harrigan during my first visit. The blundering idiot tried to get me in a bear hug, but I moved side to side, dodging him like a playful matador before a dumb bull. The first officer then reached under my arms from behind but I smashed my heel into his boot. I felt the bones bend and crack beneath the leather. Rollins reached for his baton and

I charged him like a linebacker. My shoulder barreled into his ribcage and I pinned him against the wall. He groaned in agony. The impact shook the room and sent implements and instruments crashing to the floor.

Limping with a broken foot, the first cop leapt at me. At the right moment I spun Rollins around and their heads collided with a crack. The sound of bone against bone was jarring and even made me dizzy. As the two officers stood stunned, I made for the door and sprinted down the corridor while nurses and hospital orderlies looked on in dismay. I looked back and saw Rollins close behind, reaching for something in his belt, a pistol or nightstick, I couldn't be sure. I spotted an exit sign and dove into the stairwell, tumbling down the first flight before catching my balance. When I reached the ground floor, I exploded through an exit door and into the cold light of the morning sun. I was blinded by its glare.

Abandoning the Valiant, I ran through the lot, dodging parked cars and leaping over potholes, and stopped at the sidewalk. Hunched over and drooling from exhaustion, I scanned the lot but the officer was nowhere in sight. As if nothing happened, I turned and started down Harrison Avenue. I ducked into the first side street and slowed to catch my breath. My shoulder throbbed from the fall in the stairwell, my ribs hurt from the scuffle. I pressed my hand against the damaged parts to feel for broken bones. When I felt well enough to continue, I pulled the hood over my head and walked on. The cold wind whistled through the bare trees and dead flower gardens of the brick Tudor row-houses. It was a beautiful bleakness. Looking around, I reached into my belt for the .38 and unlocked the safety.

BOOK TWO

CHAPTER EIGHT

⁓

In the dream I was lost in a cold, barren place of empty streets. It was a colorless land of misty grays and shadows, illuminated by sudden streaks of light that faded as quickly as they came. The only sound was the patter of my feet against the pavement and the gentle rattle of the rain. On my lips I felt the words, repeated like a mantra, "more air, more air." What was I running from? Where was I running to? My heart pounded under my ribcage and my shoes sloshed in the puddles. I was breathless and thin, a scrawny beggar driven by terror, tempted by possibility. The moment I was ready to give up, to collapse face-first on the asphalt and drowned in the gutter, her image appeared in the distance like the flag of a rescue ship on the horizon.

A thin blue dress clung to her body like a wet veil, accentuating each curve and revealing the soft texture of her body beneath. Her white arms and legs were covered with goose bumps and her hair hung in long clumps of wetness. She beckoned to me, smilingly, and with gentle urgency. I ran to the vision with the unsteadiness of an epileptic, tripping on soaked shoelaces and stumbling every few yards. When I got close her face was a maddening blur. With arms outstretched, I leapt towards her but in an instant she was gone.

⁓

The morning sunlight warmed my face and my eyes flickered as I slowly awoke. I felt uneasy, calmly startled as the fleeting images of that dreamland faded and the dimness of reality set in. My neck ached and my body was covered in a cold and clammy wetness that caused a sudden chill. Huddled in a bed of damp weeds, I could barely move.

"You gonna eat that?"

A gruff voice called out and I turned to see someone looming above, arms akimbo and with a bearded face that peered down at me like a scolding father. I held a hand to my forehead and squinted to see. He was a shriveled old man, hunched at the neck and dressed in soiled rags. His wrinkled face suggested a man in his early seventies. With a winter tan and yellowed teeth, he appeared nothing more than a harmless vagrant. As I sat up, I looked around and recognized the place instantly. I turned to the old man with a subtle sneer.

The brick watchtower on Fort Hill had the warm familiarity of a child's tree fort or secret hideaway. Situated at the crest of Fort Hill, it was the highest point in Roxbury and from it could be seen the entire city, harbor and beyond. I had come here with Marty Mirsky many, many years before. During the hurricane of '38, with the entire institution on lockdown, I pried through a hole in the fence, met up with Mirsky and together we escaped to Fort Hill. The streets were empty as we skipped across overflowing gutters and climbed the muddy grass precipice which led to its tower. High winds lashed our faces and anything not tied down flew in tornado-like circles through yards, streets and lots. Mirsky hoped that we might spy the eye of the storm. We huddled together at the base of the tower and looked out to the misty city and imagined the furies of heaven. We felt like kings that afternoon.

"If you ain't gonna eat it, I want it," the old man said, pointing to the ground beside me.

I stood up, dusted myself off and struggled to recount the previous night. It was bitter cold and my bones cracked with every movement. I felt something at my feet and looked down to see a green duffle bag with black stamped lettering; JOSEPH H. BRAE. And beside the bag, nestled in the dead grass was a half-eaten sandwich wrapped in tin foil.

"It's all yours," I uttered.

The old man reached over and took the sandwich. I grabbed the green bag, nodded goodbye and walked away. I reached the edge of the small park that encircled the watch-tower and laid the duffle bag on a rock. There I stood motionless, gazing out across the city, as immovable as the structure behind me. Below, a continuous stream of cars and trucks raced along Columbus Avenue, beeping, swerving and spewing exhaust in the rush-hour frenzy. The sun was excruciating; the wind relentless. I felt like the battered ensign on a splintered mast, idling across an ocean of solitary endlessness. It was a loneliness I knew too well.

I thought back to that brisk night many years before when, having returned from Korea in one piece, I landed at a dock in San Francisco to a half-hearted welcoming parade of hobbling veterans and mothers of KIA's. There were no photographers, no politicians. Americans were sick of war and had grown tired of welcoming home heroes. The Second World War had given the country its fill of rallying optimism and righteous outrage, the result of half a decade of destruction and a half million body bags. No one cared about a tiny peninsula on the other side of the world.

So when I stepped off the gangplank the night of my return and wandered into the dusky streets by the docks, I was struck by a strange disconnectedness from all things. I had forgotten how I got there, my standard-issue field jacket offering few clues other than my name and even that I questioned. I staggered through the shadows of dark streets as whores and swindlers called out to me. When a street cop asked if I needed help, I took off running like an outlaw. The lights, sounds and scents of an unfamiliar city circled around in a dizzying mash of disorder as I slipped gently into madness. Finally I came upon an alleyway beside a corner diner and collapsed next to a dumpster, tears pouring down my cheeks, my lips quivering like a dying fish. I felt like I was slipping off the edge of the world.

Now that same dank desolation had returned and I again found myself running through the world like a naked child, with no past and no present. Thoughts, images and emotions swirled chaotically in a mind that had become a broken machine, short-circuited and misfiring. One moment I shook from rage and the next I was as numb as a block of wood. The only thing I was sure of was that I had to get to Ruth. She was the one absolute, the one person I trusted and the only one who could save me from myself and the world.

"Everything alright soldier?"

Startled, I spun around to see the vagrant behind me, his bony hands up high and approaching with the nervous caution of a surrendering combatant. My fists were clenched and I snorted like a boar. One wrong move and I would level him. But as we stood facing each other, he reached into the pocket of his overcoat and held out the crumpled sandwich. I was suddenly shame-filled and looked down at the grass, shaking my head.

"No thanks. Just trying to sort some things out."

Despite his civilian rags, I knew the man was a soldier. I didn't have to ask when he served, which branch of the service, or if he had earned a purple heart. I didn't need to hear his life story. A soldier's voice was unmistakable and had a soft humility, a faint sadness that only someone who had experienced the horrors of warfare could detect. He could have been at The Marne, Normandy or even Inchon. The war was a detail, the plight was timeless.

"You can't give up that easy soldier," he said, reaching down for the duffle bag, "you still have miles to go."

Beneath the tangled beard, his smile was hidden yet visible like a fawn in the woods. He held the bag out to me and I took it. I patted the old man on the shoulder, smiled and walked on.

"Don't give up the fight," he shouted as I scurried down the side of the hill.

I made my way to Columbus Avenue and flagged down the first cab. When I reached Ruth's apartment building, I lingered on the front steps, unshaved, disheveled and covered in moldy dirt. I hesitated then tapped the knocker. Within seconds I heard feet descending from within. As the door opened, there was a muffled cry.

"Jody, what happened?"

"Ruth, I am being hunted." I said gravely.

She put her around me and ushered me into the hallway. When the warmth hit my skin I began to shiver.

"My god. Jody, you are freezing."

Ruth stood beautifully in a long yellow bathrobe, her hair still damp from the morning shower. She smelled of fresh soap and her eyelashes were bunched together from wetness. It was hard to imagine Ruth without makeup and perfume. And seeing her so unadorned was like seeing her stripped down to her essence. She was raw, natural and sensual. She took my arm and helped me up the stairs. When we got to the apartment, I threw the duffle bag to the floor and collapsed on the couch.

"I went to see Harrigan, they…"

"Who are they?"

"The cops—the ones guarding his room. They have orders from Lovell. I can't see Harrigan."

I gasped with each word, overcome by exhaustion and fever. With each passing minute my body grew colder and colder. My teeth rattled as I spoke. Ruth ran into the bedroom and came out with a white wool blanket. As I tried to explain, she stood over me and listened, her lower lip curling, her face wide with worry. I spoke hysterically, blurting out half sentences and stumbling over words like a frightened child recounting a nightmare. Ruth was silent. With her eyes averted and head tilted, she gazed towards the kitchen wall with a tortured expression of sadness, confusion and regret.

"What?" I asked.

"There are rumors."

"What kind of rumors? What do you mean?"

"I don't believe them…"

"Ruth, tell me!" I shouted. "Shh," she said, holding a finger to her lips. She paused and then continued. "I was told you went to the hospital and attacked two officers."

"That's absurd!"

"You tried to pull out Harrigan's breathing tube and IV."

"Oh my God," I blurted out in a hushed cry.

"You tried to pull out your gun. The officers stopped you."

I put my head back into the couch and ran my fingers through my hair. I felt the urge to jump up and start smashing things. I wanted to put my fist through a wall. I stomped my foot on the floor; the lamps and bookshelf shook. But I couldn't let my actions validate the lies. I had to control myself or the anger would kill me. Exasperated, I held my arms out and faced her.

"Ruth, do you think I'm crazy?"

Tears filled her lower lids like the water in a half-empty glass. Her arms were crossed tightly, defensively and she stared down to the carpet, tapping one foot and shaking her head back in forth as if torn between disbelief and uncertainty. I waited for a response.

"No, Jody, I don't. But…"

"But what?"

"When you came by last week. You said you were at a fire?"

"Yes, I told you that!"

"People are talking. They say that you are suffering from mental illness; that you are obsessed with fires…"

I jumped up from the couch, took her by the shoulders and shouted, "What? That I am starting these fires?"

Ruth backed away and wept openly.

"That you've been spotted recently, that you show up at the scenes acting strangely," she cried, waving her arms around and gasping with each word.

All I could say was no, no, no as she hysterically recounted the gossip and lies she had been told. I circled around her as if trying to dodge the words, each revelation stinging like the hot pierce of a needle. I felt defenseless and wilted as I watched the last person I trusted lash me with skepticism, pummel me with doubt. In an instant I was a young boy, huddled in the corner of the institution yard, sobbing from the gut-wrenching barrenness of abandonment. I was sick to my stomach and had I not kept moving about the room, I would have collapsed.

But then suddenly the shouting ceased. The room became so quiet I could hear the buzz of the lamp. Ruth and I stood still and facing each other, eyes averted, knees buckling, only feet away but miles apart.

"Do you believe them?" I whispered. "Do you?!"

Tears trickled down her cheeks and she panted for air, drowning in the torment of her own ambivalence. She reached for me but I backed away. She walked towards me but I took her wrists and held her back. I fell back to the couch, seething, and stared out the window at melting icicles that hung from the gutter. Ruth stood in her bathrobe, her eyes pressed closed, her sobbing reduced to short spasms. I was suddenly calm.

"I don't know what to think, Jody..."

"Give me a few days," I pleaded quietly. "I need to stay here."

With her forefinger and thumb, she pushed the tears from her eyes while nodding continuously. I reached for her free hand and held it close.

"Someone is trying to silence me. I don't know who's involved. I don't know the motive. But I know it involves the department. There's no other explanation."

Ruth was still nodding when I pulled her to the couch. I put my arms around her and felt tremors throughout her body. We sat in an embrace for several minutes, quietly, the only sound the lamp, the traffic and the gentle lapping of our breaths as they gradually returned to normal. Then Ruth looked up and into my eyes.

"I am with you," she whispered and I pulled her closer.

"But you can't tell Jackson or anyone else you've seen me. You don't need to lie. Just don't mention anything until I have more information."

She nodded smilingly and pushed the last tear from her eyes. Curled beside me with her arms limply by her side, I shuddered at her beauty and was at once renewed. As I let her go, she looked at me one final time.

"I love you. Please don't get hurt."

I sat frozen, my mouth agape and clinging to the cushion. But before I could reply, she hopped up and rushed into the bedroom to finish getting dressed. There I waited, pasted to the couch and staring at the walls. The desperation of the morning, in all its homeless isolation, vanished with three short words. It was the best and worst day of my life.

I had no memories of anyone ever saying they loved me, especially a woman. There had been brief bouts of imagined love, whispered or shouted under white sheets in a drunken stupor. But with Ruth it was different. I was torn by a strange mix of sadness and joy and a vague guilt at having brought someone into my dark and twisted life. Now that I was in danger there was a sense of urgency about our relationship. Maybe she was trying to give me a boost, hope, or a reason not to throw in the towel.

Ruth stepped out of the bedroom like a Moroccan princess, dressed in beige from head to toe; a beige skirt, beige blouse, beige stockings and beige stiletto shoes. She paused in the bedroom doorway and looked at me, her head tilted and smiling bashfully. I rose from the couch out of politeness.

"I'm going to shower and go see some people. Is there a rear exit?" I said.

"Go to the end of the hallway on the first floor. Please be discreet. If anyone asks, say you're visiting from Utah."

"I'm not sure I can fake Mormon," I said with a smirk.

"You'll be fine. Just don't let anyone see you smoking or drinking coffee…"

Ruth reached for her purse on the coffee table.

"There're eggs in the refrigerator. Coffee and tea in the cabinet. I should be home around 5:30."

Before she walked towards the door, I took her hand and kissed her on the cheek.

"You don't know how much this means. Thanks."

She leaned in and kissed me on the lips. Without another word, she took her coat and walked out the door. I listened to her footsteps as she descended, heard her heels click as she walked out the front door. The smell of perfume lingered and I imagined her lovely figure strolling along the cobble stones as she made the half-mile journey to headquarters. I kicked off my shoes, laid on the couch and tried to gather my thoughts. My mind raced in a flurry of frustration and confusion. In moments I fell into a deep and unrecoverable sleep.

When I awoke the room was pitch black and for a moment I forgot where I was. I glanced over to a clock on the mantel, the moonlight cresting through the back window just enough to make visible the hour and minute hands: 5:32. She would be home any minute, I hoped. I reached for a small lamp in the corner and twisted the switch. The room was illuminated by a soft glow and as I looked around, I observed, as if for the first time, all the things that comprised Ruth's world. A ceramic teapot on the stove was painted with a courtesan kneeling before a blushing maiden in what I imagined to be a thistle in some Medieval English forest. My eyes continued to sweep the room with an almost sentimental curiosity. On a chair beside the kitchen window hung a purple woolen scarf, partially frayed but carefully folded. To the left of the window was a framed black and white photograph—Ruth and some friends—smiling on a snow covered peak, their eyes squinting in the sun, in what I guessed was a college trip to the Swiss Alps, or perhaps the Rockies. All these little artifacts, most which wouldn't fetch a few cents at a second-hand shop, were pieces of Ruth. And just being among her things, I felt mysteriously close to her despite her absence. I turned to the side, burying my head in the cushion, when my eyes caught the front cover of the morning Herald. I felt the world erupt inside when I observed a small headline, beaming in bold, black print;

LABOR UNIONS ENDORSE CHIEF LOVELL FOR MAYORALTY

I reached for the duffle bag on the floor, pulled out a wrinkled pair of pants and a shirt and changed furiously. In seconds I was creeping out the back door and into the moonlight of the frigid night. I thought back to Sam's last word—Levinsky. The name was meaningless, as generic as a character in a Cagney film, but I would seek him out and make him significant even if he wasn't.

When I got off the trolley in Mattapan Square, it was like disembarking at a foreign port. The last stop within city limits, the area was the Jewish Boston version of Times Square. Dignified couples strolled along the avenue, mischievous boys lingered on corners and hungry patrons packed into a well-lit diner, warming up with a bowl of clam chowder, coffee and a good yarn. I hadn't been down this end of Blue Hill Avenue in months, possibly years. Being stationed at headquarters, I never had reason to visit the outlying neighborhoods of Boston.

Mattapan kept to itself. Having one of the lowest crime rates, it was the golden child of the city, good schools, good neighbors and a damn good assignment if you were a patrolman. Many would beg to work this precinct, but it was mainly reserved for older cops who were biding their time. And since Mattapan was the last stop before the leafy suburbs of Milton and beyond, it was a fitting metaphor for officers who had reached the end of their careers and had one foot in the lush lawns of retirement bliss.

But there was a darker side. Mattapan was the last neighborhood along Blue Hill Avenue that was predominantly white and Jewish. Although most walked around like it was still 1940, you could sense a restless uncertainty as residents quietly gossiped about how long it would take for the black ghettoes just north to spread to Mattapan. As muggings became more commonplace and the tenement fires nearer, residents suffered the gradual loss of the safety and stability of their little ethnic sanctuary. And much like Parisians on the eve of the German invasion, they celebrated life with bittersweet abandon.

I walked past the shops and stores, a few blocks up the avenue, scanning the names from side to side. Mattapan Square was a self-contained world, with butcheries, grocers and kosher delicatessens. There was an old Oriental theatre, reminiscent of Vaudeville, and a small hotel that offered monthly rates. When I reached the end of the block, I came to an intersection and saw on the opposite corner, shining in muted yellow neon, Gropen's Pool Hall. The building consumed an entire city block and was so rundown that at first glance it appeared closed-down or vacant. Dried weeds covered the property and what could be seen of the painted brick façade was weathered and peeling. I waited for the last car to pass and then crossed the intersection.

I pulled the handle of the front doors and they were locked. I leaned over and peered between the cracks but there was no light. Crouching in the shadows, I followed the side wall of the building towards the back and crawled down a small knoll that led to a parking lot with a dozen automobiles. It was dark and quiet, the only light being an occasional car passing along the street above. I spotted a rear door, cracked open and emitting a smoky light. Within I heard the muffled sounds of laughter and music and the rattling of glasses. I shimmied along the back wall towards the door like a prowler when suddenly it swung open. I dove back to avoid being hit and ducked into the bushes. I held my breath as two men swaggered out, either drunk off wine or consumed by arrogance. They wore long dark overcoats and hats pulled down over their ears and eyes. They walked halfway across the parking lot and stopped beside an automobile, speaking in low tones and smoking cigarettes in short, fitful drags. The taller one did most of the talking while the other nodded.

As I waited, headlights from a passing car burst across the lot and there, as plain as the moon, stood Rollins, his pug nose and wide forehead illuminated like a clown's face. As I recalled our scuffle at the hospital, I reached to my belt and caressed the .38. A battle on conscience erupted within as I alternated between discretion and revenge. If it weren't for Ruth I would have leapt from the hedges and unloaded the revolver into his head and chest, ending my plight, my career and possibly my life. Yet something kept me grounded long enough for Rollins to hop in the car and race out of the lot and into the night. The other man lingered for a few minutes, finishing a cigarette and looking around. When he turned in my direction, I thought he had spotted me crouched against the white brick wall, poorly concealed behind leafless bushes. But then he too flicked his smoke, got in a car and sped off.

I stood up and brushed off my overcoat. I reached into my coat pocket, grabbed a cigarette and walked to the rear door. It opened with a creak and I walked inside. The first thing I noticed were pool tables, dozens of them, lined across the room and all in use. They were old, with faded felt beds and worn leather pockets. But their condition didn't discourage the men who gathered around them like roulette tables, sipping bourbon from tumblers, smoking cigars and calling bad shots. Along the wall to the right was a long, hand-carved bar, stacked to the ceiling with bottles of cheap liquor. Counting the bartender and waiter there were perhaps two dozen men in the room, but not a woman in sight. I was surprised when no one looked up and so I stepped over to the bar like a regular.

"What can I get for you, partner?"

A short and plump man in his forties looked up from behind the bar. He had a fat, friendly face and a gut that bulged through his white apron. His thinning black hair was slicked back with either hair grease or the perspiration from long hours pulling taps and shaking drinks. A patron at the other end of the bar yelled for a drink.

"I need a glass of water and Levinsky."

The bartender looked down hesitantly, fumbling with a couple of glasses and wiping the counter with a towel. He seemed suddenly ill-at-ease, as if busying himself with small tasks to delay a response.

"You can have one or the other," he said peering up with a forced grin.

"I ain't too thirsty, brother."

"Who's asking for Levinsky? You a cop?"

"I'm not sure."

He gave an ironic look then did an about-face and reached for a phone on the wall. I tried to listen but the noise of pool sticks and half-drunk laughter was distracting. I tried to watch his lips, but he held the receiver to his mouth with a cupped hand. After a few words and a few nods, he placed the phone down and turned to me.

"Go through there and up the stairs."

The bartender pointed to a door at the back of the hall next to a cigarette machine. I nodded in thanks and walked away. Although only thirty feet, the door seemed miles away and I felt strangely self-conscious, almost frightened, by having to pass so many dark and unfamiliar faces. Someone in the room had to have known me. Gropen's was too clean to be a criminal hangout, too obvious, but it had an unsettling atmosphere and the patrons seemed a little too cute. They dressed and acted as stereotypical locals, out for drinks after a long day driving a cab through slushy streets or scalping tickets at the Boston Garden. Whatever my reluctance, leaving would have aroused more suspicion than continuing on.

I took a deep breath and started across the floor, maneuvering around pool tables like crossing a minefield. I kept my head down and my pace up and looked straight ahead. A few faces looked over through the cigar smoke. I felt the stare of one player as he leaned across a table with his cue poised perfectly. Crack! Some players cheered while others moaned and I heard the unmistakable sound of money changing hands. It wasn't the first time I was saved by a good shot. Relieved, I walked the last few steps to the door.

I glanced back once and then opened the door. I climbed a narrow staircase and stopped on the second floor landing before a large metal door. The sounds from the pool hall faded and were replaced by voices from within the room. I reached to my belt and felt the grip of the revolver. It was my one escape ticket if things went wrong. I paused for a moment, thought of Ruth and opened the door. The tension vanished instantly as I stood before three old men, smoking cigars, sipping Brandy and passing cards around a small table. A single light hung from the ceiling, just above their heads, and shone down upon a pile of crumpled ten and twenty dollar bills.

Not one of them looked up. I waited in the doorway, watching with the safe curiosity of someone looking through a one-way mirror. They played furiously, their eyes fixated on both the cards and the cash that each coveted secretly. Two of the men sat to the left and right of the table while the third was plopped in the center, facing me and hunched over. He was plump, perhaps sixty-five years old, with a bald head that shone like a cue ball under the dangling lamp. He had unusually broad shoulders for a man his age and he sat so firmly that I wouldn't have been surprised if he stood up and was a giant. He didn't blink and he barely moved, grasping his cards with powerful hands that bulged with veins and muscles. They were gray and subtly frail, like an old man's, but had the lingering strength of a retired stone mason or dockworker.

The old man was motionless, the only expression a slight quiver at the corner of his upper lip, an ironic smirk that indicated neither win nor loss but only the intention to keep on playing. I hoped he would look up, but he never did. As another hand was dealt I admired him like an ancient statue, measuring and marking each wrinkle on his face, noting the movement of each eye. He was unreadable, a hulk of mystery, with an expression that revealed nothing but suggested all. He was undoubtedly the boss.

The other two sat like minor characters in a Shakespearean drama, artificially placed to enhance the tension, to further the plot. If only I knew what role I played. The longer I stood the more the scene felt remotely reminiscent. It was a vague déjà vu, the feeling I had been there before although I knew I hadn't. As the silence and stillness of the room persisted I hoped for someone to move, to make a sound, to acknowledge me with an insult. I felt like I was on display.

"Have a seat young man," the old man grunted, not taking his eyes off the card. As I walked slowly towards the table, the wood floorboards creaked. I took the empty seat, opposite the old man, and sat. Still, not one looked up for a moment and I felt like a welcomed ghost, present but unobservable.

"What can we do for you?"

"I'm looking for Levinsky."

"How do you know?"

I squinted in confusion.

"Pardon me?"

"How do you know you're looking for Levinsky?" The old man looked up for the first time. His glossy yellow eyes peered at me through the cigar smoke and I got a sudden chill. Then he looked back to his card hand.

"I've been told he can help me solve a riddle," I said coolly, leaning back into the chair, spreading my shoulders.

"A riddle or a crime?"

"Is there a difference?"

"A crime can put you behind bars. A riddle can haunt you." he said, blowing smoke through his hands and slapping two cards on the table.

"If I can solve one, I will. If I can solve both, I will."

"Well, young man. You can have one or the other."

"I'm hardly young."

"You were once, Brae."

When he spoke my name I was suddenly dizzy. I gripped the chair seat and clenched my teeth. The desperation of recent days had tricked my senses. Exhaustion had lulled me into a hallucinatory semi-stupor. I imagined things that weren't there. Was I dreaming? But I had long before learned to trust my senses in the same way pilots favor instrumentation over the disorienting haziness of their own perception. The smoky stillness of the room taunted me like celestial solitude. I felt a sudden urge to jump from the chair, spin around and run. But something kept me fixed.

"I was never young, my friend. I was a child. Never young," I said.

"You've made a remarkable success of yourself."

I looked down to my filthy, wrinkled shirt and pants. "If you call this success."

"You've been tidier. But you've been more soiled, Brae."

One hand held the cards and the other was pressed against his chin as he sat deep in thought. The other two men were expressionless, almost lifeless, except for an occasional exchange of cards, cash and cigar smoke.

"How would you know my habits?" I said.

The old man chuckled, the first sign of emotion I had observed. "I know a lot about you. You were an Eagle Scout. You begged your overseers to let you join. You walked three miles to the nearest troop meeting, sometimes in the rain. The Knights of Columbus in Mission Hill, if I'm not mistaken."

I froze. I wanted to speak but couldn't. I stared at the far wall like a monk, my mind blank and body numb as if trapped in a daydream. The old man continued.

"You joined the Marines. Went from Private to Lieutenant in the time it takes most to finish boot camp. You saved your platoon in Korea. Ran across a frozen field, overtook a Goryunov and blew your attackers to pieces. Got a battlefield promotion to captain, right?"

My eyes grew heavy, the words were hypnotic. I could do nothing but listen.

"When you joined force, you went from street cop to detective to senior detective in four years. A mighty accomplishment, I'd say."

Levinsky summarized my life like a broadsheet obituary, noting the achievements, omitting the failures. Although I had known him only a few minutes, I resented him more than anyone I had ever met. He was vile and hunched, like a crippled ox. I flexed my arms and legs, took back control of myself and my name and lashed out.

"I don't measure myself by ranks Levinsky."

"Don't discount your accomplishments, young man. The ranks of Jody Brae make Eisenhower look like a meter maid."

When Levinsky chuckled, the others laughed too.

"What do you want from me?"

"You came to me, remember?"

I held my breath and crossed my arms. "I need to know who's burning down Roxbury."

The man to my left raised an eyebrow; the other blew smoke from his nostrils. Something had startled them both.

"How would I know anything about fires? I don't even light my own cigars," Levinsky said, looking to the others.

"I was told you know something about everything that goes on in this town."

"I am sorry…"

"Don't bullshit me! I've travelled a hard road to get here. I ain't leaving without some information."

Levinsky was suddenly offended. His gentlemanly calm turned to outrage in an instant. He dropped the cards and pounded the table with his firsts, sending a few bills floating to the floor. The other two men stopped the game. Levinsky looked at them, waved his hand and they continued playing as if nothing had happened.

"Look here Brae! Don't come here and start giving me orders. This is my business."

"Someone is torching Roxbury. That is my business."

"Take your business elsewhere. You've no customers here!"

I got up from the table and looked down upon Levinsky. He picked up his cards and focused on the table, ignoring me entirely. One of the men collected the cards, shuffled the deck and started to deal a new hand.

"People are homeless Levinsky. There were children shivering in the snow, watching their god damned home burn to the ground."

Levinsky dropped his cards for a second time. He took his cigar and stamped it out on the table, the ashes falling to the floor. His jaw tensed up and he gazed at me with a burning fierceness. The tendons in his neck pulsated and he spoke without moving his teeth. I had awoken a sleeping lion.

"Listen to me Brae and listen carefully. In ten years all the old Jewish wards will be black ghettos. The shvartzers are slowly coming down Blue Hill Ave, devouring everything along the way like a filthy lava stream. Look what they've done to Dudley Square. When my parents came over from Lithuania, my father worked two jobs. We lived in a coldwater flat. But we had dignity, class."

"You saying people don't have dignity because they're poor?"

"I am saying they reap as they sow! If they want to turn half the city into a stinking wasteland, they won't do it at my expense." Levinsky stopped abruptly, as if his anger had overcome his senses. "Look at Andre," he said, nodding to the man on his left. "He spent his entire life in Roxbury. His folks are in their eighties. They were attacked last year by a gang of black thugs. His mother's hair was pulled out for God's sake!"

Andre nodded. There was a knock at the door and the bartender poked his head in.

"We need Cohen and Rolfe downstairs." Levinsky looked up, mildly disturbed, and waved one hand in the air. The two men dropped their cards, got up and swaddled out the door like obedient ducks.

"Take a seat Brae, you make people nervous."

"How the fuck do you know me?"

Levinsky was silent.

I continued, "Connections in the force? Pull my records? Track down an old girlfriend, perhaps? "

"That would be a tough task," he said sarcastically. "You yourself said I know something about everything. Maybe they were lucky guesses. And watch your mouth. Your parents would be ashamed."

"I don't have parents. Don't you know?"

"Everyone has parents, Brae. Even you."

"Nope." I shook my head, side to side, defiantly.

"Then who gave you your name?" Levinsky asked.

"You tell me."

I was unsettled, quivering, and the room swayed in large thrusts and heaves like a ship's galley. Yet Levinsky sat unmoved and unmovable, his vast hulk the center of that little universe around which all things orbited, towards which everything was drawn. His magnetism was inescapable. He spoke with the authority of a Talmudic prophet, retelling my past and foretelling my future. Had I the strength I would have leapt over the table and gouged his eyes out, slew the dragon. But my armor crumbled and like a frightened child I began to cower in the chair, my legs pressed together, my back hunched, my hands on my gut.

"My name was given to me by The Home."

Levinsky leaned in closer and whispered. "What if I told you that's not true?"

"I would say you're a liar!" I spat, my eyes averted.

Levinsky sprung back in the chair. "What if I could prove it!?" he shouted.

I was nauseated and fever-struck and leaned over like my appendix had burst. Levinsky rose slowly and, keeping one hand fixed to the tabletop, walked around to me. As I stared to the wooden floor, I heard his heavy breathing, felt his presence. I closed my eyes and waited for the end, defenseless and squirming. When he put a hand on my shoulder, I felt a spasm and watched as streams of yellow vomit poured from my mouth, steaming and acidic, across the floor. Levinsky patted my back like a kind uncle.

"There, there."

"What the fuck do you want from me?"

"I want what you want. Now go find the apartment building, the one that bears your name. Find that place and then come back to me."

The door opened. Cohen and Rolfe walked in and stopped when they saw the puddle on the floor.

"Get someone in here to clean up this mess. Our friend isn't well." They nodded in unison and left down the stairs.

Levinsky held me by the arm and lifted me from the chair. My mind fought to resist but my body was too weak. I floated with his guidance in a woozy and hypnotic trance, my eyes sagging and my body as limp as a ragdoll. Everything was a blur, but I smelled his warm cigar breath and tangy cologne that was cheap but not vulgar. I felt oddly safe in his arms and had an urge to hug the old man like a grandfather. When we reached the door, he gently nudged me towards the stairs. I clutched the handrail and turned one last time to see his face.

"Find your name, Brae."

CHAPTER NINE

One of my earliest memories was eating crabapples on a picnic in the Berkshire Mountains while on a summer excursion with the Home For Stray Boys. Although warned to stay away, I indulged with the same mischievous delight as Eve. In minutes I was overcome by stomach cramps that left me rolling in the grass, clutching my abdomen and writhing in agony. I heaved constantly. My half-digested lunch dripped from my lips, stained my shirt and trousers. When it was over, I was covered in sticky warmth but felt a relief that was almost ecstatic. Since that day I could never look at an apple without feeling a sudden, overpowering revulsion. I gravitated towards warmth with the same life-sustaining imperative as oxygen, instinctively, irrationally and with a clinging desperation. That was the only way I could explain how I felt about Ruth.

"What are you thinking about?"

"Nothing."

"Tell me. I want to know," she said.

"I can't see her face."

"Do you want to?"

"I don't know." I stared at the ceiling, counting the cracks, finding pictures in the patterns of disrepair. "Maybe I don't want to see her at all."

"Does she call to you?"

"She waves. I don't hear anything. Just 'more air, more air.'"

Ruth lay hunched on one elbow, smiling prettily and looking into my eyes.

"I need your help," I said, turning towards her.

"Anything."

"Go to the Assessment Department. Find anything you can about my name."

"Jody?"

"No. Brae. Find an owner. Or find a building with my name on it."

"What do you mean? A building with your name?"

"Etched into a fresco. Carved into a molding. Maybe in a stained-glass window. I don't know."

"I don't think they keep records like that," she mused.

"Start with the owner's name, Brae. They're alphabetical, right?

"Yes, but…"

"If not, see if there are records on building markings. Check with Maggie. She's the head clerk. Say you're a friend of mine but don't say you've seen me."

"I will try."

When I awoke, my best guess was that it was early evening that same day. My body tingled from exhaustion and I drifted back to consciousness as if waking from a coma. If I had been asleep for a week, I wouldn't have been surprised. I lay in Ruth's bed battling the urge to fall back asleep. My arms and legs were numb, my back ached. A hazy dimness filled the bedroom and the soft sounds of traffic, rush-hour I assumed, hummed in the distance. I crawled to my feet, stretched, and walked to the kitchenette to light the kettle.

I reached for a small radio on the counter and turned it on. The ringing harmonies of The Beatles enlivened the room as I sat, half-naked, and sipped tea on the couch. I tapped my foot, softly so no one could hear, but with an uneasy restlessness. Above the melody I heard Levinsky, speaking to me, directing me to some damning yet irresistible destiny. I had already forgotten what he looked like, but heard his voice with the clarity of lightening. Each word was an image, each half-truth a picture, or fragment of a puzzle. I recalled our meeting with the vague perceptions of a flu survivor, with flash-visions, voices and foggy impressions somewhere between real and imagined. Levinsky, whether a god or devil, had infected me with something that was part triumph and part despair and I knew my life was redirected. His mysterious knowledge of my past had given me a new hope.

In all my life, no one had ever spoken my name without knowing me first. Born into solitude, I had created from scratch any personal connections and relationships I ever had. I had no past—no family, no distant relatives, no uncles, no doting grandparents. As a result, no one made assumptions about me because they knew an aunt or had gone to school with my father. And while I lacked the advantages of family ties, I also didn't inherit the dishonor of a bad parent or relative. My life was my own, a blank canvass, and any beauty or color on it was the result of my efforts. People knew of me only what I decided to show them. Now there was Levinsky. His insights, his knowledge, the little details of my life were all beyond coincidence. I resented him for it, hated him, but was grateful all the same.

Keys jangled in the lock. The door swung open and Ruth walked in, her purse in one hand and a bag of groceries in the other. I felt the urge to jump up and help her. But she looked so lovely in her clumsy determination that I just sat back.

"Hello," she said quietly.

"Can I help?" I said reaching for the bag. She smiled and turned away.

"No. This is a surprise." She marched to the kitchen counter, put down the bag and reached to turn the radio down.

"Sorry."

"I'm going to cook for you tonight. But it's a surprise."

"I've had a lot of those lately."

"This place smells like a chimney."

"Must be the fireplace."

"There isn't one," Ruth smirked. "Please don't smoke in here."

"Sorry."

She unbuttoned her overcoat and it slid off her body like a negligee. She walked over to the door and kicked off her shoes. With faded makeup and wind-blown hair, she was completely irresistible. I could only watch.

"You naughty boy," she said, turning back to me as she hung the coat on the coat rack. "Don't look at me like that."

I blushed like a schoolboy and looked away. When she walked into the bedroom to change, I sat tapping my finger against the teacup. I was weak, lethargic, and needed a good meal to strengthen my body and my resolve. If my stomach hadn't growled, if Ruth hadn't brought groceries, I might have forgotten to eat altogether. In Korea I lost thirty pounds by accident; I forgot to eat. I needed duck tape to hold my fatigues up. When I fainted one night on watch, they put me on an IV for two days.

I heard a forced cough and looked to see Ruth, standing in the doorway wearing a mischievous smile and nothing else. She was completely unclothed. Her white skin glistened and the only shadow was the crease beneath her breasts. I felt a giddy excitement, as much from humor as from arousal. There was something funny in seeing a woman naked so unexpectedly.

Ruth kept her eyes on me with a seductive half-smile, her lids lowered, cheek buried in her shoulder. With one hand on her hip, she caressed the doorframe with the other. Her long red nails slid along the white trim like an erotic scene from a B-movie.

"Want some dessert before dinner?" she murmured.

I walked over, pulled her waist to mine and kissed her like a bride. She gasped. She pulled me into the bedroom and pushed me down to the bed.

I awoke in a damp sweat, breathless and blinded by the dark as the thought of her lingered in my mind, only to fade away like the spots from a camera's flash. Moments before, I was sprinting under a heavy rain through a land of endless geometric streets. I had gotten close to her, closer than I ever had. She waved in the distance, a faint vision of glowing femininity, calling to me silently, beckoning with wind-swept arms. 'More air, more air,' uttered from my lips. Raindrops pelted my eyes but I ran undeterred towards the image until I was steps away. In one last Olympic leap, I hurled myself towards her, staring at a face that was a blurred approximation of what I imagined it to be. I couldn't see her. The moment before she vanished, I observed the slightest form of her eyes, a glassy blue, the shape of kindness, a fragment of possibility that renewed me for the next chase. I collapsed to the pavement and woke up in Ruth's bed.

"Has Jackson said anything to you about me?" I wondered aloud.

Ruth shook as if startled, waking suddenly at the sound of my voice. She turned over with the bed sheets wrapped around her body and looked at me in a groggy daze, half-listening, alert yet still sleeping.

"Huh?"

"Jackson. Has he mentioned me?"

Her eyes popped open and she lifted her head from the pillow.

"No. Not to me. But he wouldn't confide in an intern."

I sighed. "I wanted to keep you out of this," I said, turning to her as if for the first time. She hesitated, staring across the dark room at the emptiness, thinking silently to herself and searching for the right words. It was early evening and dinner sat in cold packaging on the kitchen counter. But it felt like midnight on the edge of the galaxy, with only us.

"Jody." She paused. "I don't know what's happening. I'm scared, very scared." She pulled the covers to her chin and watched me with frightful, girlish angst.

"I know, I know." I whispered, patting her knee. She then sprung up and put her hands on my shoulders.

"I forgot to tell you. I found out something about your name!"

"What?"

She got out of bed and ran to the living room. When she returned, she turned on the light and waved a piece of crumpled paper. I squinted to see.

"You'd never believe it. I went to Building Records at lunch. I told the clerk I was looking for any owners, alive or deceased by the name of Brae."

"Maggie?"

"No. But as the woman was showing me how to find ownership records and liens, I mentioned that I was really looking for a building with the word 'Brae' carved into it. She said she had seen it!"

I got out of the bed and stood facing Ruth. My knees shook and my heart raced and I felt a strange anticipation, something between hope and dread.

"I couldn't believe it," Ruth continued, "It took her a few moments to remember. Then it struck her. A building on 'Boo-do-in' Street…"

"Bowdoin Street."

"Yes. At the corner of Mt. Ida Road," she said, reading the scribbled words.

"That's Dorchester."

"Yes!"

Ruth was overjoyed. She knew nothing of its meaning but everything of its importance. I took her into my arms and kissed her on the cheek. "This is huge. Thank you."

"What does it mean?"

I held her hands and pulled her gently to the edge of the bed, where we sat side by side. "I'm not sure yet. I was checking out a lead, a washed-up wise guy. He didn't give up any information on the fires, but he knew something about my past. When I challenged him, he told me to find the building that bears my name."

"He knew who you parents were?" Ruth whispered.

"I don't know."

"He wants to help you?"

"I can't say."

I leaned over, grabbed my pants from the floor and began to dress. Ruth put her hand against my back.

"What are you doing?"

"Going out for a few hours."

"What about dinner?" she moaned.

"Keep it hot. I shouldn't be long."

I kissed her on the lips and left the room. I got my coat, reached under the couch for the .38 and walked out the door. I descended the hill to Charles Street and flagged down a bus just as it was pulling away from the curb. Life without the Valiant had its inconveniences but public transportation was the safest way to travel. Here, crouched in a rear seat with my collar up and head down, I was a nobody, a faceless rider among the anonymous masses. If Lovell's men were after me, this was the last place they'd look.

When I changed buses at Dudley Station, I glanced out the fog-covered window to see a man spread across a metal bench. His body was twisted and bent in every direction as if he couldn't get comfortable. Next to him was a canvas bag, covered in torn plastic and bulging with things. As the bus pulled out of the station, his head popped up and I recognized the kind face of the vagrant I had met on Fort Hill. Unless I was hallucinating, he lifted his tired arm from the bench and waved. I smiled and nodded.

I got off the bus at Columbia Road, in the heart of Dorchester, just after ten o'clock. The temperature had nose-dived and it was bitter cold. I stuffed my hands into my coat pockets and turned down a side street, towards Bowdoin Street a few blocks east. I walked fast, into the wind, wincing from the chill but determined nonetheless. The streets were barren, nothing but block after block of quiet multi-family houses. They were uniform, identical, except for variations in shingle color or vinyl siding and they had the bland sterility of government housing. Some were well-kept, but most were rundown, with sagging porches and crumbling asphalt roofs. Dorchester had changed in all but name. When I was a child it had teemed with families, the newly arrived and the long established and although most were poor, there was a sense of hopefulness that had long since vanished.

The streets were familiar if not the names. My own turf, Roxbury, a short mile to the west, was so closely intertwined with Dorchester that few could point out where one began and the other ended. Municipal borders meant little, however, since neighborhoods were defined by the ethnics that occupied them. In my youth, an invisible line somewhere between Columbia Road and Bowdoin Street had marked the change from Jewish to Irish. But the era of tribalism had vanished and the area had become a slum, a no-man's land of poor blacks, a few poor whites and a smattering of businesses that stayed afloat with small change and iron grates.

The deeper I got into the neighborhood, the closer I got to Bowdoin Street, the more evident the neglect. There were vacant houses, cluttered with overgrown grass that seemed glad to be dead. Litter was everywhere, on the sidewalk, in the gutter, on front lawns and in alleyways. In the darkness, I almost tripped over a ragged couch, torn open to expose a bulging wad of dried cushion like the innards of a slain beast. At the corner of the next street was an abandoned automobile, its tires, trim and mirrors neatly stripped. The murmurings of human defeat were everywhere.

I reached Bowdoin Street, only one block from where it intersected Mt Ida Road. I turned left and picked up the pace when suddenly I felt a sharp pain and looked down to see a rusted shopping carriage, upended in the middle of the sidewalk. My knee throbbed but I continued onwards. I walked a few more yards when I saw, sparkling beneath a streetlamp, a field of glass spread across the sidewalk, the shards of a broken bottle. In the silence of the street, I was struck by a superstitious fright, imagining that someone or something placed obstacles in my path. I shook it off and walked around the glass.

As I approached the intersection, my thoughts turned from the past to the present and then to the past again. I heard the words of Levinsky, felt his hand on my shoulder, smelled his sour breath, his rank cologne. His mystical presence was nearby, lingering, hovering, creeping behind a mailbox, peering from behind a parked car.

I reached the corner, stopped and stood still. I breathed heavily from the walk, the steam from my mouth bursting into the beam of a street light like a fogbank. I reached for a cigarette, lit it and smoked nervously. Every few minutes headlights broke through the darkness as a solitary car whizzed by. Aside from that, it was only me.

All was silent, a quiet and muffled world of shadows interrupted only by streetlamps. I was alone but felt strangely accompanied, led by some mysterious hand, guided by a presence unseen. Although anxious, I was overcome by an unnatural calm. As I flicked the cigarette my gazed swept a brick apartment building on the opposite corner where, illuminated by an indistinct light, I observed a cement fresco over an arched entranceway. The words were faint but clear: HARLAN-BRAE. I leaned against a street pole aghast, staring like a curious monkey. I smoked a cigarette and then another, looking away and then looking back as if trying to disentangle my mind from an illusion. The longer I stared, the less real it seemed but the more real it was.

I stepped on to the street and started to cross, my eyes focused on the engraving and nothing else. When I passed the median line, there was sudden rush of wind and I saw lights. Honk! I jumped back just in time as a small dark car raced by, missing me by inches. It vanished into the darkness as quickly as it had appeared. I held my breath and continued on. When I reached the opposite sidewalk, I gazed up to the fresco, my arms out wide, and repeated the words; Harlan Brae, Harlan Brae, Harlan Brae. It may have been a single name or two last names, the juxtaposition of the original owners or construction firm. The first, Harlan, was almost foreign sounding, possibly Southern, like Harlow Atkins, a private from Louisiana I had known in boot camp. Brae, however, was unmistakable, a rare Celtic surname, nearly extinct, whose conflicting origins wavered between the bogs of Ireland and Scottish Highlands.

Yet more than the words on its fresco, the building itself struck me as something familiar. I dug into the well of my mind, searching the memories, the moments, the events, as if slowly rewinding a movie reel. But nothing clicked. The shape of the structure, three-stories and square, with a flat roof and flanked by wrought-iron fire escapes, was no different from the hundreds of apartment buildings constructed in the early nineteen-twenties. Some were workmen's lodgings, their hallways lined with three-room cold-water flats. Others were more genteel, with marble stairwells, large windows and expansive apartments. They were all built to meet the demands of a city that swelled with returning veterans, immigrants, and families. These buildings were everywhere, on every corner of every street in every neighborhood and were so common they blended invisibly into the urban landscape. They were the same apartment buildings that now were burning down.

I stepped on to the dried grass of the narrow front yard and looked up the wall with a mountain-climber's awe. I felt an almost magnetic pull and had an urge to pry open the door and rummage inside. But it was impenetrable, boarded up and vacant, a hollow skeleton of brick and mortar. The front door hadn't been opened in months, possibly years, a fact indicated by the dirt and frozen leaves piled against the doorstep. I tiptoed to a front window and peered through a crack in the plywood but saw only blackness. I turned and put my ear against the hole. Within, I heard the whistle of the breeze, eerily echoing as it wended through the rooms and hallways. As lifeless as a graveyard, I thought to myself.

As I went to walk back to the sidewalk, I was knocked to the ground. My first thought was I had tripped, somehow caught my foot on a tree stump or rock. Within two seconds, however, I knew it was worse. I had fallen too quickly, too abruptly, and a sharp pain ran from my knee and down the side of my calf. I was plastered against the sidewalk, flat on my back and staring at the sky. The pain was so strong it rippled through my body, although I knew it was localized. I convulsed, writhed, and flipped like a caught fish, my jaw clenched and will paralyzed. I had been shot. I felt the warm blood seeping from a hole in my leg, rolling down my knee and dripping on the sidewalk.

There was a second shot. A bullet smacked the sidewalk, sending shards of pavement across my coat and into my eyes. Stunned, I blinked wildly and tried to roll off the sidewalk and into the shadow of the building wall. The last shot was a tracer, I guessed, and the next one would end it all. Then I heard another shot followed by a sharp ding, as the bullet ricocheted off a metal fencepost just inches from my head. I reached behind to my belt for the pistol but I had lost it in the fall.

By now I could smell the blood from the leg wound, that sour but subtle odor known only by experience. As I pressed my eyes together and waited to die, the most trivial thoughts crept into my mind. It was about time I bought a holster, I reminded myself. Who was going to clean up the blood, I wondered. I thought of Ruth and the dinner that waited for me in the warm apartment miles away. The last thing she would remember was that I stood her up for dinner to seek out an empty building and get executed. As I lay beneath the streetlamp like a cornered convict, I decided that I finally believed in fate. I resisted no more. I rolled on to my back, spread my arms out like Christ and awaited the coup de grâce .

But the moment I put my head on the pavement there were three more gunshots, crack, crack, crack, one after another. I knew they weren't aimed at me. If I had developed anything in combat, it was a sixth sense about gunfire. I could tell by the report whether shooting was enemy or friendly fire. Just as bats navigated by echo location, I knew by sound the direction of a bullet. I could even envision its trajectory, knowing whether it was accurate or not.

Someone fired again, this time from a different direction than the last. The exchange continued for another ten seconds and then all fell silent. I lifted my head to see what was happening but the street light above blinded me from the surrounding darkness. I heard the screech of tires as an automobile sped away, down Bowdoin Street, the rumble of its engine fading into the night. When everything was quiet again, I felt more vulnerable than ever.

"Get up Detective! Quickly, we need to leave here!"

A strong hand grasped my arm and hoisted me to my feet. The blood rushed to my head and I was dizzy. The world spun around, the buildings, the street signs, fire hydrants and post boxes. I must have been in shock because I no longer felt the pain in my knee. I limped to the other side of Bowdoin Street, my arm hunched over a broad shoulder that stabilized and guided me with each step. As I was ushered into a car door, I turned to see Harrigan.

I leaned back into the sofa chair and rested my leg on a footstool. The pain had returned and my knee throbbed like I was just hit, although it was several hours later. I laughed at the irony of having to return home and wait a decade before finally being wounded. I had fewer bumps and scrapes in Korea than in all my life. I had been in several firefights, had watched friends pulverized in front of me by machine gun or mortar fire. Yet the closest I ever came to injury was when a two-inch piece of shrapnel from an explosion a half-mile away bounced off my shoulder. I had been hit harder by acorns.

"Ouch!"

"Don't move Detective."

"Am I dying?"

"You're in heaven already."

"God is a black man?" I chuckled.

"Are you surprised?"

"The Nation of Islam is right."

He leaned over, tore a roll of gauze with his teeth and then tied the ends. I looked down for the first time to see that my knee looked like a lace-covered bowling ball.

"You were lucky Detective," Harrigan said. "The bullet went clear through. Missed the bone and cartilage. A miracle, if you want to know the truth."

"Who ever wants to know the truth," I said, leaning forward and reaching into my coat for a cigarette.

"Please, no smoking, Detective. My mother hates it."

"When will you stop calling me Detective? I'm not sure if I'm even still on the force."

"Then we're in the proverbial same boat."

We sat in Harrigan's mother's apartment, sipping tea in the half-darkness and lingering under the uncertainty of an approaching new day.

"What the hell were you doing out there?"

"I've been tailing you for three days Detective. Someone is after us. Someone doesn't want us investigating those fires."

"That's obvious," I said, looking down to my knee. "But who?"

"Not sure."

"Who shot me?"

"Couldn't tell. I lost you at Columbia Road. It was just luck that I pulled up to Bowdoin Street. You were already on the ground. They were in a Chevy, newer model. Dark. That's all I could see in the darkness."

"Did you hit anyone?"

"Don't think so. They were parked on the side street. Hidden but with a clear view of the sidewalk. I'm sure they could've killed you if they wanted."

"If that was a warning, I'd hate to see the punishment."

There was a short silence as I thought back to the incident.

"Why did headquarters stop me from visiting you?"

"Don't know."

"But you handed me a note." I said, raising my voice.

"Ssh, please. No one knows we're here. I want it to stay that way."

Harrigan looked down, one hand on his knee and the other holding the tea cup. He was shaken and tired and I saw under his eyes, across his cheeks, the faded purple of healing bruises.

"You see, I was heavily sedated."

"They said you were in a coma…"

"I'm not sure. I don't remember much. I was certainly unconscious for periods of time at the hospital. But there were days I couldn't move a muscle but was still able to hear and see. It was the oddest sensation. I think…"

Before Harrigan finished his sentence, the apartment lights went out and the room went dark. As if by instinct, I reached to my belt for the .38 but it wasn't there.

"Don't worry, you're weapon is under the couch," I heard Harrigan whisper, although I couldn't see his face.

Harrigan opened the blinds on two large bay windows and a soft moonlight filled the room. When my eyes adjusted to the dimness, I glanced outside to a postcard scene of warm familiarity. The apartment looked out across Franklin Park, that vast urban oasis where I had spent so many days as a child, wandering among the oak and maple trees, climbing its small hills and sledding down its valleys. When Harrigan had brought me to the apartment I drifted in and out of consciousness, a condition I attributed to both the shock and blood-loss of being shot. In a sense he had brought me home, only blocks from the institution and yards from the park, nestled in the heart of Roxbury. I couldn't escape the fact that somehow my life had come full circle. If the shot had been more accurate, if it had punctured an artery or pulverized an organ, I wouldn't have wished for a more fitting location to die.

There was something soothing about the blackout. Crouched in the apartment, sipping hot tea, I felt hidden in the shadows of a city gone mad. For the first time in weeks I felt safe and could rest easy. I leaned back and sighed. But the moment Harrigan left to get candles, I heard the sound of sirens in the distance. Somewhere out there another inferno was underway, tearing through rooms, blazing down hallways, consuming and devouring. I scanned the horizon for smoke but saw none.

Harrigan returned with two wax cylinders, fat and oily, the kind of candles used by miners a century ago. He lit a match, held it to the wick and instantly they came to life with a dull but persistent glow. With nothing to do but wait, I looked around the apartment, scanning the walls, examining the décor. It was a sparse and simple place, with the rustic charm of a peasant's cottage. On the far wall hung several framed black and white photographs. One showed a middle-aged black couple, short and stout, arm in arm, grinning for the camera with a quiet dignity. The woman wore a floral dress down to her knees. The man had on dress pants with suspenders and a tilted bow tie. Behind them was a wooden house, a small one-roomed hovel, whose whitewash exterior glistened in the sun. And behind that, miles of hillside, so green and lush I could almost smell their dampness.

Harrigan placed the candles on a table beside the couch.

"Damn electrical grid," he said. "Third time this week the power has gone out."

"You've been here all week?" I asked.

"Well, no. I got out three days ago and came here. My mother told me about the blackouts," he explained.

"Those your folks?" I wondered, nodding to the pictures.

Harrigan looked over then looked to the floor smiling. "No, that's my aunt and uncle. My mother won't have her picture taken. She's superstitious."

"Are you superstitious?" I asked. Harrigan rubbed his chin, took a sip of tea and glanced out the window.

"I'm rational. And I know that someone wants us silenced," he said.

"What do you mean?"

He paused.

"Like I was telling you, I went in and out of consciousness at the hospital. One day, maybe shortly after I arrived, I overheard some things."

"What kinds of things?"

"Two men were talking. I heard one say you knew too much, you had to be kept running."

I nodded as I listened.

"The other said you were suffering delusions, you were nuts. No one would believe you. The conversation was quick and vague. I only remember because they said your name."

Through the grim darkness I watched Harrigan, his glazed eyes staring out the window, over Franklin Park and to the vague horizon. His eyelids twitched like a man in distress. He was scared and unnerved, a haze of desperation in his normally tranquil expression. With each sentence, he stuttered and with each movement he trembled. He turned, looked at me and spoke as if uttering his final words.

"I don't want to be involved, Jody."

I worried he was collapsing inside and tried to talk him through the terror like a platoon leader.

"Why?" I asked softly. "It's your job. It's our job."

"I'm a Black man. If they want to make an example out of anyone, it will be me."

"Tell me about the note," I said, trying to keep him focused on concrete things. Harrigan ignored my questions and continued on, speaking in short spurts and long gasps. In his eyes I observed a trembling disillusionment.

"I was, I am scared, Jody. The attack, the police protection at the hospital, the things I overheard. I am going to be straight with you..." He hesitated.

"Go on," I whispered.

"I think they're burning the buildings down..."

"Who?"

"The cops. Lovell. The mob. Maybe they are all in cahoots. I don't know. All I know is what I heard."

"Then we need to get them?"

"I don't want to be involved. I'm only on the force six weeks. I don't want any trouble."

We both sat with a cautious stillness, facing each other in the shadow of the candlelight, two figures conversing in the dark. I understood his reluctance. Harrigan was one of only a handful of blacks on a white force and was, in a sense, more at risk than me. If it could have been any other way, I would have let him walk. But our fates had become entwined and we were each dead without the other.

"You're already involved."

"We could just walk away from this. Tell Jackson we found no evidence of wrongdoing. We could back step out of this whole mess before one of us gets hurt."

I shook my head at the irony.

"You were almost beaten to death."

"Maybe that was a warning," he replied.

"What if I told you someone tried to run me off the road?"

Harrigan winced in surprise. "Seriously?"

"Seriously. I left my car near the scene of a fire, just around the block, on Elm Hill Ave," I said, pointing my hand over my shoulder. "I noticed a car tailing me. When I tried to lose them they almost ran me into a wall."

"Are you certain?"

"Certain? My Valiant looks like the Titanic."

"Any idea who they were?"

"None. I was trying to stay alive. I caught a glimpse of the driver before I turned down a side street. A black guy." I thought back, recalling the excitement, the chaos, the flash images etched in my brain from the adrenaline-soaked fury of near-death. But so much had happened since that day.

"I saw a scar."

"What kind of scar?"

"No, not a scar. A birthmark. A patch of discoloration around his eye. That's what I saw."

Harrigan's teacup fell from his hand, bouncing off a small coffee table and rolling to the floor. His mouth hung open, his eyes were agape and he sat with a face of blank astonishment, something between torment and ecstasy. For a second I thought I might have described his own brother.

"Birth mark? I remember, I remember!"

Harrigan rose to his feet, clenched his fists and stomped his feet. "That's the man who attacked me…"

"The kid from the mosque?"

"No, no. The man from the mosque met me at the building that night. He took me inside with a flashlight. We went through the basement door on Intervale Street, the one I had pried open. I remember the smell of the soot. I was nervous, jittery even. We climbed the stairs to the first floor and stood in a hallway. Someone approached us. A black man. He had a large birthmark across his face. That's the last thing I remember."

Harrigan was ecstatic. It was as if I had given him back a piece of his soul. Amnesia was a form of mutilation. In Korea, I had met soldiers who suffered massive head trauma. Although the physical injuries healed, they were haunted by the memory loss, the ghost pains of having a section of their lives expunged from their brains. Some spent their final years trying to recapture those lost fragments, forever worried about the integrity of their mind and living under the paranoia that, at any moment, they might suddenly forget their wife, parents, kids, or past altogether.

The lights flickered and electric power was restored.

"Ah, the epiphany," I said sarcastically.

"Are you superstitious Detective?

"I believe in fate."

CHAPTER TEN

I had learned years before that a Brae was a hillside along a river. When I was a child, there was an old Scottish woman named Tess who worked in the kitchen at the Home. She was a superstitious old crow and saw hidden meaning in all things, particularly names. Whenever she encountered a word that was unusual or uncommon, she made it a point to explain its meaning and origin. Most of the children in the institution were hopelessly incurious about such obscure facts. The world we knew was bleak and harsh and, if anything, meaningless. We lived day to day and so were focused only on things we could touch and feel. So when Tess approached me one morning in the breakfast hall and told me what my last name meant, I shrugged my shoulders with typical seven year-old indifference and took a seat on the nearest bench, cold and hungry as I was.

Shortly before she died, Tess caught up with me in the yard after a game of handball and told me that whenever I felt alone, I could know that I had a home among the soft grass on that hill overlooking the river. She urged me to imagine this place, to make it my own, and to always go there when I needed to. As I grew older, I never forgot the advice. In Korea, when my platoon had taken a battery on the crest of a hill overlooking the Yalu River, the first thing that came to my mind after I stuck my rifle in the dirt was that I had finally arrived there, as cynical as it was. When I hit the streets as a rookie, I kept the vision in the back of my thoughts, retreating there from time to time when the tension became unbearable. My partner and I once cornered a bank robbery suspect in an alleyway on Bunker Hill, the assailant dying in a hail of gunfire after he decided he wasn't going peacefully. Although I thought the horrors of bloodshed behind me, I looked down from Bunker Hill to the Charles River and thought again of this gentle refuge. The idyllic setting my name described seemed to express itself in the darkest variations.

Harrigan snored. It wasn't typical snoring, but rather long, drawn-out grunts that began somewhere deep in his chest, followed a course through his larynx and reached a whinnying crescendo at his palate. It sounded like a jet airplane taking off along a runway. So far it had been the first uncouth thing I had seen in Harrigan, the dark-skinned island gentleman who spoke like a prince and dressed like a prime minister. As he sat spread out on the cushioned chair beside the window, a sleeping giant, I laid on the couch in a restless semi-sleep as first light broke between the trees on the farthest hill of Franklin Park. It was a new day.

My throat was dead dry and I saw a small kettle on the stove. As I leaned to get up, a jolt of pain shot up my leg and sent me falling back to the couch. I looked down to the swelled kneecap and cringed like a newly crippled. I bit my lip to keep from shrieking in agony, knowing that the more rested Harrigan was the better for both of us. I sat on the couch, seething with energy but immobilized by injury. Lying for so many hours in one position had made the wound stiff and the joint cold. I could either work through it or be crutches-bound for weeks. Feeling too vulnerable to even stand without protection, I reached under the couch for the .38. With my other hand I pushed on the couch and lunged forward, using the momentum to rise, while careful to put the weight on my good leg.

The moment I was on my feet, the front door swung open with a loud whoosh. Instantly, I held the gun out with both hands, pointing it at the door with my feet spread shoulder-length in military firing position. If it was one of Lovell's crew, I was ready to blast him. I heard a moan and looked over to see Harrigan's eyes flick open. He looked at me in terror just as a small black woman, her arms wrapped around a bag of groceries, hobbled into the apartment. As I stood with the poise of an assassin, she smiled and walked to the kitchenette.

"Now put that pistol down son," she said, "I'm no common burglar."

Harrigan leapt from the chair and positioned himself between me and his mother.

"What are you doing Detective?"

With a slight delay, I lowered the gun and tucked it in my belt.

"I am sorry Ma'am," I said, looking down in shame.

"Don't be sorry young man. You was startled. Would you like some tea?"

"You read my mind."

"I've always had that ability," she replied as she unbagged her things.

I looked at Harrigan. "I told you she's superstitious," he said, his face glowing in relief.

Harrigan's mother was a sprightly woman of about sixty, barley five feet tall, with a round, loving face that seemed frozen in a constant smile. Despite her tired eyes and hunched back, she carried herself with an easy and dignified grace. She had an accent that was impossible to understand, yet everything she said was clear. Her words lilted gently and she spoke with the ho-hum cheerfulness of anyone's grandmother. I loved her instantly.

"Detective Brae, meet my mother," Harrigan said awkwardly.

"My pleasure Ma'am," I said and reached to shake her hand.

In minutes the small apartment was filled with the exotic aromas of a Caribbean carnival. There were eggs, papaya and Caribbean dumplings made of cornmeal and bacon. I washed it all down with endless cups of hot tea. I was so satisfied that the soreness in my knee seemed to all but disappear, perhaps a reward from a body that had been undernourished for weeks. Harrigan and I sat on the couch, laughing like newborns, as contended as cats, while Mrs. Harrigan quietly went about her business, stowing the leftovers and cleaning the dishes. I was so overjoyed that I forgot to offer to help, a lapse made more shameful when she put on her coat and made for the door.

"Where are you going?" I asked.

"I am staying at my boy's place until you sort out your troubles."

Harrigan looked at me and nodded.

I leaned to get up, "I want to thank you, sincerely…"

"No need," she interrupted. "Just be good and be safe. Take care of my boy." With that, she smiled, waved and shut the door, vanishing as abruptly as she had arrived.

"I've asked her to stay at my place tonight," Harrigan added, "If anyone comes looking for me, she'll say I'm in St. Kitts."

"What about Jackson?"

"I called him twice, he never called back. I left a note at the office. I'm entitled to recuperation leave. It's all official, you see?"

"You haven't told me. How'd you get out of the hospital?" I asked.

"I woke up Monday morning. The guards were gone. At least, they weren't in the room. I pulled the wires out of my arm and walked out. Who would notice a six foot two black man leave a hospital in Boston?" he said with a sarcastic grin.

"You're in this as deeply as me," I said, rubbing my chin.

"I guess we have to crawl out together."

I held my hand out and Harrigan took it firmly.

By the time I got back to Ruth's house it was dark. I crawled up the back staircase and saw light through the bottom of the apartment door. Ruth was home. I stood on the balcony, reluctant to knock, pausing in the silence of the dark stairwell. I was stuck in the moment, unable to move forward but afraid to go back. My knee throbbed and my throat itched. I was blindsided by indecision, a paralyzing doubt that began in my mind and rippled through every limp. I was at a crossroads. Something deep within tempted me to turn and flee, to leave Ruth out of it, to save her innocence from the madness of my broken world. I fought the urge, repelled the angst, caught between the desire to do what was noble and what was best.

The door swung open and there stood Ruth, looking up and half-smiling, as if she knew and was not afraid.

"Jody," she whispered and took me in her arms. She glanced down the hallway, pulled me in and shut the door. "I was scared to death."

"I am so sorry."

"Why didn't you call?"

"I couldn't."

I hobbled to the couch, but Ruth couldn't sit. She fretted, moved side-to-side, walked over to turn on the kettle then spun around. Her arms were crossed, her legs unsteady and the nervous twitch at the edge of her lip suggested a woman torn between fear and confusion. Before she said another word, I reached down and pulled my pant leg up. The thick gauze was stained with dried blood and formed a misshapen white ball so enlarged that my legs appeared thin and frail, as if held together only by the dressing. The moment she saw it, Ruth's expression changed from concern to panic. She rushed to my side and leaned over to inspect the wound like a worried mother.

"Oh my God, what happened?"

"Ruth, sit down, please," I begged, patting the couch cushion.

She sat beside me, unable to take her eyes off the injury, until finally I pushed my pant leg down to cover it.

"I need to tell you something. I need you to be strong."

She turned to look at me, her red lips quivering, her face as pale as ivory. When I tried to put my arm around her, she squirmed and moved away. In her unsteady breathing I detected a fear beyond words.

"I got shot last night."

"What...happened? Who...who did this?" she cried.

"I found the building, the one with my name. I think it was a setup. Someone was waiting for me."

"Someone followed you?"

"Someone knew I would be there. But Harrigan was also there." I paused. "He saved my life, Ruth."

"Harrigan?" she said, looking up in surprise.

"Yes, Harrigan."

"My God, Jody, haven't you heard?

"Heard what?"

"There's a warrant out for his arrest. He's been charged with arson."

When I walked out of the apartment, Ruth screaming for me to come back, I had nothing but my jacket, wallet, and gun. I couldn't convince her of something she was unwilling to believe; that Harrigan was innocent and, like me, was being targeted. He had been accused of taking bribes and altering evidence of the Arson Unit. The fact that he had been spotted off-duty at the scene of so many recent fires fit conveniently with the terms of the indictment.

Ruth was willing to believe me but she couldn't extend her trust to a man she hardly knew. When she hesitated, the moment I sensed her skepticism, I picked up my things and left. Ruth was loyal but, as a young woman, not trustworthy. She was fickle and impressionable, a prisoner of emotion, with a big heart but no backbone. I had learned long ago there was a big difference between loyalty and trust. A loyal friend would watch your back while a trusted one would risk as much as you. Harrigan I trusted.

As I limped along the side streets of Beacon Hill, into a headwind of fresh falling snow, I knew that I had made a decision to leave Ruth for the time being. It was getting cold, brutally cold. I kept my hands in my pockets and my collar up and walked as fast as my bum knee would allow. When I came to Charles Street, I ducked under an awning and lit a cigarette. My mind raced as I struggled to decide what to do next. The snowflakes pelted my eyes and headlights from passing cars blended with streetlamps into a dazzling blur. Paranoia set in. When a car lingered a moment too long at an intersection, I panicked, scurrying past closed shop fronts, looking back every few seconds for a phantom pursuer.

It must have been past midnight. The only traffic was an occasional cab creeping through the white storm. I stood under the shelter of a doorway, lighted my last cigarette and debated whether to live or die. My hands were blue and frost clung to the scruff of my chin. I looked and felt like a weary Everest climber from an ascent gone terribly wrong. My wartime training kicked in and I held one wrist to feel the slow, erratic thump of my pulse. I wasn't sure if it was my mind or body that was succumbing, but I knew I could have crouched then and there and slipped gently to a hypothermic death. It would have been so effortless, I thought.

In the shop window, feet from my face, was a promotional poster for Ireland, with a small thatched cottage, bleached white, and landscape of rolling green that faded towards a distant shoreline. At the edge of the foothills were the remains of a castle, grey and crumbling, that blended so seamlessly with the countryside as to appear naturally formed. In the foreground stood a young woman, a tourist, a knapsack over one shoulder, with long chestnut hair that fluttered in the breeze. She smiled in the sunlight, her teeth glistening, as awake and alive as the earth and fields around her. Across the bottom of the poster was written, IRELAND: LAND OF ENCHANTMENT. I brought my face nearer, so close my breath fogged the store window, and I inspected the poster like a laboratory scientist. The sunlit optimism of the faraway scene had the uncompromising perfection of Eden, or heaven, or some other tranquil place I had imagined but never seen. When my eyes reached the woman, I thought of Ruth.

I crumpled the butt of the cigarette in my palm, pulled my collar up, and charged back into the storm. I turned at the next side street and approached the first automobile, a black Ford Fairlane, parked halfway on the sidewalk and covered beneath a slab of snow. I looked up and down the street. Except for a few gas lamps, it was dark and barren. Without hesitation, I reached for my pistol and whipped the steel butt against the wing vent window. The shatter of glass was muffled by the snow and sounded no louder than the thud of a snowball against a wall. I reached my arm in and, holding the pistol, stretched just far enough to raise the door lock with the tip of the barrel. Once inside, it was dark and cold. I felt around under the dashboard and pulled down a clump of wires. I unsheathed them with my fingernails then sorted the colors, working with the cautious fury of someone defusing a ticking bomb. I identified the ignition wires, coupled them, and there was a quick spark. The engine sputtered once, then again, and then started. I slammed the car into drive, floored the gas pedal and sped off the curb.

I raced down Beacon Street as snow from the hood flung into the windshield, blocking my view until the wipers strained to clear it. I drove with a single purpose, to get to Harrigan's apartment and warn him that he was wanted. The streets were desolate and the only challenge I faced was maintaining traction. The temperature had dropped and what had been slushy snow was fast turning to ice. With each corner I swerved; at every intersection the rear wheels fishtailed.

I soon came to Blue Hill Avenue and waited at a red light when suddenly, from out of nowhere, came two fire engines, sirens on and lights flashing. They charged through the intersection just as my light turned green. I cut the wheel right and followed. As I neared the rear truck, I was blinded by a cloud of snow kicked up from its massive tires. Nevertheless, I stayed close to his bumper and followed the white lights.

The fire trucks blew through two more red lights and turned at Seaver Street, just across from Franklin Park. They drove for half a block then stopped so unexpectedly I had to slam the brakes to prevent from sliding into their steel backside. I skidded out of control and bounced off a parked car, landing in a snow bank only feet from a wall and inches from a telephone pole. I sat for a minute, caught my breath and let the adrenaline of near-death flush itself out of my bloodstream. I reached for the handle, opened the door and crawled out. I immediately smelled a chemical odor and assumed the radiator had cracked or a brake line had come loose from the impact. I circled the car to inspect the damage. The passenger's side was entirely crushed, but the Fairlane was intact and the engine idled like a baby.

The shock from the crash subsided and I looked towards the fire engines to see a large brick apartment building, engulfed in flames, flumes of black smoke ascending into the whiteness. In an instant I knew the location and my heart dropped when I realized it was the building where Harrigan's mother lived. I couldn't, for the life of me, recall if she was still staying at Harrigan's place. I rushed towards the scene, fixated on the apartment window on the third floor where I feared Mrs. Harrigan lay trapped. On the sidewalk stood a crowd of neighbors, panicked and pointing at the smoking roof. When I reached the first fire truck, I heard a two-way radio and looked to see officer Rollins, standing beside a cruiser. As if repelled, I leapt into a hedgerow and sat quietly beneath a quilt of snow. There was nothing I could do.

The structure burned for hours. I lay behind the hedges, buried under a coldness that numbed my body. I rubbed my nose and was surprised when it had no sensation. The snow had made its way into every corner and crevice of my body. I felt it under my socks, at the tip of my toes. It penetrated my collar and rolled down my back. All the while I peered through the bushes and watched as streams of hose water soared into the air, dousing windows and doorways with little effect. I heard tiny voices and looked to see three small black children, dressed in pajamas, gathered on the sidewalk in shivering terror. Police and fire officials stood nearby, offering neither help nor hope. Despite the cold, my body burned with rage at the sight.

I crept out of the bushes and followed the fence back to the car, keeping my head down to avoid being spotted. When I jumped into the Fairlane, it was still running. I slammed it into reverse, backed out of the snow and spun around. I sped down Blue Hill Avenue and the smell of smoke faded.

I felt deflated, helpless, overcome by a weakness I had never known. The vision of Harrigan's mother tormented me. I imagined her soft humility and the way she smiled. In minutes I was struck by nausea that left me incapacitated. I rolled down a side street, clutching my gut and heaving like an asthmatic. Finally, I hit the brakes and, with the car still rolling, I threw open the door and puked into the snow. When I was finished, I closed the door, leaned over the steering wheel and, for the first time since childhood, sobbed uncontrollably. It seemed like hours although it lasted only minutes. And when the emotion had run its course, I looked up to the rearview mirror at myself and felt a strange tranquility.

My eyes flickered open. With my trench coat over me, I lay curled in a ball in the backseat of the Fairlane. The windows were covered by a thick, dense whiteness. The wing vent I had smashed open prevented my suffocation under the all-consuming blanket of snow. I knew I should get up but the silence was soothing. I waited still for a few minutes, peering out from under my coat like a mole. My pistol dug into my lower back, branding me with its cold steely impression. My head pounded from lack of food and water and I felt an irritable exhaustion. When I could sit no longer, I grabbed the front seat, pulled myself over and crawled behind the steering wheel. I reached for the ignition wires and touched them together. The engine sputtered a few times, sounded like it was catching but then fizzled out. I looked at the dashboard and saw the gas needle tilting as far left as it could go: empty.

My memories of the previous night were scattered and colorless, like a bad dream. The smell of smoke was on my hands, in my clothes. I even tasted it. Reluctantly, I pulled the door handle and pushed but it didn't budge. I put one foot against the dash, another on the floor and counted to three. I thrust my shoulders into the door with the last few bits of energy I had left. Woosh! It burst open and I landed back-first in a snow bank. I crawled to my feet and wiped the snow from my arms, chest and face. It was a white, windless morning and I stood on the sidewalk of a city street, a nondescript block of three-family homes, lined with cars buried up to their tires. In was as familiar as it was foreign, a typical urban setting that could have been any part of town. I trudged along the sidewalk, down another side street, searching for any hints of my location. I peered between houses, looking for a landmark, something I could use to get my bearings. Finally, I came upon a street sign, tilted from a collision, but readable nonetheless; Poplar Street. I was instantly oriented. I walked faster, down one street, then another, until I came out to Roslindale Square, a bustling commercial village of nickel-and-dime shops and barrooms. I crossed Washington

Street to a payphone beside a Greek Market. Everything was closed, either because of the snowstorm or the early hour. In the quiet barrenness of an area usually so vibrant, I felt like the lone survivor of a nuclear holocaust.

I got to the phone, dropped a nickel and dialed. Ruth would know whether Harrigan's mother had been killed. It rang for almost a minute before she picked up. I was startled to hear her voice and had the urge to hang up.

"Hello?"

"Ruth."

"Jody? Jody, where are you? I've been worried sick."

"I can't tell you."

"What?" she cried.

"Listen, please, just listen. Last night there was a fire on Seaver Street, at Harrigan's mother's building."

"I know."

Then I remembered it was Harrigan and not his mother that was staying there. I stood silently, clutching the receiver and banging my head softly again the payphone.

"Jody, Jody, are you there?"

"It was Harrigan. He was staying there."

"He's safe," she said quickly.

"Safe?"

"They arrested him last night. He's in custody at the Charles Street jail," Ruth explained.

"My god," I said, holding the phone out, "These fires are killing people, Ruth."

"No, they are killing you Jody," she sobbed.

"What the hell are you talking about?" I shouted.

"You said the Fire Department was neglecting the victims, leaving children on the sidewalk in the cold!"

"I am telling you what I saw, Ruth! They are burning down buildings and leaving the families out in the cold."

Ruth tried to restrain her sobs, her voice dry and cracking in the receiver. She stopped for a moment and then spoke with a somber steadiness.

"They are vacant buildings. All of them—Warren Street, Brunswick Street, Blue Hill Avenue. I saw the files. There were no occupants, Jody. They were completely empty."

I stood at the payphone, as thin as a ghost, struggling to stay up against the morning breeze. I let the receiver fall from my hand and I stared blankly at the dial. Ruth called my name, over and over, her voice squeaking through the phone as it dangled from the cord.

CHAPTER ELEVEN

~

When I reached the backside of Mission Hill, it was near-ly noon, the sun glaring through the overcast clouds dead-center in the middle of the sky. Traffic was light and I had walked the four miles under the cover of snow banks and mailboxes, little worried about being discovered by one of Lovell's henchmen. Huge plows passed me, spreading rock salt and scraping the roadside to restore a city besieged by snow. Life was in low-gear as many residents just now began to creep from their lairs to examine the aftermath.

I followed a small street to the top of the hill, then ducked into a yard, hopped a fence, crossed another yard and finally ended up at the tall picket fence behind my apartment build-ing. I reached up, pushed with one foot, and dove to the other side, landing on the side of my knee, which, although padded by layers of gauze, stung like a whip. I lay in a pile of snow, clutching my leg and biting my tongue. I got up and went for the back door, when I saw Demetrius, the landlord, peer-ing from the basement window. I was less concerned with secrecy than I was with the fact that I was late with the rent. When I opened the door to the back stairway, he stood before me, stout and stoic, with a scruffy beard and wide grin.

"Hey D."

"Detective," he nodded. "Lose your way?"

"Fell asleep in a snow bank. Ain't that obvious?" I smirked, looking down at my wrinkled coat and soiled pants.

"In that case, you lucky you woke up," he grunted under a thick accent. I frowned and tried to pass, up the stairway, but his girth blocked my way. "If you don't mind, I have to go change."

"It's too late," Demetrius said.

"Huh? What do you mean?"

"You're date is left, gone," he added, trying to be clever. I turned around and looked him in the eye. "Who left?"

"Black Plymouth that was out front all night. Gone!"

"How do you know it was for me, D?"

"I don't, but you do," he said, shrugging his shoulders with a grin, holding an arm out to bid me pass. Demetrius was no fool and had lived too long and too hard to be naïve. Someone had stalked me, he had taken notice and now he warned me, not as an open informant, but with a Mediterranean subtleness.

"Thanks pal," I said, patting him on the shoulder as I walked up the stairs to my apartment.

"Be careful Jody Brae."

I reached above the door for a spare key that rested on the molding under a veil of dust. It wasn't the cleverest place to conceal it, but I had few items of any value. I opened the door slowly. The hinges creaked and I peered in to see that everything stood just as I had left it a week before. I half-expected to see it ransacked, with drawers flung open, clothes and newspapers strewn across the floor. I undressed with the speed of a prostitute, ran to the tub and turned on the hot water. I pulled off the gauze and looked at my naked injury for the first time. It was swollen and blue, with two tiny red spots, one to the left of the kneecap and another behind my thigh, the points of entry and exit. I got in the tub carefully and was soon enveloped in a bowl of warmth, as my tired muscles quivered and popped in little spasms of relief. I titled my head back and let the water soak deep into my hair and head.

I was so fatigued that I barely made it from the tub to my bed and lay naked for the next ten hours on a damp mattress. When I awoke it was dark again. I made tea, had some old bread and cheese and was soon revitalized. I moved quickly but didn't rush, preparing myself with the ritualistic grace of kamikaze pilots on the eve before the last flight. I put on clean pants and shirt, dusted off a black cardigan sweater and buttoned it up for warmth. Leaning under a lamp, I inspected the .38 for cleanliness, blowing through each chamber, knowing that any misfire might be my last on earth. I tossed the old bullets and replaced them with new, shiny brass slugs from a box under the sink. There was only one place to go, only one man who could explain the madness. When a cab arrived, I hopped in and told him Gropen's Pool Hall, Mattapan.

The streets were cleared and the night was crisp, with a cloudless sky of a billion stars, dimmed by city lights but determined nonetheless. We drove along Blue Hill Avenue, passed closed shops, boarded up homes and vacant lots. There was something strangely unfamiliar about this area of my youth, as if I was returning centuries later and nothing remained but the vaguest outlines of former streets and buildings. As the cabbie talked, I sat silently and hissed at the passing desolation. We came to Gropen's at the right moment, not a minute too soon. Everything unfolded like an ancient plan, executed seamlessly, as unstoppable as the rising sun. If Levinsky didn't reveal what he knew about my past, who I was and where I was from, I would blow his brains out. Either way, I would get something out of him.

When the cab pulled into the rear parking lot, I handed the driver a $20 and got out. As I walked towards the back door, he called, "sir, sir, sir," the astonished cries of an honest man who had just been given three times the fare. I ignored him and he sped off. I reached the door of the building, grabbed the handle and yanked it open. The lights were low and the smoke was thin. In the distance, five or six men played pool while a few lingered beside the bar. All heads turned when I entered and walked across the room. I nodded to the bartender and headed to the stairwell door, as simple as a saint, as shameless as a sinner.

The bartender followed and tried to intercede as I ascended the stairs. I held my hand to his gut and shoved him away, whipping out my gun as an afterthought. He scurried away, bumbling through the door, his bald head gleaming. I got to the top of the stairwell and waited. I breathed deeply, counted to three and kicked the door. It swung open to reveal Levinsky, fixed to the same wooden chair, chomping a cigar and clutching a hand of cards. His henchmen jumped from their seats, startled but not frightened. Had I given them a minute to think or act, they may have come at me. But I walked right over, grabbed the edge of the table and flipped it on its side. Crash! Cards flew into the air, glasses shattered on the floor. I held out the .38 and pointed it at Levinsky, right between the eyes.

"I want answers!"

The old man seethed with a helpless rage, his temples pulsating and his nostrils flaring. I moved the pistol in three quick motions, just to watch all three men flinch.

Levinsky held his hands in the air. "Son, calm yourself. You have a lot of balls coming in here!" he said nervously. I pointed the barrel within an inch of his nose and he began to sweat.

"You send me on a search to find my name? Then try to execute me?"

"What the hell are you talking about?" Levinsky shot back.

"Don't play games old man!"

"You better start talking sense kid. You might kill me. You'll never make it out alive!"

Suddenly the man on my left lunged. I ducked, turned and smacked his forehead with the butt end of the pistol. He backed away, swayed for a second then fell to the floor. I turned back to Levinsky.

"Next one who tries anything gets shot!"

"Alright Brae, you have our attention."

"I found the building," I continued. "Bowdoin Street, right? HARLAN-BRAE, right? I show up and get shot!" I said, pulling up a pant leg to reveal a blistering bulb of pink and blue.

"That wasn't me. If I shot you, you'd be dead!"

"I want answers or you'll be dead!" I shrieked. "I've got a hole in my leg and a partner who was nearly beaten to death!"

Levinsky held his hands out, nodding and rolling his eyes. "Listen, Brae, I have no idea what happened to you. Sit down, please." He turned to his right, "Cohen, get us some drinks. Be quick!"

"I don't drink Levinsky."

"Get Mr. Brae some water."

He looked back to me and continued.

"Brae, please, let Andre get us some drinks. Let's talk this over." As he spoke, something clicked. Andre Cohen. A. Cohen.

"Come back Andre!" I screamed. "You're A. Cohen?"

The man shrugged his shoulders.

"Tell me why your name is associated with so many properties that have burned down in Roxbury?"

Levinsky looked at Cohen and nodded, as if giving permission to reply.

"There're lots of A. Cohen's. Who's to say it's me?"

"You listed your address as 1476 Blue Hill Avenue! This building," I said, lying with a straight face.

Cohen stood quiet, reluctant to speak or act, and I knew I had struck gold.

"Brae, if you sit down and have a drink, I will explain everything." Levinsky held out his hand graciously. I backed away and took a chair. Cohen walked over to a small cabinet bar and I watched him obsessively. If he reached too quickly for a glass, rattled the ice, or stirred to fast, I might have shot him in the back. He handed Levinsky a bourbon and soda water and me ice water. I took a huge gulp and stared at Levinsky, my arm still and the pistol pointed.

Levinsky turned to Cohen, "Thank you. Now get out. And take sleeping beauty." Cohen walked over, heaved his unconscious cohort over one shoulder and dragged him across the floor, through the doorway. The door slammed shut and the room was quiet.

Levinsky wiped his eyes and looked at me. "You have to understand the way things were years ago."

"Get to the point."

"Brae, what do you know about your childhood? Please, tell me."

"I remember the Home For Stray Boys. Nothing before that."

"But who were your parents?"

"As far as I'm concerned, I don't have any."

Levinsky's expression softened. As he spoke he held the glass between his middle finger and thumb, waving it like a concert conductor.

"Listen son, I'm an old man. I don't have much time left. I play a few card games, have a few drinks, maybe smoke one too many cigars. I am going to make you an offer…"

"I'm not here to make a deal."

"And I'm not offering one. What I have I'm selling at a premium."

"What might that be?"

"Knowledge."

"You'll have to do better than that. Every guy on the block thinks he knows something no one else does."

"This is your chance Brae. What I can tell you no one else can. But if I die, if I am thrown in jail, then I'll go to my grave with your past as well as my own."

"My past is the Home."

"You had a mother."

"I understand biology. And a father?"

"That I'm afraid, I can't answer."

"If he were here, I'd put a round in his head too."

Levinsky's voice lowered to a whisper and he leaned in close.

"I can tell you who she was."

The gun began to quiver, my hand shook and my eyes lost focus. The words were hypnotic and I was transported beyond the tension of the bare room, out of the present, and to a realm of past images, impressions, thoughts and visions. I saw a young child, toothless and cold, as awkward as an ostrich, running through the streets of Roxbury with a wool coat and no socks. In his hand was a screwdriver, in his pocket a bag of peanuts. Flash forward and I saw a young man, cynical before his time, in soiled fatigues and standing beside barracks with two friends, smirking while they smiled. Next there was snow and mountains, stretching to the horizon. Machine gun fire cracked in the distance, disturbing the tranquility, mocking the solitude. Bloodied soldiers, young men if not boys, passed on stretchers like corpses in waiting. The young child returned again, crouched in a hallway, concealed by a shadow, listening to the silence and remembering the last birthday and the five candles that burned out before the wish was wished. It was a life relived and I watched with the fascination of a quiet observer, as lurking and detached as scientist, if only to prove a theory but achieve nothing.

"What do you want from me?"

"A trade."

"What could I possibly trade with you?"

"Your past for my future."

"I have neither."

"Brae, you're nothing if not determined. No one has counted you out yet. When the hammer drops and heads start rolling, I want to be left out of this mess."

"What mess is that?" I asked, prying for information, hoping for a confession. Levinsky took a deep breath and held the glass out, pointing his finger at my chest.

"I need your word that any criminal investigations, any indictments don't get to me."

"Do you deserve any trouble?"

"I don't know what I deserve. Sure, I've made my mistakes. But I am asking you kindly. Keep me out of this and I'll tell you who you are."

"Let's hear it."

"I need your word," Levinsky said, squinting and staring into my eyes so fiercely that my soul burned.

"You have it."

CHAPTER TWELVE

~

"**P**artner, get up!"

A large hand took my arm and shoulder and pulled me from the ground. I was groggy and semi-conscious, a stream of drool tethered to my lips, frozen to my five-day scruff. Everything spun suddenly as I was hoisted over a shoulder and carried off. With my eyelids frozen shut, I experienced everything by sound and sense. Two voices conversed, one familiar and one strangely accented, as plain and direct as a drill-sergeant's. I finally could open my eyes and saw the glare of siren lights, flashing wildly, somewhere near. All other forms and figures were blurred. I clutched the shoulder of the man who held me and prayed for salvation. If I had been captured, at least I would know, finally, who sought me. Whether Lovell, Levinsky, the force, the entire city or even the world itself, I would know. I braced for anything.

"How long has he been there?" I heard.

"Don't know. He's breathing and conscious."

I was lowered into the backseat of a cruiser, unmarked and plain, a black Plymouth, the same car Demetrius had warned me about. The door slammed shut and I pressed against the window, shivering from cold, sweating in fear. As the car started to move, I peered through one eye to the streets beyond, searching for a landmark or any sign that might indicate our position and direction. I hadn't even bothered to look to the front seat, since I was always more concerned by where I was than who I was with. But then a voice behind the wheel called to me.

"You almost died out there partner."

"What were you thinking?" the passenger said.

I peeled my face from the window, turned and looked into the rear view mirror to see a large round face staring back. It was McQuillan. When he smiled, I felt suddenly at ease and whatever happened next was a little less uncertain. If I knew anything, it was that he wasn't one of them. I leaned deep into the seat, closed my eyes and knew I was safe.

I woke up on my back, lying on a bed, my knee as sore as the night I got shot. A corner lamp, glowing yellow through a tasseled shade, illuminated the empty room. On the walls were faux paintings and elegant wallpaper. The floor was covered by commercial carpeting and beside the door was a buzzer for room service. Although the curtains were pulled shut, I knew it was a hotel room somewhere downtown. I heard footsteps and looked to see McQuillan, walking in with a tray of food and coffee. Next to him was a man, middle-aged, slight and fit, with dark thinning hair and even darker eyes. He wore a proper suit and shining shoes. His expression was blank and he stood with the rigidity of a toy soldier.

"Hey partner. How are you feeling?" McQuillan asked, "Take a couple of these and drink some coffee."

I took the aspirin and swallowed it dry. McQuillan placed the tray on a side table and helped me up from the bed. The smell of fresh coffee was intoxicating. I grabbed a slice of toast and cantaloupe and devoured them whole.

"What happened," I asked, my voice cracking.

"You tell us."

"I don't remember. Who's your friend?" I said nodding to the stranger.

"Funny you should ask," McQuillan smirked. "Detective, this is Paul Deitz of the FBI."

I stopped chewing, looked at McQuillan, and then looked at the man. He nodded and I leaned forward with my arm outstretched. As we shook, I stared to see if he flinched, hoping to call their bluff, wondering if it was all a joke.

"My pleasure, sir," I said. "How was I lucky enough to be accidently rescued by the FBI?"

"It was no accident," Deitz stated, "We've been following you for weeks."

"You didn't happen to try to run me off the road last week, did you?"

"That wasn't us, I'm afraid. But we know who it was."

"That's encouraging," I said, sipping the coffee.

"Jody," McQuillan said, "I will start from the beginning. This is strictly confidential. Any breach would be a Federal offense."

I nodded.

"The FBI has been building a case against Lovell. We will have a federal indictment within days."

"You?"

"Me. I've been doing field surveillance for the Bureau since I left the service. Mainly internal investigations, bribes, abuses, etc."

"And I thought that was my job."

"As Stalin said," Deitz interrupted, "Who will police the police. This is fairly routine. We've been monitoring departments across the country for over a decade. You can thank Senator McCarthy for that."

"Lovell is dirty," McQuillan continued, "He's been involved in a number of scams throughout the years. We have him on arson, insurance fraud, and possibly murder."

"Why are you telling me?"

McQuillan took a seat on the bed.

"We know you are investigating the fires in Roxbury. Lovell is organizing them and getting kickbacks from the property owners on the insurance money."

"I was taken off the case."

"Why?" Deitz wondered.

"No stated reason. Jackson said I needed a break."

"Why were you running down Blue Hill Avenue last night?" McQuillan asked pointedly.

"I said, I don't remember anything."

"Why were you at Gropen's Pool Hall?" Deitz barked.

I shook my head and stared at the wall as if in a day-dream.

"Do you know a Wilmer Levinsky?"

"Maybe…"

"Well, he's named as a co-defendant on the indictment."

"Look, Jody," McQuillan said, "This isn't an interrogation. But we've got a Chief of Police who will most likely be the next mayor. He's got a lot of power, the cops, the labor unions, the construction firms. We need to dethrone him."

"How can I help?" I asked.

"Start by explaining everything that's happened to you in the past few days," Deitz replied.

"We need your help in this. Please," McQuillan pleaded.

"Where's Harrigan?"

"He's has been arrested for arson. They say he torched a building on Blue Hill Avenue…"

"That's a fucking lie!" I shrieked, "We were both there that night. Why the hell would an officer torch a building?"

"Several Nation members are named in the indictment, including the minister. They've been doing Lovell's dirty work. Breaking into the buildings—dousing the basement and hallways with acetone, dropping the match."

"Nation members?" I said in astonishment.

"The minister has a long history with Lovell. They grew up together in the South End. In '28 they were arrested together, along with some other hoods, for robbing meat trucks by Fort Point Channel." McQuillan added.

"We know your partner was attending services," Deitz said.

"Harrigan had only been to a few meetings. He'd just moved back to town for Christ's sake."

"He was seen leaving the premises ten minutes before the fire," Deitz added, "There's a witness. A Sam…"

"Sam Kagan." McQuillan added.

"Sam the hatman?" I asked. McQuillan and Deitz looked at each other.

"They found a charred doll in his apartment, a keepsake from the fire. It was identified by a former resident."

"Former?"

"The building was vacant," Deitz explained, "In the process of being sold when it burned down. Residents were evicted months ago. Some were allowed to store things in the basement until they relocated."

McQuillan went on, "Harrigan was also spotted trying to break into a vacant building on Bowdoin Street."

"Bowdoin Street?"

"Yeh, from the report, he was ordered to halt. He turned around with his weapon drawn. Shots were exchanged. No one was hit."

I laughed to myself, wanting to tell what really happened, but I let them continue.

"Then his own apartment building burns," Deitz went on, "The department claims someone tipped him off that he was being investigated for arson. So he torched his own place to seem an unlikely suspect. A bit ironic, huh?"

"What do you think?" I said, looking to both of them.

McQuillan looked to Deitz, then to me. "We think a black man is an easy scapegoat."

"Unless we can nail Lovell first, that is," Deitz said.

"What do you need from me?"

"Simple," McQuillan said, "We need you to keep running. We know Lovell's men are after you. Not sure if their intention is to kill you. My guess is they already would have done so. I think they want to keep you scared…"

"Scared enough to keep your mouth shut," Deitz said, "They seem reluctant to get rid of you. We're not sure why. Do you know?"

"Because I can run faster than them," I smirked.

McQuillan loosened his tie, turned to me and said, "Can we count on you?"

"You want me to wander the streets like a fugitive?"

"Just continue the investigation. They know you're on to them…"

"Don't take any risks," Deitz interjected. "We've got your back. We're watching even when you don't know it."

"What about Harrigan?"

"He's safer in custody. When we get Lovell, he'll be exonerated."

"Promise?"

"You have my word, soldier."

My plight had taken on a life of its own, a scandal that burst beyond the confines of parochial Boston and into the limelight of Federal scrutiny. Each turn had become more unbelievable than the previous and every minute seemed more urgent than the last. Before we left the hotel room, McQuillan handed me a new outfit, wool pants and navy sweater, compliment of the Feds. He had overestimated my size and the clothes hung from my shrinking body like a sheet over a skeleton.

We got into the Plymouth and I asked for a lift to Blue Hill Avenue to settle some business. Deitz agreed and followed McQuillan's directions like a confused tourist, blowing through stop signs and stopping at green lights. As we passed through Roxbury, he drove with a nervous caution, repulsed by the dilapidation and blight that contrasted so bleakly with the handsome boardrooms of the Bureau offices in Washington. The Feds were the government equivalent of corporate management, clean, polite, God-fearing and ruthless. Observing Deitz's discomfort made me a little less intimidated.

"Pull over here." I said.

"Right here?"

"Yes, at the corner."

I got out, shook McQuillan's hand and walked down the sidewalk in the noonday sun. Despite a shower and new clothes, I was exhausted. I passed some homeless men, sitting against a wall beside a liquor store. They waved as I passed, curious that a smartly dressed white guy would be walking down the sidewalk. I quickened my pace until I came to the block of shops where Sam's store was. Witness intimidation was the last thing that concerned me in my quest to avenge Harrigan. With the FBI on my side, I felt a new sense of invincibility that made me as bold as it did foolish. Sam was going to answer for his lies. I looked up and down Blue Hill Avenue and then approached the shop door. It was locked, closed, with a small note taped at eye level:

DEAR PATRONS. AGNES AND I WOULD LIKE TO THANK YOU FOR THIRTY YEARS OF LOYALTY. WE HAVE DECIDED TO CLOSE THE SHOP AND PURSUE OUR DREAM OF RETIREMENT IN FLORIDA. THANKS FOR THE CHERISHED MEMORIES. AGNES & SAM.

Sam the hat man had made his escape, had fled like a thief in the night, leaving behind the friends and enemies he had cultivated for over half a century. Gone was another character from old Roxbury. I was frustrated, disappointed even, and ripped the note from the door, crumpling it in one hand and tossing it to the breeze. Sam had gotten the last word, or at least the last laugh and I imagined him reclining in the sun with a straw hat, sipping from a glass of salty ice and cheap liquor. Maybe he would be subpoenaed, but it was unlikely.

I walked alone, half-discouraged, thinking of the past and wondering about tomorrow. I skipped over potholes, kicked up trash and wandered through my old neighborhood with no fear, no reluctance. I wasn't sure if I was at a dead end or new beginning. All I knew was I was killing time, staying alive until the Feds had enough evidence to bring down the house of Lovell. I came to the apartment building on Blue Hill Avenue that had burned weeks before. It was unchanged, except for the snow that covered its roof and the small pitched overhang along the front, the remnants of a ground-floor shop from years past. I crossed Intervale Street and stopped into a corner store for a pack of cigarettes. When I came out, I stood on the sidewalk smoking one after another, staying alive by killing time, an irony I couldn't overlook. Behind the charred building, on Intervale Street, I spotted a blue awning above which was written, Masjid al-Qur'an. The Mosque was in an old Victorian house, converted a few years back by adding a brick anteroom with a large arched entranceway. Along the right side was an alleyway leading to the door of the food bank where Harrigan had met his informant. A portion of the sidewall was burned, the roof eaves severely damaged and two windows boarded up, the unfortunate result of the building fire next door. The flames must have followed the dry brush of the yard between the two buildings, eventually reaching the Mosque, quelled only by the mercy of their savior, a sign that would surely encourage the fledgling congregation.

I crossed the street towards the building. The scent of damp ash was still in the air, a smell that now seemed to follow me wherever I went. I reached the front steps, stood under the awning and looked at the wooden double doors with a curious hesitation. I didn't know how to knock, wasn't sure where to enter. Was this the entrance to their prayer room or their administrative office? The truth was I knew nothing about Black Muslims. They swept into Boston behind the hordes of Blacks that poured into the city after the war in search of jobs and homes. I didn't know their worship times or whether there was activity during off-hours. The sect was as mysterious as my childhood, and almost as hostile. I walked up the granite stairs and knocked when, as if on cue, the door opened and a middle-aged black man stood smiling. He was tall and well-dressed, with black-rimmed glasses, close-cropped hair and two rows of large, glistening teeth.

"How may I help you young man?" he said with a wide grin.

"I'm Detective Jody Brae. I was hoping you could answer some questions."

He stood for a moment, his face unflinching, as if caught off-guard but to cool to let on. "Please, come in." He held the door open as I entered. "I am Dr. Thaddeus Muhammad," he said, extending a hand. As we shook, I nodded with a cautious reverence.

I followed him down a narrow hallway and into a small office, a sort of scholar's study, with random sized bookshelves against every wall, stuffed with books and binders. One wall commemorated the congregation with gold-framed pictures of weekend outings, summer picnics and service work. There were file cabinets and end-tables, a student's desk and wooden boxes stacked too high. Everything in the room was either donated or purchased at a yard sale.

On the other wall were two tapestries, hung from the ceiling, bearing inscriptions in Arabic on yellow parchment paper, much like Egyptian artifacts. In the corner stood a globe supported by a decorative bronze stand, tilted to reveal Africa and the Middle East. At the center of the room was a large oak desk with turned legs and claw feet. Behind that, next to the window, was a short flagpole draped with an American flag and, on the wall, a framed citation from the Boston Patrolmen's Association for civic activism.

The man offered me a seat on an old ladder-back, another antique, which creaked and wobbled when I put my weight on it. He walked around and sat behind the desk, leaning forward and gazing with an almost smug politeness.

"I've been expecting you Mr. Brae."

"That's strange. I hadn't given it a thought of coming by until ten minutes ago."

He leaned back into the chair, put his arms behind his head and chuckled. His fingers were lined with brass rings, a gaudy indication of status in a neighborhood where what you had was who you were.

"But you had to come. Your partner is a brother of ours. That makes us related, in a way?"

"My partner was given false information by someone in your church…"

"Mosque, if you would please, sir…" he interrupted.

"Mosque. He was lured next door and beaten, almost to death."

"I know that Detective. And I am sorry."

"Do you have something to be sorry about?"

The man raised an eyebrow, startled if not insulted by my boldness. He dropped his hands to the desk, leaned forward and paused.

"You see, Mr. Brae, compassion is fundamental to Islam. Despite how we are portrayed in the media, we do good works."

"I know. My partner was here to drop off donations the day he was beaten," I said plainly.

"That's unusual. Our donation center has been closed since the fire next door damaged our supply room." He frowned. "We, also, suffered from the fire."

"Harrigan met a member of yours here the same night. He wouldn't lie."

There was an uncomfortable silence. The man put two fingers to his lips and looked up, thinking or contriving, a suspicious delay for someone with nothing to hide. I kept my eyes fixed on his expression, searching for any signs of hesitation, duplicity, the slightest hint that he was less pious than his markings and manners suggested. He laughed to himself, as if replaying scenes in his mind, wrestling with notions and ideas, plotting his next move, the proper response.

"Are you afraid, Detective?" he asked, looking through his glasses with an iron gaze, a sudden transformation from the shallow formalities of moments ago. The question was so vague I felt stumped. I started to speak, then stopped, then began again.

"No more than I've always been."

"Then why have you come here?" he wondered.

"I need answers."

"In the Koran it says, 'Fear God and he will give you knowledge.'"

"In my life, I've feared nothing except God."

"We all live with fear. Some of us just mask it better."

"Is that what I am doing?" I asked, turning his philosophy back at him.

"No," he said, leaning over the desk and lowering his voice. "You don't hide. Your heart and soul are written across your face, plain as day."

"I blush easy, if that's what you mean?" I snickered.

"No Mr. Brae, you're much more revealing than that. I can see you are not here to inquire about prayer services," he added with a grin.

"I thought you might be able to help me."

"I will try. Sincerely, I will."

"It's Harrigan."

"Brother Harrigan. What can I tell you?"

"How well do you really know him?"

"Well, let me see," he said, folding his knuckles and wincing in thought, "He's been visiting us for a few months now. He seems a bit distant, a bit tentative, perhaps a little troubled. We all are, of course."

I put my hands on the desk and leaned towards the minister, staring fiercely into his eyes.

"Would he be capable of burning down buildings?"

Dr. Muhammad's eyes flickered and he was suddenly fretful, pushing aside papers, organizing pencils. As I watched him he looked away and when I smiled he smirked. He turned towards the window and looked through the shade, crossing his arms and humming a strange tune. I felt his uneasiness and his nervous silence was evidence enough of something sinister lurking beneath his bowtie, from behind the academic pretense of his bulky glasses. I had him cornered in his own room.

Finally, he sighed, the relief of having made a critical choice, one that wasn't easy but was perhaps the easiest. He turned to me and spoke.

"Harrigan struck me as unstable." I smiled within but kept a straight face. "And as reluctant as I am to turn on a brother, I worry more about the consequences…"

I broke him off mid-sentence and blurted out, "I have information that Harrigan is directly involved in the rash of fires that's been plaguing this area,"

"Oh dear, Mr. Brae," the minister said, his lips quivering, a reaction of disbelief that was poorly acted. I kept the pressure on, lowering my voice to a whisper, "We are preparing to make an arrest. But we need to be sure."

"It's not my business to know how your fine department manages its affairs. I can say only that brother Harrigan was troubled."

The minister was hesitant to finger Harrigan unjustly but feared more that his congregation's involvement in Lovell's crimes and cover-ups would be discovered. I laid before him the ultimate test of criminal ethics, to see whether he would guarantee his own freedom at the expense of his coconspirators. The phone on the desk rang and the minister snatched it up in relief. Someone spoke and he nodded. He then held the receiver to his shoulder, mouthed an apology and suggested we speak at another time. I stood up and spoke loudly, interrupting his conversation.

"Before the department makes a move, I need to know."

The minister looked up, mildly disturbed, listening to the caller yet focused on me. With his hand covering the receiver, he whispered with the cringing reluctance of someone forced to a confession.

"I do, unfortunately, believe that Harrigan would be capable of such actions."

When I discovered the back door was locked, I knew my entrance was going to cause a stir. Ruth's apartment building was only one in a continuum of attached brick buildings along Chestnut Street. To get to the front, I had to walk along a narrow garden corridor and cut through an alleyway three blocks away, only to walk back up the street to her doorway.

I knocked three times and waited but there was no response. There were no lights on in the windows and the hallway was dark. I never needed a woman like I did that moment. Evening set in and the temperature began to drop. I sat on the stoop like a vagrant, with only a few dollars and nowhere to go. I was at a dead end, too proud to stay and too stubborn to leave. I could have taken a three dollar cab ride to my apartment, but with Harrigan's arrest, it was too risky. For all I knew, Demetrius was part of the scandal also. Nothing would have surprised me, no news, good or bad, could have altered my distrust. If someone had told me Pearl Harbor was attacked again, I would have believed it. It was easier to believe the unbelievable than to go on trying to make sense out of the senseless.

When I finished a cigarette, I tilted my head down and stared at the granite steps. I felt my eyelids close and did nothing to resist. I stopped shivering and sank into a drowsy sleep, dreaming of warmth and imagining beach days. Just when the last flicker of the present moment was about to vanish, restoring me to the dreamy solitude of sleep, the door swung open behind and I jumped. I turned to see Ruth, dressed in a white nightgown and wool socks that were too big for her feet. She looked out before looking down and might have missed me entirely if it weren't for my sudden movement.

"Jody," she said and burst into tears. She leaned over and put her arms around me, trying to warm me although her clothes were much thinner. Crouched on the stairs and unable to move, I clung to her like a life raft. I felt her hands press into my back as tears rolled down her eyes onto my cheeks. She pulled me inside and we tiptoed up the stairs to the apartment. I collapsed to the couch with Ruth still in my arms and waited for the feeling to be restored to my limbs. A room never felt as warm as it did that night. And although the chill took several minutes to subside, I sweated profusely.

"Where have you been? You look awful," she cried.

"I've been everywhere," I said, wondering at her smudged mascara.

"You need to get out of these clothes. They're filthy," she cried as she unbuttoned my shirt and belt, tending to me as she did always when I showed up at her doorstep in the cold. The longer I rested on the couch the worse I felt, as if my body began to realize the extent of its deprivation. Soon I couldn't even move. As I alternated between chills and fever, Ruth worked to adjust the room temperature. I faded in and out, hearing things that weren't there and not seeing things that were. A slow and constant ached permeated my entire body, a paralyzing soreness that felt like it was everywhere and nowhere at the same time.

The vision of Ruth's face wavered in and out of my field of view and I wondered what was happening to me. For a moment I recalled Harrigan's hospital experience and I even wondered if Ruth was drugging me like they did him. Regardless, I was at her mercy, whether she would have me live or die. All I could do was moan.

"Jody, wake up!" Ruth shrieked, shaking my shoulders and slapping my cheeks. I opened one eye to see a small leather bag beside the couch. Ruth reached in and pulled out a stethoscope and blood pressure monitor. She held the chestpiece against my heart and listened. When she wrapped the cuff around my bicep, my arm hung limply off the couch. If McQuillan was with the FBI, maybe I would learn Ruth was really a doctor, I wondered fancifully.

"You going to operate?" I whimpered.

"I was in nursing school before I got into forensics. Open up and say "ah."

When she took the thermometer out and read it, I watched her face collapse in disbelief.

"My gosh, you have a temperature of 104! Your heartbeat is rapid. You're burning up. We need to get you to a hospital," she cried.

"No, Ruth, I can't. If they find me, I am as good as dead."

"Who, Jody? If who finds you?"

"Please Ruth, you need to trust me. Don't believe anything you've heard."

My pleas were the last thing I remembered before drifting into a hazy semi-consciousness. I awoke sometime later—maybe hours, maybe days—to a jarring chill of coldness, so deep that every muscle trembled. When I opened my eyes, I found myself immersed neck-deep in a bathtub of water and ice. Ruth leaned over from above, caressing my forehead with a towel. My hands and feet were numb from cold and my skin was blue. Yet I felt strangely relaxed, as cold as I was, and the headache that had followed me since my troubles began, was gone. I drifted back to sleep.

Later I awoke in bed, face up and shaking violently. My bones ached and my head throbbed. Again, Ruth sat over me, smiling softly and wiping my face and brow. She reached across and gently pushed my eyelids closed.

At some point later I heard the sound of rain and knew I was there again, running through streets without end in the dark, scared and haunted. I ran though I was winded, my heart pounded under my ribcage. I tried to turn left, to run right, but my direction was predestined and all I could do was not resist. Raindrops rolled along my cheeks, bounced off my shoulders. I shook my head to clear the water from my ears when suddenly I spotted the vision of her, looming in the distance, as fixed as a tree yet swaying gently. "More air, more air," I mouthed as I ran faster and faster yet. She was within yards, the glowing image beckoning to me, tempting

me like an angel from some past world where only goodness reigned. As I began to close in, she was just beyond my
grasp and didn't move. I yearned to see her face, to speak to
her and hear her voice. I wanted to ask her about Levinsky. I
wanted to say that finally, after all these years, I understood
and wasn't angry.

I jumped up in bed like a spring board, startled as a
mouse, and looked around the room with wide, gleaming eyes.

"Jody, please, lay down," Ruth said, caressing my shoulders.

"What happened? What time is it? Where are we?" I
shouted between breaths.

"You've been sleeping a long time."

"How long?" I said.

Ruth was silent.

"How long, please?"

"Five days, Jody."

My mind was murky, my thoughts were someone else's,
fleeting, random, beyond my control. I lay lethargically, as
disoriented as a coma patient twenty years later. I looked
through the shades of the window and saw it was evening.
I lay back into the mattress and experienced the sensations
and impulses of being alive. It was euphoric.

When I had finally calmed down and my breathing returned to normal, I turned to Ruth, who lay beside me with
the patience of a mother.

"I saw her again."

"Did she speak to you?"

"No. Just stood there, in the rain."

"Does she scare you?"

"I don't know. What happened?"

"You showed up last Monday. You had a fever that could have killed you. You said you couldn't go to the hospital. I was scared but it's alright."

"Thank you."

Ruth smiled and proceeded to message my neck as we spoke. She ran her fingers through my damp hair and didn't take her eyes off me.

"I need to get to McQuillan. I was supposed to meet him Tuesday."

"Jody," Ruth said softly.

"Yes?"

"I need to know."

Ruth had waited like a soldier's wife, patiently, quietly and with unwavering support. I owed her the world and everything in it, or at least an explanation.

She continued, "I was told you're suffering from mental illness."

"Do you believe that?"

She gasped and looked at the wall blankly. Then she looked back to me, shrugged her shoulders and wondered.

"No, I don't. My father lost his mind. He spent his life dragging us across the country, from place to place, trying forever to build a bigger and better career. His ambition always outpaced his achievements. Years of drinking turned him into a bitter old man. His demons were of his own making."

"And mine are not," I said, looking her straight in the eyes. "But it's a long story. And it begins thirty years ago."

"I told you before I have time," she smiled.

CHAPTER THIRTEEN

The Boston Public Gardens contained a network of small footpaths that wound along some of the lushest arrangements of flowers and bushes in the city. Woven throughout were narrow streams and rivulets that collected at a central basin, over which stretched an ornate arched footbridge. As a child, I had been brought here every summer with the Home's annual city field trip. The moment I walked through the wrought iron gates, I was overcome by the perfume scent of the endless flowers. I would lean over the embankment and stare into the lily pond, reach mischievously for the long neck of a swan that hovered near the shoreline. For a child whose world was enclosed by brick, cement and mortar, it was paradise. Each year the bridge and walkways seemed smaller and less magical, but they never lost their charm.

By now the flowers were dead, the swans were gone and the pond was a murky black pool. Children passed by with their parents, hand in hand, pointing at statues and looking for swans, which had been relocated for winter. I would have mentioned it to them, but I was focused on bigger things. The small trees and hedges, although bare, provided enough cover for me to blend into anonymity as I waited for McQuillan and Deitz. I sat on the bench in the cold midday sun with my collar turned upright, reading the newspaper. I reached into my coat pocket for another cigarette, the fifth one, while awaiting a meeting that was long overdue. I heard three quick honks of a horn and turned to see a car idling along Beacon Street, the unmistakable figure of McQuillan in the driver's seat. He must have had enough of Deitz's driving, I thought, as I walked through the park gates towards them.

We drove for a block in silence, speeding down Beacon Street away from downtown to a destination that was irrelevant.

"What happened to last Tuesday?" McQuillan said, looking at me in the rear view.

"The flu happened. I'm lucky to be here."

"Any new information?"

"Harrigan is clean. There's no question."

"You're sure about that?" Deitz asked, looking back.

"I am sure. I met with the minister of the Mosque. Told him Harrigan was a suspect."

"And?" McQuillan asked.

"He turned on Harrigan like a dog."

"Good. We need to be sure."

"We're sure."

We drove through Kenmore Square and into Brookline. I was about to mention we were leaving our jurisdiction when I remembered the Bureau had no boundaries. They were transparent, borderless and everywhere. I felt somehow protected in the presence of Deitz, his cool and steady demeanor a refreshing change from the sloppy recklessness of city cops and detectives. He was more polished than anyone I knew, save Jackson. Deitz was likely college educated, probably at some small Southern college with a strong military tradition. I guessed he had done a stint in either the Second World War or Korea but I couldn't guess his age on a bet. He may have been forty or sixty. His smooth complexion, glassy eyes and trim physique obscured any indications of age. His dark conservative suit, perfectly pressed and impeccably tailored, gave him the appearance of the indistinguishable everyman. Deitz was an Eisenhower man without doubt, a warrior of the 50's, an era that was gone but still lingered in many forms. Behind his plainness was an almost ideological determination to defeat the three enemies of a civil Christian society; crime, corruption, and Communism.

We drove through Brookline, along tree-lined streets of Tudor homes and grand estates, a town of unspeakable affluence whose easternmost edge dipped into Boston like the hemline of a dowager into a puddle. Homes were set back, tucked away and hidden behind hedgerows as tall as streetlamps, suggesting a secluded wealth untouched by the bustle and bother of modern society. Although only a mile apart at their closest points, Brookline was continents away from the crime-infested dilapidation of Roxbury. I rolled down the back window and breathed in the luxurious air. We parked at the crest of a hill, overlooking Saint Elizabeth's hospital in Brighton and Boston in the foreground. We were safe from Lovell's influence, untracked and free from his prowling henchman. That was why we drove to Brookline.

"What's next?" I asked.

"Lovell wants Harrigan convicted. They have witnesses, evidence and a judge in the pocket."

"What about me?"

"We aren't sure. The information is muddled," McQuillan said. "Our sources think that you're either not a problem or too scared to talk."

I laughed. "They don't know me."

"We need to keep them guessing," McQuillan said.

"Listen," Deitz added, "we need you to hang on for a couple more days. Lovell is holding a press conference Friday. If everything works out we will make the arrest then."

"Why wait?"

"The indictment needs to be airtight. He's got too much influence," McQuillan said.

"We need you to contact Jackson," Deitz continued, "tell him that you had checked yourself into McLean's hospital under duress."

"Tell Jackson that I'm nuts? One call will confirm I haven't been anywhere near the place," I said, feeling irritated. McQuillan reached into a bag on the floor and handed me a folder.

"That's been taken care of. Here're your release forms. You were suffering from post-traumatic stress. Read through these and memorize your lines," he said with a restrained grin.

"We need you to go home to your apartment. Act like everything's normal. We have you covered, so don't worry. If Lovell's men make a move, we will be on them like flies on shit."

"I need to get killed so you get the evidence you need?"

"Jody," McQuillan said sternly, "It won't get that far. From one soldier to another, brother to brother. I'll have your back."

With that, Deitz put the car in drive, turned around and sped back towards the city. They dropped me off in Back Bay, down a rear alleyway used for trash collection, to ensure no one saw us. I stuffed the folder under my coat and walked along Clarendon to Newbury Street. The sidewalks were busy with college students, businessmen and the budget-conscious tourist who discovered that December was cheaper than July. I walked into Creccio's Café and took a seat by the window, the same table where Harrigan and I sat on our first day. I bought a black coffee, sat down and opened the folder to review the documents Deitz had given me. I was amazed before I thumbed through half of them. They were as authentic as a tax bill. My name even included the initial "H," the result of a typing error, I was told, by a clerk at the registry shortly after I had arrived at the Home. In her impatience, she accidently hit "H" in rapid succession, creating forever the illusion of a middle name. Except for the service, I never used the initial and so every official document, from my driver's license to my pension account, lacked this distinguishing letter. And now, ironically, it was printed on my release form from an insane asylum.

At the corner of the café was a pay phone. As I sipped the coffee, I debated calling Jackson. I hadn't spoken to him since he took me off the case and part of me wondered if he was involved with Lovell's men. But even that would have been unimaginable since Jackson above all cherished his integrity and had a sense of justice that, to him, was more precious than life itself. I had to call him, there was no other option.

The phone rang and he picked up as if expecting me.

"Captain Jackson speaking."

"Captain, it's Brae." There was a short silence and I could hear classical music playing in the background.

"Detective, you have a lot to answer for. Where are you?"

"I'm home."

"You're not at your apartment."

"I'm back in Boston."

"Do you know Harrigan's been arrested?"

"I heard."

"And you didn't contact me? I've been calling you. I sent patrolmen by your house on several occasions. We need to talk."

"I know. I should have called. I've been in McLean's for the past couple of weeks."

"I see," Jackson said with a sigh, "Well, I am glad your family's doing well. It's important to pay a visit once in a while…" I thought I had misheard him. I took the receiver away from my ear and looked at it curiously.

"Captain, I said I was in McLean's. I'm suffering from stress. I have the release form in my hand!"

"Great, Brae, a little R&R is necessary. Now get home and get some rest. I am heading to the Algonquin Club for a drink."

"Captain, what the hell are you talking about?"

"We're all glad you're doing well. Stop in next week."

Jackson hung up and I stood holding the receiver, puzzled by his attempt to mask our conversation. Someone was listening and he was being cautious. I heard a forced cough and turned to see a middle-aged meter maid standing behind me, waiting to use the phone. She smiled impatiently and I nodded. It was the same meter maid I had argued with weeks before when I had taken Harrigan for coffee. Everything comes full circle, I thought.

I paid for the coffee and headed to the Algonquin club. I walked along Arlington Street briskly, staring straight ahead and not for a moment looking to either side. I had the strange sensation of being observed, although I knew that I wasn't. The scandal within city hall and the police department was nearing its climax and I felt more vulnerable than ever. The manic frenzy of the afternoon gave me a giddy paranoia and I worried that someone would leap from nowhere and get me.

I walked fast, passing pedestrians and staying close to the wall of the buildings. When I reached Commonwealth Avenue, at the edge of the Public Gardens, I was only a few blocks from the club. I crossed into the Commonwealth Mall, a green walking path between the north and southbound lanes that ran the length of Back Bay and was studded with statues and commemorations of Boston's glorious past. I reached the club in less than five minutes, quicker than it would have taken Jackson to drive from headquarters. I stopped across from the front entrance and sat on a stone bench beside a dried flower pot.

As I gazed upon the grandeur of the building, I thought of Jackson's humble roots in Maine. It was no surprise he frequented this place. The Algonquin Club was an ancient Boston establishment, founded nearly a century before by Boston's leading businessmen. Situated in a grand bow-front Georgian townhouse in the heart of Back Bay, it was as upper-class as they come, with paneled walls, frescoed ceilings and a winding marble stairway. It was, in many ways, a monument to the Anglo-Saxon aristocracy that ruled Boston for three centuries until the Irish took over.

I had been to the club once, several years before when, after a plumbing mishap flooded the Patrolmen's Hall, the Algonquin board graciously offered their establishment for our annual ball. I never found out who got paid off or who was trying to win favor with the cops, but I was sure those stolid old gents regretted it. By the end of the night, cops were vomiting on the settees, swinging from the chandeliers and tearing up the Persian rugs for dancing. I even heard the next morning that a shot or two had been fired, probably in drunken merriment. But that incident was as absent from the morning newspapers as all the others related to police misconduct.

I had no intention of going into the Club and planned to intercept Jackson at the front stairs. I sat on the bench with a clear view of the door and waited. I didn't know what model car he drove since I only ever saw him in the office. In fact, I wasn't even convinced he drove.

Jackson lived in the Back Bay, somewhere close, in a one-bedroom apartment he had been renting for twenty years. No one I knew ever visited; very few even knew the address. I imagined that it was much less a home than a place to hang his hat and take a shower. Jackson spent as much time as he could in Cornish Maine, in a country house he built by hand, nestled on a hillside a few hundred yards from the house where he was born. When work was stressful, when Jackson and I worked late reviewing evidence from impossible cases, he often started talking about his place in the hills. He described the flowers at springtime, the low mountains and the farmer's marketplace in town. After five minutes, I forgot the bitter details of some back alley murder or decapitated body found floating in the harbor. And as Jackson drew his pipe, we both imagined the sultry serenity of his Shangri-La in the backwoods of Maine. In moments, I was nearly lulled to sleep by sweeping images of white spruces and red pines, of orchids waving in the breeze and blueberry patches that stretched forever.

"Brae!"

I heard my name called from somewhere in the near distance. I turned on a reflex, although I really couldn't tell the direction it had come from. I was sure, however, it was Jackson's voice, that distinctive baritone, gruff but refined, something between lumberjack and legislator. From the sound I knew he was near, but not too close. He shouted with a whisper, like he too was scared about our meeting.

"Psst. Brae!"

This time the call seemed to come from another direction. I turned the other way, looked towards Commonwealth

Ave. northbound, until my eyesight adjusted. There I spotted Jackson, stopped in the passing lane, waving furiously, his glasses hanging at the tip of his nose like a confused professor. He leaned halfway out the window of a black sedan, squinting in the sun with a wrinkled gaze that suggested he thought he saw me but couldn't be sure. Behind him was a line of cars, some honking, others swerving to get past. A cabbie rolled by, shouting profanities with a fist in the air. If I didn't get to Jackson soon, he was going to get lynched by a mob of enraged drivers. I turned my head, took one last look at the Algonquin Club and sprinted over to him. When a passing car pulled up to insult us, I whipped out my badge and shoved it in the driver's face. The horn-honking ceased and those waiting behind Jackson were suddenly patient. I hopped in and we drove off.

"I didn't know you were a member of the Algonquin."

"I knew it was one landmark we could agree on."

"I see."

"Are you alright, Brae?" Jackson asked.

"As good as can be, I guess."

"So you know about Harrigan?"

"I know he's in custody."

Jackson drove on in silence. He looked tired, his skin was dry and he seemed much older in the sunlight of the afternoon. We drove down Beacon Street, through Kenmore Square and passed Fenway Park. I looked out the window and then to him, wondering where we were going, what he knew and how it would all end or if it would. I couldn't watch Jackson without feeling pity, a sentimental reverence for a man that was almost naïve with idealism. He looked funny in the driver's seat, a lanky white-haired bachelor, leaning into the wheel, grasping it tightly like the helm of a ship. He was as serious as a minister, with none of the piety, and he squinted at the road ahead. If he knew about Lovell's criminal activity, he certainly didn't let on. Sadly, Jackson's belief in the department, and government in general, blinded him to the dark possibilities of corruption. His was an us-versus-them world, where goodness prevailed and evil was always apparent. He was as smart as a whip, there was no doubt, but he viewed things with a scientific simplicity that bespoke his hard, rural upbringing. I wanted to pat him on the back and let him know the universe hadn't changed.

"Where are we going?" I asked.

"We are getting out of Dodge," he said, turning to me with a tight smile. "Let's head to Jamaica Pond and have a chat, shall we?"

"Mind if I smoke?"

Jackson nodded ok and I reached into my coat. I felt something inside, made obvious by the emptiness of the pocket, and pulled out the note Harrigan had passed to me weeks before. I rolled it in my fingers, crumpled it into a ball, went to toss it out the window but then refrained. The note was a token, a little keepsake of the trust between Harrigan and me. At the same time it was central to the volcano of corruption ready to erupt across the city. I stuffed it in my pocket, as much for a souvenir as for evidence. Jackson peered over curiously but unaware, his sixth-sense having little effect outside his office room. If Jackson needed to know then he already would have.

We reached the Jamaicaway, a winding two-lane road that runs south from the city, along the border between Boston and Brookline. I hadn't been out this far in years and was surprised how little it had changed. The massive trees, arched over the road in a natural tunnel, had hardly aged. They still stood as grey and accident-scarred as they were when I was a boy. Beyond, in the distance, the reflection of Jamaica Pond appeared gradually between the trees and small hills. We pulled to the side of the road and parked under the shade of a spruce. The air was cool and the breeze heavy and we walked down a shallow embankment that led to the paved walkway that encircled the pond. The water was alive like an ocean, with small whitecaps splashing and splattering in the wind. I stepped on a pebble and my knee buckled, sending a bolt of pain up my thigh. I froze and gritted my teeth. Either it was suddenly sore or had always been but was numbed by the distraction of trying to survive. I had watched soldiers in Korea riddled with bullets and spitting blood return to camp unfazed, not knowing they were hit and moving about like hyped-up athletes. All the while they were dying a gradual death obscured by the adrenaline of combat.

As we walked, I limped slightly but tried to hide it. Nevertheless, Jackson slowed his pace and we strolled along the path like two old friends. We passed an elderly couple, hand-in-hand, and then a young girl with a Golden Retriever. By the time we reached the far side of the pond, we were alone. Jackson stopped and turned.

"Brae, I need you to be honest with me."

"I'll try Captain."

"What do you know about Harrigan?"

"I know he was setup."

"And Chief Lovell?"

"He's not going to be around much longer."

My response either shocked Jackson outright or confirmed what he already sensed. He kept a straight face and continued to walk. I felt his distress and knew his brain was grinding through the facts and fiction of a situation beyond anything he had experienced or imagined. Had it been weeks before, I might have spilled my guts, revealed all I knew and all that had happened to me. But the case had escalated beyond even Jackson's jurisdiction. With my life at risk and a force that was half-faithful and half-corrupt, and not knowing who was who, I had to be vague. As much as I respected him, Jackson might be a liability.

"I was asked to take you off the case." Jackson said remorsefully.

"That's what I hoped."

"After Harrigan was attacked, I was told that you might have been involved." His words slowed. "That you might have set him up."

"That's crazy, Captain."

"I know. Lovell called with orders to arrest you. When I questioned him, he did everything but threaten me. I knew something wasn't right."

"He's desperate."

As we walked, Jackson stared ahead, looking up to the trees, gazing over the pond, focusing on everything but me. It was the long, solemn walk of a father and son, years after the man returns, when the apology is what's left unsaid and the burden of past mistakes is lifted by a handshake. I didn't resent Jackson for taking me off the case since he, like many, was only following orders. I understood the tension between command and conscience, directives and discretion, the dilemma of receiving orders that defied reason and disregarded morality. I thought back to the night I was instructed to take a battery to the top of a small hill along the Nakdong River, within sight of Pusan. I hesitated like a schoolboy, knowing the enemy had heard us when a green second lieutenant dropped a grenade into a water well he mistook for a pillbox. Hunched in the snowy grass beside my radioman, I ignored the static-ridden pleas of Major Bradshaw to proceed, an order that would have had my unit marching into a wall of aimed Degtyaryovs. I pretended not to hear and so the lives of many were saved.

Jackson probably thought he could have done more, we all did, but he could be blamed no more than Harrigan could for getting assaulted. We were all bound to an inscrutable destiny, acting out roles, taking our punches but giving some back. Life had taken on new meaning and shined with a mystic clarity, like a bright day between storms. I understood and I forgave him.

I stopped and turned to him.

"Captain, I had no part in the fires. I had no part in Harrigan's beating. I've been on the run for days. I couldn't even go home."

Jackson could only nod, just once, but enough to let me know he understood and he believed. With his hands stuffed in his coat pockets, he sighed nervously and backed away to allow a midday bicyclist to pass. We stood inches apart, our eyes averted like reacquainted rivals, although that was hardly the case. I looked at Jackson and saw spider veins at the tip of his nose, across his cheeks. They were purple and swollen, indications of stress or too much alcohol, enhanced by the sunlight he was so seldom exposed to. Beneath the long trench coat he trembled.

"What's your take on this?" Jackson asked.

"Lovell is going to be brought down. Within days. I can't say any more. I'm sorry Captain."

He looked up to me with sad eyes, "Are you sure?"

"Yes."

"The Feds?"

"Yes."

"Are there things you can't divulge?" he asked.

"Unfortunately."

It was a hard thing for him to take, learning that a higher authority had intervened, that his control had been trumped. I knew it would break his heart, but he had to know. The lines of jurisdiction fluctuated like the national borders of Eastern Europe and it was anyone's guess who was in charge. As it stood, Jackson could have arrested me on the spot for assault on a fellow officer. Lovell had given the orders; the warrant was active. For all I knew, I would remain in custody until the Feds had served their indictment and made their sweep. I might have sat in the same cell with Harrigan, kept awake by his snoring.

"I am sorry I let you down, Jody. Truly sorry."

I looked across the pond, face to the wind, as snow-covered branches, frail and spindly, moved in unison like the world itself swayed. There was a beautiful emptiness, a holy solitude in the heart of the city. Despite the cars and passersby there was a silence that only a child could remember. I heard Levinsky's voice, distant but not faint, and the last conversation we had, the promises exchanged, my past for his future, a covenant kept and not wasted. After all these years, it was finally my turn.

My apartment hadn't changed since this last time I was home. When I walked in the front door of the building, I tripped over a stack of mail. I crept up the stairway, each step bending with a creaking familiarity as if to welcome me home. I flipped through the mail; oil bill, electric bill, phone bill, advertising circular from Sears Roebuck. It was reassuring to know some things continued normally. I got to the apartment door, slipped in the key and opened it. I tossed the mail on the coffee table and collapsed to the sofa. Before I got too comfortable, I reached behind my back, grabbed the gun and slid it under the couch. I had never felt so glad to be alone in my cramped apartment.

I turned on the television and the nasally voice of Walter Cronkite broke the silence. I hadn't showered in days and smelled like a wet dog. So I rose from the couch, grabbed a dirty towel from a pile at the foot of the bed and made for the bathroom. I peeled off my clothes, got under the shower head and let the water run through my hair and over my face. As the steam rose, I inhaled it like an intoxicant. I was so relaxed I could have fallen asleep standing up.

I let the shower run until the hot water ran out. Half-naked and holding the towel, I tiptoed to the bedroom leaving a trail of water and suds behind. There was a sudden knock at the door and I stopped. I stood as still as a fox, holding my breath and listening. After ten seconds there was another knock. Had it been Demetrius, he would have left after the first. I hoped it had been Ruth, but the force of the knock was anything but female.

I was literally caught with my pants down, against a corner, trapped in the apartment with no escape. I peered from the bedroom to the door when a third knock, harder than the last, rattled the rusting hinges and sent a chill up my back. My heart raced but I remained still.

Finally I couldn't stand the tension any longer. If it was a hit, or an arrest, I was either going to die clothed or die fighting, but I couldn't do both. I leaned down and crawled to the couch with the stealth I learned in boot camp; ass to the ground, knees outspread and pulling with the fingertips. I got to my gun and the second my finger touched the trigger, there was another knock. I stood up and faced the front door, pistol pointed and ready for anything. Since I had left it unlocked, the next move was his.

"Come in."

I let go of the towel and it dropped to the floor, leaving myself exposed but not vulnerable. I clutched the pistol grip with both hands for dead accuracy and spread my bare feet against the hardwood floor. My left eye ran along the barrel, fixated on the front sight and the imagined target beyond. I was impressed by my own steadiness, a physical calm that contrasted with the shaking terror in my mind. Then the knob began to turn, slowly at first, until the bolt clicked and the door was free. I pulled the hammer back until it cocked. As the door swung, I saw the edge of a man in the darkness, the outline of an arm, then a shoulder. The door was half-way open when the shadow broke and there was McQuillan, smiling mischievously, one hand in his pocket and the other holding a brown paper bag. I sighed and lowered the gun.

"You weren't going to be taken with clothes on?" he cracked.

"Get the hell in here Mac," I said, waving him in. I knelt down, grabbed the towel and wrapped it around my waist.

"Is that water or did you piss yourself?" McQuillan joked. I looked down to a puddle on the floor, bathwater or urine I couldn't be sure. He slapped my back, sat on the couch and kicked his legs up on the coffee table. Bare-assed and shivering, I scurried into the bedroom to dress.

"You're lucky I didn't blow your head off. What the hell are you doing here?"

"I wanted to make sure you're alright."

"Where's the stiff shirt?" I said, coming out of the bedroom and buttoning a shirt.

"Deitz? Staying at a hotel in Quincy until his assignment is over."

"And when will that be?" I wondered.

"Soon. How's that knee?"

I bent over and pulled my pant leg up. The bruises were fading but the bullet entry points were still blood-encrusted and weeping a white, transparent puss.

"Healing. Can't you tell?"

McQuillan had little sympathy for leg wounds, having himself been disabled by a side tackle that crushed his meniscus like an egg yolk. He leaned back into the couch and reached into the paper bag for a beer. When he crack it open, the sour smell of carbonation filled the room. As I walked over to lock the door, he grabbed another can and tossed it to me. I instantly caught it with both hands and threw it back.

"No thanks, Mac."

"Still don't drink Jody?"

"Not on Thursdays," I snapped back.

"Well, today is Wednesday."

I paused for a second. "Not in Korea."

"Fourteen hours ahead, right?" McQuillan asked. "Are you still over there?"

"Sometimes. You?"

"Just when I'm alone," McQuillan said, taking a big gulp.

"If that was me, I'd be there permanently," I snickered, taking a seat beside him.

"What about that little gal from headquarters? You still seeing her?"

"Ruth? Yeh, but she's pretty shaken up about things."

McQuillan frowned and turned to me. "She's got to know this ain't your fault Jody."

"She's a simple girl from California. Corruption, arson, shootings. She probably feels like she's trapped in a James Cagney film. They see everything in terms of Hollywood out there."

"You ain't no Cagney, Brae," McQuillan said in a low, gruff voice, as if he had to belch but couldn't. He smiled and took another swill.

"What's next?"

"I'm doing a double tonight. Officially that means I'm on duty. Unofficially, I'm watching out for you."

We sat on the couch like crotchety old war veterans, talking old times and arguing over everything from film stars, to women, to who made the best pizza in town. But as a die-hard Democrat, McQuillan loved nothing more than to talk politics. His father had been a teamster, raised in the working-class slums of Lynn. So McQuillan was raised in a home where the Democratic Party was second only to the Pope as savior of mankind. I was indifferent. Politics to me had always been like a chess game. It was interesting to observe the back and forth and the occasional checkmate as an opponent is backed into a corner. But ultimately it was a pastime for union laborers and aristocrats. I had lived through the war years of Roosevelt and the prosperity of the Eisenhower era and neither seemed to have affected my life in any meaningful way. I admired that McQuillan was passionate about the world. But his beer-infused tirades against the elites and the enemies of the common man seemed nothing more than an attempt to achieve in conversation what he had sought before his football injury years before; another win. I held my hands to my ears and forfeited the game.

I awoke on the couch hours later. The television was still on and hummed with after-hours network static, a glaring screen of garbled gray and white lights. As I got up, I accidently poked McQuillan in the eye. He jumped like a startled bear, leapt over the coffee table and stood in the center of the room, fists out and circling with the hypnotic grace of a martial artist.

"Shh,"

I waved my hand and snapped my fingers and, as if awoken from a trance, McQuillan was instantly sober. I pointed to my ear and then the door. He held up his thumb to say ok. I walked over and placed the side of my head against the wall, beside the door and just below a light switch. I had learned in the academy how sound travels through a house or building. With an ear against a stud or beam you could detect sound and movement from several floors above and below. But with one cheek pressed against the wall, I heard only my heartbeat and the low rumble of the boiler in the basement. I nodded to McQuillan, shrugged my shoulders and backed away. But then there was a noise, a heavy and gritty shift, like someone dragging a workbench across pavement. It was faraway but unmistakable, distant yet distinct, a movement somewhere within the house. The old building was full of holes and cracks and the acoustics were as deceiving as an echo in a canyon. Smash! This time it was louder. McQuillan gasped and I turned to see him holding a gun the size of my foot, a .357 magnum, non-standard, with a wood handle and gleaming steel barrel. I motioned for him to lower it.

We heard voices below, the shuffling of feet and then a scream, a woman's voice, a cry of terror. I hit the light switch and reached under the couch for my .38. My nose hairs tingled and I tasted a faint but familiar saltiness. A strange odor grew stronger and stronger.

"It's smoke!" McQuillan shouted.

Doors flew open and the panicked voices of other tenants sounded in the stairwell below. The smell was undeniable, it was smoke. The building was on fire.

"Quick, let's go!" I screamed.

When I opened the door, the hallway was filling with thick black smoke. I ripped open my shirt and pulled it across my mouth. With McQuillan behind, we descended the stairs. I groped the wall, found the banister and held it firmly for balance. When we reached the second floor, a burst of scalding heat stung my eyes and caused me to jump back. McQuillan pushed me onward with his massive hand, down the stairwell and into the blackness, both of us choking but determined to live. We landed on the bottom floor and I saw a dull light, soft burgundy and green, that shone through a stained-glass window like a guiding star. In a split-second I decided that if the door didn't open I would dive through the panes. As I hesitated in the smoke, McQuillan reached around, turned the knob and we ran into the cold openness of the night. We scurried down the front steps and stopped on the sidewalk, hunched over and gasping for air. Even in that brief exposure, my lungs burned. Other tenants, people I had passed in the hallway but rarely acknowledged, were huddled on the street in pajamas, arms crossed and shivering in morbid silence. In the distance I heard sirens and between the spaces and yards of the houses I saw the flashes of approaching lights.

I looked around but didn't see Demetrius. The basement windows smoked like the bowels of a hearth and I started to walk towards the alley, imaging the old man flailing in the poisoned darkness, knocking into things and dying a slow death.

"My landlord!" I shrieked, pointing at the basement door.

"We have to go!" McQuillan shouted, yanking my shoulder.

There was no hope and I knew it. The building burned from the basement up, evidenced by the thick black smoke that poured from the foundation windows. The intensity of the heat was greatest down there and even if Demetrius had been awoken by the smoke, he was surely asphyxiated and nearing cremation. Regretfully, I pulled myself away and ran down the street with McQuillan at my side. We turned down the first side street and out-of-view just as a ladder truck came around the corner. We sprinted for half a block and then stopped, winded and coughing up black spit. McQuillan, bent over and panting, turned to me and smirked.

"Thank god for the parking problem around here."

We were at his car, two blocks from the apartment, wedged between a fire hydrant and work van. He unlocked the doors and we got in. As we neared the end of the block, I spotted a shadowy figure, hunched low, dart across the street like an oversized rat. It was so fleeting that I would have missed him with a blink. Luckily the headlights nicked his ankle just before he vanished between two cars, thereby confirming what we both saw. McQuillan and I looked at each other.

"Hit it!" I yelled.

The tires chirped and we sped for a few yards. McQuillan slammed the brakes and we hopped out with guns drawn, scanning the sidewalk and peaking under parked cars for a vision that was gone. Standing under the hum of a streetlamp, we stood silently and listened for the slightest crunch of snow, the pitter-patter of feet. The street was lined with massive three family homes, separated by narrow alleyways and surrounded by chain-linked fences. The homes were so close together, spaced by only five or six feet, that the street lights didn't penetrate the side and back yards. He could be lurking anywhere, I thought.

It was so quiet I could hear my own pulse and the windless silence created a chilling calm. We split up. I headed down the steep slope of the street, towards the next corner. McQuillan went up the hill in the opposite direction. As I walked along the sidewalk, I looked left and right, searching for movement and hoping for the slightest quiver of life. When I reached the mailbox at the next cross street, I turned and looked up the hill at McQuillan, who stood with arms up and palms out, gesturing in frustration. He had abandoned the search. I tucked the pistol into my belt and walked back leisurely, the salty, damp stench of fire apparent everywhere. Everything I owned, all the tiny treasures I accumulated over a half-lived lifetime, were burning in the distance and I could do nothing. It was beyond the mystery of coincidence that my building caught fire on an evening I was home. The sirens in the distance seemed to tempt me back, to show up at the scene, where my sudden appearance would be evidence enough for Lovell that I was torching buildings.

As I lumbered up the sidewalk I saw the flashing lights of the ladder truck reflect off the night sky. Without warning, another fire truck rumbled up the hill behind me, lost and searching for the apartment building. I looked straight ahead and aimed towards McQuillan, who was twenty yards away, leaning against his car. I counted to three and turned away from the street, just in time, hiding my face and holding my breath. The truck rolled by with its sirens and lights blaring. When it passed and turned at the next corner, I felt relieved.

I looked back up the sidewalk and didn't see McQuillan. I began to run, slowly at first, then in full sprint. I got to his car but he was gone. Then I heard a groan and saw his dark frame spread between the curb and front tire, hidden in the shadow, one arm extended and holding the gun. When I knelt down and put my hand on his shoulder, he trembled. It took all my strength to roll him on to the sidewalk and under the streetlight so I could see what was wrong. His eyes were glassy and distant, rolling up into the sockets like lifeless cue balls. Guessing he had fallen, I felt along the back of his head for a bump but there was none.

"Mac, what happened?!" I shouted.

McQuillan's arm slowly rose and pointed at his chest, where, to my horror, blood pulsated from a hole in his black leather jacket. He was shot. I unzipped the coat and tore open the shirt to see, just below his ribcage, a silver-dollar sized entry wound. I frantically felt around his stomach and along his back for other bullet holes. Behind his right kidney I discovered the exit, a large hole of torn flesh and fatty tissue, blood trickling but strangely clean. Quickly I heaved his three-hundred pound body over my shoulder, opened the passenger door and lowered him on to the seat. I reached into his jacket pocket for the keys, fired up the engine and took off.

"Hang in there Mac." I begged.

When I got to the foot of Mission Hill, I turned right on Tremont Street and raced towards Boston City Hospital. McQuillan was bleached white, his eyes flickering enough to let me know he was alive but in shock. With each abrupt turn he groaned. In a panic, I tore a piece of his shirt with one hand, crumpled it up and pressed it against his chest wound. He looked at me desperately, taking the compress and holding it himself.

I got to Mass. Avenue, only a half mile from the hospital, and aimed the car like a missile towards the towering grey building of lights. I rolled down the window for air when suddenly my head hit the steering wheel. Ugh! I looked in the rearview mirror and saw a dark car, driving erratically and attempting to pass. It had rear-ended me with the force of a battering ram. I punched the gas and flew down Mass. Avenue, passing the hospital in a fit of confusion. The other car raced into oncoming traffic to pull beside me but as it did, I cut the wheel and blocked him.

McQuillan slumped in the passenger seat, his head tilted back and his eyes almost closed. With one hand, I reached over and pushed him down and out of view. The other car swerved side-to-side, accelerating every few seconds and smashing into my rear bumper. With each collision we were thrust forward and McQuillan moaned.

I blew through a red light at the next intersection and cross-traffic skidded to a halt. I bore left on Southampton Street, through the industrial slums of South Boston—fish wholesalers and meat packing companies—passing rows of parked tractor trailers that I prayed would not back out. I screamed for McQuillan to hang on, begged him to keep breathing but he only smiled. We approached a narrow bridge that crossed the Southeast Expressway. Halfway across, the other car made a final attempt to pass, pulling into the on-coming lane until we were neck-in-neck.

It was then I saw the birthmark, the same man who chased me weeks ago, sneering from behind the driver's wheel, alone and seething. Our eyes met for a single moment when suddenly I heard the blare of a horn and was blinded by headlights. If my pursuer hadn't looked over to me for that half-second, he might have lived. But before he could hit the brakes and return to the safety of the right lane, an approaching truck, as unstoppable as a meteor, plowed into him head on. The impact was explosive and my car was lifted in the air. Metal and glass rained down on the trunk and rear window like shrapnel from a grenade. As I came over the end of the bridge, I glanced into the rearview to see lights, sparks and smoke.

I wound through the back streets of South Boston with the panicked aimlessness of a bank robber. Each time I looked over to McQuillan, he stared back with a subtle smirk. Although he couldn't speak, he seemed stable. Two police cruisers raced by, responding to the accident and the tangled mix of steel and body parts, blood and motor oil. The next time I looked at McQuillan, he was frothing at the mouth. His breathing was labored and I feared he was losing too much blood. I drove onward, speeding through the streets of Boston. My mind went blank and some deeper instinct took hold. As if on autopilot, my arms steered and my foot pressed the gas while I sat back and observed. When I pulled down Chestnut Street, to Ruth's apartment, McQuillan was still alive.

"He's very badly injured."

"I know."

"We need to get him to a hospital."

"I know."

Ruth leaned over the bed and held a wet towel over McQuillan's forehead. His breathing had normalized and some of the color returned to his face. Nevertheless, I couldn't look at him. The glassy emptiness of his eyes stirred memories of death that I long suppressed. As a detective, I had witnessed the dead and dying like most experienced rush-hour traffic; frequent, expected but never something you got used to. But unlike in war, being a cop didn't mean watching friends suffer. I had had colleagues killed on duty over the years. There was an order to society that was entirely absent in battle. On the street, most civilians were on your side while in Korea you never knew who your enemy was. One day local villagers might offer your platoon food and water and the next they would send a messenger to the Chinese, informing them the Americans, lying in the sun and drunk from complacency, were over the next hill. In war there were no rules and no laws. So watching a comrade die on a dusty cot, blood spewing from an artery like a water fountain, was acceptable. I was able to handle the things that were expected, even things that were possible. But standing in a poorly lit room with a friend that had a tunnel through his gut was too much to bear.

Ruth shouted orders like a field nurse. Once she had cleaned the wound and covered it with gauze and a compress, she injected McQuillan with morphine. In seconds he relaxed and his eyes were responsive. Had I never met Ruth, had I never pushed aside my cynicism and asked her out, Mac might have been a corpse on that bed.

We waited in the bedroom, the three of us, like the last people on the planet. I paced the room while she leaned over and tended to McQuillan. Every few moments I looked over and watched the white sheets rise as he struggled to breathe. We had to get him to the hospital but I was incapacitated by fear.

"We need to go now," Ruth pleaded.

I held my finger out.

"Please, I need a few more minutes."

"I'll take him without you," she threatened.

I reached for a cigarette and Ruth motioned for me to smoke in the other room. My head pounded just behind the eyes and I couldn't think straight. For the first time in my life I was afraid to act. As McQuillan clung to life, I feared for my own safety and the risk of showing up at the hospital.

The demons of paranoia circled me and I imagined Lovell's men observing, watching, waiting, and lurking from every street corner, behind every parked car. I didn't know when the Feds would move in to make their arrests, but something told me the madness of the past weeks was nearing a conclusion. Life was ironic and I only imagined being cut down the moment before the sweep, seconds before the FBI showed up with warrants, agents and guns. I would be the lone hostage slain before the rescue, if only out of spite.

"I am taking him in."

Ruth peered from the bedroom door with smudged mascara and sad eyes, a look of postponed hysteria, contained by crisis and crippled by urgency. She waited for a response but I said nothing. I felt her quiet pleas and the stare of those delicate watching eyes, begging me to act before it was too late. I gazed at the wall, as empty as an attic, with a lifeless apathy, screaming without making a sound, sobbing without tears. When, finally, she stomped her foot in frustration, the floor shook to the mantle of the earth. My legs buckled but I regained balance as if caught by some invisible hand.

"Jody!"

Something inside me was finally awoken. In those scattered seconds I relived an entire life. The night I told Ruth how my mother died, she held me as I wept. Levinsky had kept his half of the bargain, recounting a tale that began over three decades before with a street corner gang of petty thieves and sidewalk criminals.

Levinsky, Lovell and Dr. Muhammad grew up in the South End when it was a featureless stew of ethnics and ethnicities—Jews, Irish, Blacks, Italian, and Lebanese—as unclaimed as the Wild West and often as lawless. Drawn from the slums along Fort Point Channel, they lived in cold-water flats of crumbling brick and fetid basements. In winter they scavenged for coal in the foundry yards along Massachusetts Avenue. During the summers they stole fish from icecarts, robbed storehouses, ran craps games and engaged in penny extortion. In time, the mischief turned to misdemeanors and the misdemeanors to serious crime. It was with great irony that Darren Lovell, a convicted felon by age sixteen, made the police force through either an error in judgment or bad record-keeping.

When they turned to arson during The Depression it was at the hire of property owners with apartment buildings or warehouses too devalued to sell and too decrepit to repair. With Lovell as lookout, 'Rags' Levinsky would crawl inside a basement window or bulkhead and litter the place with strips of torn cloth, soaked in gasoline. With the flick of a match, the building was engulfed. Lovell's influence as a cop was just enough to delay the arrival of the fire department and so most buildings burned beyond repair and the insurance money was paid-out. The scheme was airtight and no one got hurt, the one condition being the property was either vacant or unoccupied. That was, however, until one cold March night.

Levinsky had nothing to gain by telling me what he knew. I could only guess he sought that last-minute redemption, larger than forgiveness, so common to people approaching the end of their lives. As I sat facing him, he had spoken with a slow intensity and his words trembled with a shaking regret. I listened:

> *We got a job on Bowdoin Street, Dorchester, at the HARLAN-BRAE apartment building. It was a little before midnight. Lovell and I met in the alleyway next to the building. Together we soaked strips of cloth in gasoline. Then he sat in his car on the side street, guarding the firebox on the corner street pole, in case someone*

tried to pull it. We waited until after midnight, when Lovell's connection at headquarters started his shift. He would delay any calls long enough for the building to burn thoroughly.

I entered through a rear door, left open by the owners. It was an old building, dry and musty. I laid the rags across the stairs and hallways of the first floor. I lit the match, tossed it and ran. Poof! The place went up like a tinderbox. I'd never seen anything like it. But when I got outside, I heard a woman scream. I tried to run back up the stairwell but the smoke was too thick.

I ran around the corner to Lovell, who was waiting in the car, ready for the getaway. I screamed that someone was inside but he scoffed. He said it was impossible. In a panic, I ran for the firebox on the corner. Before I could get to it, Lovell jumped out and tackled me, breaking my ankle. We wrestled for a few minutes, until I broke free and hobbled to the street pole. The moment before I pulled the alarm we heard the cry of a child. We looked up to see you, Jody, clinging to a fire escape beside an open window. Smoke poured out and I knew we only had seconds. Lovell ran up the stairs, took you in his arms and brought you down. I have to admit I had never seen much humanity in that man until that night, and not much since.

We drove to Thad's apartment in Roxbury. His father was a Baptist minister. Everyone knew him. Thad arranged to have his father drop you off, no questions asked. We said your mother had died and your father was unknown. When Thad's father asked if you had a name, the first thing that came to Lovell's mind was HARLAN-BRAE, the building we torched.

That's all I know, son. I tried to help her. My own father died in the Chelsea fire of 1908, when I was six. I too, have been scarred by fire. I pulled the alarm, that's all I could do. The fire trucks arrived shortly after. I was able to save the building but not your mother.

The visions of that day, half-remembered and half-imagined, haunted me every minute since my last meeting with Levinsky. Until that point I had had no memories of my childhood. It was as if I was born at age four, my earliest recollections being a smiling house matron at the institution, washing me like a prized dog. I gravitated to her warmth like a mother, reaching to touch her face, moving to suckle her breasts, not knowing she would soon be replaced by another, then another. Those years were a kaleidoscope of faces and femininity that left me groping for love like a blind man would a wall switch. As a result I withdrew into my mind, that solitary shelter of darkness over which I alone ruled. With the exception of Marty Mirsky, I made few friends and even fewer enemies, choosing instead a life of detached indifference that allowed me to like without loving, to experience happiness without joy. It was a bitter freedom.

The war had given my life a new purpose, a sense of destiny that explained the desolation and justified the apathy. I was so enthralled by the new me that I feared the war might end and I would have to return to Boston. As a result, I acted with a certain recklessness, something between valor and sloppiness, that heightened the risks, that tempted the danger, and made my return all the more unlikely. I wasn't suicidal but I acted with a blind enthusiasm that made gung-ho sound tame. As my tour of duty neared the end, I grew more daring and my platoon thought I had a death wish. One night while taking small-arms fire I leapt from the brush and sprinted across an open field to commandeer an enemy machine gun. I could still recall the faces on my men when I turned the weapon and blasted the enemy with their own artillery. I got a field commendation for that act although I should have gotten a month in the brink.

When I returned from Korea I was something of a lost cause. I wandered the streets of San Francisco for weeks with no aim, drinking in barrooms and sleeping in hallways. I spent the last of my money on a hooker named Geraldine who had immigrated from Scotland only weeks before to escape the advances of her drunken step-father. We shacked up in a cheap motel near the docks and unloaded each other's woes and disappointments like scared runaways. We clutched to each other day and night, naked and drunk. When we were tired of sex, we drank. When we grew weary of drinking, we made love. When the money had run out, I awoke alone in a bed of piss, with empty bottles of cheap wine and brandy scattered across the floor. Geraldine was gone and so was my wallet and watch.

That was as close to a woman as I had ever been and the experience had been my model for intimacy ever since. As a rookie, living alone and drinking without cause, I spent every weekend and many weekdays trying to rediscover Geraldine in every woman I met. Eventually the hangovers and foggy mornings became too much. I woke up one Sunday morning in May, my head pounding and my throat as dry as lint, and gave up alcohol.

Ruth was the first woman that both terrified and fascinated me. In all those places where I was weak, she was strong. As I wavered she stood firm. I brought McQuillan to Ruth because she was the only person that could fix the broken mess of my past and his present. I abandoned myself entirely to her, bowing at her beauty, begging for her to forgive a lifetime of hardened indifference. With McQuillan dying beside me in the passenger seat, I had become a child once again, cold, scared and shivering, baffled and unknowing.

"Let's go."

I walked into the bedroom, fighting to hold back the tears that dripped down my nose. I was weak and light-headed but something empowered me to carry on.

"Lift him off the bed. I'll help," she ordered.

We lifted McQuillan to his feet and, although in pain, he was silent. I looked at him and a dry, blissful smile broke across his face, that same look of final acceptance I had seen on dying soldiers right before the end. He put an arm over each of our shoulders and we carried him down the stairs. Outside it was dark and raining heavily. We dragged McQuillan to the car and leaned him against the door as I searched my pockets for the keys. I tried to put them in the keyhole but my hands shook uncontrollably. Ruth swiped them from me and opened the doors. I pushed McQuillan into the back seat while Ruth pulled his coat from the other side. His frame was so large I had to bend his legs just to close the car door. Ruth ran around to the driver's seat and started the engine.

The roads were a deathly mix of ice and snow and the rain so intense we could barely see with the wipers on high. Ruth drove with cautious haste, focusing on the road and grasping the wheel with both hands. When we reached an intersection, she turned to me and I nodded left or right. We passed the Boston Common, drove down Tremont Street and through the South End towards Boston City Hospital.

I looked back to McQuillan who lay cramped along the cold vinyl surface. When we rolled over a pothole, his eyes popped open and he grinned, his parched lips murmuring words of quiet delirium. My eyes swept the rear window and

I observed headlights hovering unnaturally close to our bumper. With each turn, at every stop, they remained as fixed as a hitched trailer. I was overcome by the warm tingle of paranoia that left me gripping the seams of the seat. Yet I couldn't be sure of anything. From the muted calm of the car interior, it was difficult to see what was happening in the misty world of neon and streetlamps beyond. I kept my mouth shut and looked to the back seat as if keeping an eye on McQuillan.

The closer we got to the hospital, the more I felt an end approaching—the end of Mac, the end of Lovell, the end of me, or perhaps the end of Ruth and me. Whatever it was, it was culminating and I felt a vague sense of imminent conclusion that was neither welcomed nor dreaded. Either the Feds were going to make a move or I was going to blast the next person that got in my way. I only hoped Ruth would accept any outcome. I looked through the rain to the city lights and thought of how crazy this world was. I had seen the worst of society and had lived in its underbelly. Since I was a child, all I had ever known was filth, coldness, destruction and deceit. Maybe I had grown too comfortable with those things. Yet I always believed there was a brighter place and maybe that was why I kept close to my heart that vision of the hill overlooking a winding river. I could have sat there for eternity, counting the lilacs, watching the river flow lazily towards the horizon. The vision was mesmerizing. In minutes I was half-asleep, my chin in my chest and dreaming as the rain pattered against the windshield.

"Jody, wake up!"

I came to as we rolled to a red light on Massachusetts Avenue, the intersection I was chased through only hours earlier. The engine sputtered a few times and then stopped. I looked to Ruth, but she stared ahead, her hands on the steering wheel and tears rolling off her cheeks. Something was wrong.

"We're out of gas," she cried.

Directly across the intersection was the main entrance to Boston City Hospital. Behind the gate was a large roundabout and behind that, the main doors. Cars and ambulances pulled up day and night with the sick and injured, dropping off and picking up at one of the busiest transfer points in the region. We had to get McQuillan through those doors and to the safety of an emergency room. Ruth convulsed from desperation, her face in the steering wheel and turning the ignition key over and over again. The engine moaned like a dying widow. I looked back and saw the headlights of the tailing car, hauntingly still and lurking. When the traffic signal turned green, there was a sudden chorus of horns as impatient drivers swerved around us to pass. We were alone and trapped.

I looked across to the hospital entrance and spotted police cruisers parked like centurions on either side of the gate. Beside the cars were two officers, dressed in long parkas and holding flashlights. With each arriving visitor or ambulance, they would peer in to inspect the occupants. There was no urgency to the searches, no method to their task. They simply held out their flashlights, leaned over to look inside and then waved the vehicle through. I marveled at their boldness, hunting for a suspect in one of the most visible places in the city. It was vanity to think they were there for me, but I had no doubt. I reached for my gun, unlocked the safety and put my arm on Ruth's shoulder.

"Let's carry him."

Ruth leaned into the dash, her forehead against the steering wheel. When she turned to me, I saw a face of utter bewilderment. Her mascara was streaked across her face and her hair a tangled mess yet she was as beautiful as ever. She looked like a heartbroken girl whose world had been shattered with a letter, a kiss. Her innocence was not lost.

"Ruth, please."

I leaned back to check McQuillan, who lay as lifeless as a sedated bear. His eyes were half-open but unresponsive and his cheeks glistened with sweat. Every few seconds his chest rose in shallow, awkward breaths. In the paleness of his graying skin color, I watched the life slip from his body.

"Ruth, now, please!"

I leaned across, kissed her on the cheek and opened the door. The rain lashed my neck and arms—the wind blinded me. But I opened the rear door and pulled McQuillan out. Ruth ran to my side and together we heaved him on our shoulders, pausing to balance the weight. With my right hand, I took the gun and let it hang by my waist. When I looked back, passing headlights illuminated the windshield of the other car long enough for me to make out the bloated gaze of officer Rollins. I waved my pistol but he was unmoved.

We limped across the intersection like a wounded fire squad returning to camp, one grueling step at a time, over puddles and around piles of slush. Passing vehicles skidded to a stop at the sight of our maimed and hobbling figures. In the darkness under the streetlights we were an image of brutality. McQuillan's jacket was open and his white shirt soaked in blood. With his arms slung around us and his chin hanging down, he must have appeared crucified. I tried to walk steady but my injured knee buckled with each step, sending an electrifying sting up my thigh. I slid on black ice and almost brought three of us crashing to the pavement. Ruth tripped on a manhole and broke her heel. Yet we continued on, our eyes fixed to the front entrance like the gates of heaven.

When we were halfway across the intersection, I observed a third figure standing between the officers. He wore a black fedora, pulled down low, and a long trench coat, hands tucked into the pockets. I couldn't see his face but I felt his stare as he monitored our approach. He stood with the passive confidence of a baseball catcher, knowing the pitch and waiting for us to land in his glove. I didn't have to see him. I recognized the posture—I knew the frame. I didn't have to guess. It was Lovell.

"Freeze! Drop your weapon!"

The two officers stood with pistols out. Yet we stumbled on, disheartened but not deterred.

"Who do you work for?" I shouted through the rain. The cops glanced to each other, then to Lovell, in confusion.

"Boston Police. Drop the god damn weapon!"

We were only yards away when I let McQuillan slide off my arm. Ruth supported him for another few feet until two hospital orderlies rushed to his aid. With Ruth and McQuillan safe, I remained in the street, the gun at my side and my face against the merciless rain.

"Drop the gun!" the officers shrieked, their elbows shaking from either fear or anticipation.

"Drop the gun Jody," Lovell grunted. "It doesn't have to end like this."

I looked at Lovell but couldn't see his eyes. His voice was low, soft, almost comforting and had the same hypnotic allure as Levinsky's. I hated him more than anyone I had ever known. I stared with a mindless rage, jaw-clenched and frothing at the mouth. Almost subconsciously, I began to raise the gun in a gentle arc, as effortless as a morning stretch.

"It didn't have to begin like it did Lovell," I screamed, spitting rain and fuming like a melting devil. Lovell was startled by the riddle, the gentle insinuation to his part in my past. I didn't have to say anymore, he knew. Lovell instructed the officers to hold their fire and then stepped forward.

"I saved you Brae. Now you can save yourself. Give me the gun," he said, extending his hand towards me.

"You made me an orphan."

"I could've let you die. But I didn't."

"I could let you live, but I won't."

I listened to his pleas but I couldn't hear the words. The gun continued to rise. Crack! Someone fired a warning shot that passed near my head. My ears were filled with high-pitched ringing, a tormenting drone that ripped into my psyche and would have driven me to madness. Nevertheless, I held the gun and eyed the barrel sight as it swept Lovell's torso to his neck. The moment his face came into view, I would pull the trigger and be avenged.

"Jody don't," Ruth cried.

Then suddenly the buzzing gave way to a melodic hum so recognizable I almost smiled. The noise got closer each second and echoed above the traffic, buildings and rain. It was the glorious sound of sirens. The first car raced down Harrison Avenue from out of the blackness and skidded to a stop. Two men jumped out with guns drawn and shouted from behind the opened car doors.

"FBI! Drop your weapons! Now!"

I wondered if it was all a dream. Two more cars, dark and unmarked, drove up to the front entrance. Agents leapt from every door and surrounded Lovell and the patrolmen, ordering them to the ground at gunpoint. I let my gun dangle from my fingers and watched the sweep unfold.

"Brae, give me the gun. Harrigan's been freed."

The words rang out above the mayhem like the voice of God. Deitz stood before me with a reserved smile, his arm extended and waiting. He wore a fatherly expression that was demanding yet sympathetic. Ruth rushed over and took my arm, lowering it with a firm but gentle insistence. I had neither the will nor a reason to resist. My arm dropped and the gun slid from my palm like a loose glove. Ruth smiled, put her arm around my waist and together we walked towards the hospital gate. Lovell's loyalists peered from the backseat of an FBI cruiser like captured soldiers, with sulking eyes and shattered souls. Lovell was against another car, spread-eagle, as arrogant as ever and scuffling with four agents like a rabid dog. When they finally restrained and cuffed him, he was disheveled, panting and beaten, with a swollen face and blood on his nose. As Ruth and I passed, he turned his neck, straining to see through the rain and darkness.

"You're a lucky man Jody Brae," he mumbled.

"You're a murderer, Lovell," I snapped back.

"But I'm your savior. Don't forget it," Lovell snickered as two agents shoved him into the backseat and slammed the door.

CHAPTER
FOURTEEN

~

D aniel McQuillan was dead. We got the news the next
morning when Jackson called Ruth's apartment, knowing I would be there. He wanted to be the first to tell me, he
said with a trembling voice. When I hung up the phone and
turned to Ruth, she already knew. As she sobbed quietly, I lay
on my back and stared at the ceiling without thought or feeling, as cold as a fish. McQuillan's passing was no shock, since
his wound was so severe. What at first appeared a straight-
through gunshot was a pulverizing zigzag. The bullet had
ripped through Mac like he was a pinball machine, bouncing off his spine and ricocheting off his ribcage, twisting and
tearing everything in between.

McQuillan's death didn't leave me despondent. But I
did feel a wrenching hollowness, a jolt of sudden loss that
was more physical than emotional. I even experienced ghost
pains, much like amputees in Korea who had the sensation
that their lost limb was still there. For the first few days, I woke
up thinking Mac was alive and present in the world, somewhere. When I pulled into the parking lot at headquarters, to
pick up some things before taking a long overdue leave-of-
absence, I thought I spotted him walking up the stairs with
some unfamiliar men in dark suits, holding briefcases. But it
was only the FBI, visiting headquarters to take affidavits and
issue summonses. Among them was a young agent, six-foot
three and built like a linebacker, with a big head of peasant

brown hair, much like McQuillan in his youth. The chilling resemblance reminded me of how short and brutal life was.

I had never been to a cemetery for two reasons on the same day. But that rainy Monday morning I went to Mount Cavalry to serve two purposes. The first would leave me forever wondering; the second would set me free.

I walked across the lawn with Ruth by my side and holding a small black umbrella. It was unusually warm, almost mild for a December afternoon. She clutched my arm with one hand and held my back with the other as we proceeded in silence. When we reached the burial site, I looked across to hundreds of officers, dressed in formal uniforms and standing with a grim civility. A funeral for a cop was as much a show of force as it was a ritual for the deceased. When a cop was killed, every wife, sibling, mother and father of a police officer was shaken.

Ruth and I stood graveside, across from Mac's wife and two daughters. I couldn't look over to them, but I felt their agony and heard the low whimpers of the youngest one, a golden blonde four-year old, the size of a peanut and surely dad's favorite. Standing beside the family was Jackson, as inconsolable as a widower, his white mustache twitching like a feather and tears streaming down his nose. I never could have imagined him crying since he was far too rational.

After the eulogy, a line of officers marched in formation and raised their rifles for the gun salute. When they fired, I shuddered so hard that Ruth looked at me for reassurance. I was never at ease around gunfire, a quirk I acquired in the war, a reflex for self-preservation or a shell-shocked paranoia—I was never quite sure. All I knew was I couldn't go near a military funeral, firing range or even a fireworks display without feeling jumpy. So I held my breath and counted raindrops until the service was concluded.

Once the casket was lowered into the ground and the closing prayer was said, I grabbed Ruth and quickly walked away, across the damp grass towards the gravel walkway. Along the way we were stopped by fellow officers and friends who whispered condolences and kind words. The more they tried to comfort me, the harder I prodded Ruth along.

Through the crowd I saw Harrigan coming towards us, smartly dressed and a few pounds lighter. When he approached I expected a firm handshake and restrained smile. What I got was a bear hug that knocked the wind out of me. As promised, he was fully exonerated and even recommended for the police Medal of Honor for bravery. He would be taking time off until the trial when he, like many of us, would be called to testify against Lovell. For his safety, he and his mother would be staying with family in Saint Kitts. I looked up and smiled.

"I'll be waiting."

It was only later I realized Harrigan no longer addressed me as 'Detective.'

When we were safely away from the funeral crowd, we followed a small path up the hill, counting the rows of graves and searching for section 6, plot 9. The hill was much longer and steeper than it seemed from the distance of the cemetery flatlands and I was soon out of breath. I reached for a cigarette to calm my nerves, but realized the irony and decided against it.

I started to feel nauseated, exhaustion from weeks of distress. Since the Feds moved in to arrest Lovell and his collaborators, I hadn't gotten a wink of sleep. I was tired and irritable and was tempted to turn around and leave. McQuillan's wife was holding a reception at the house, perhaps I should make an appearance, I thought. As I fretted, Ruth held me tight and urged me onwards.

At the crest of the hill, the path ended at the steps of a stone chapel beside ancient elm tree. We sat for a moment and looked out across the vast cemetery grounds. Gravestones stretched as far as I could see, rolling up and down hills like millions of bobbing life rafts in an ocean of green grass. Beyond the farthest hill and floating on the horizon was the Boston skyline. I took out a cigarette, cupped my hands to light the match and inhaled. Ruth sat silently at my side and looked out dreamily.

When I finished the smoke, Ruth took my hand, looked at me and nodded. It was time to continue. We walked to behind the chapel, to the location that the caretaker promised was just behind the elm tree. When I spotted a small white placard, section 6, I let go of Ruth's hand and began to search. My heart pounded and I felt a strange exhilaration, almost euphoria, that was part hope and part hopelessness. I ran between the rows clumsily, as ravenous as a wolf, my feet squishing in the wet grass. I tripped on a small American flag beside a grave and knocked over a vase of dead flowers next to another. I smashed my shin against a small black headstone obscured by weeds. As I read the endless names and dates, they murmured from my lips.

With Ruth waiting quietly in the distance, I got on my hands and knees and scoured the rows. My pants were soaked and my hands black from mud and when a pebble pushed into my wounded knee, I winced in pain. I was a soldier again, low to the ground and creeping among the weeds, hunting the ghosts of my broken past. My elbows dug into the lawn and I peaked between two gravestones like a sniper. Then I felt a hard surface and looked down to see a small flat grave marker, faded and hidden, covered by soil and grass and leaves, no bigger than a pauper's plaque. I pushed aside the debris with my fingers and scraped away the dirt with my nails. I knew it was her. The light mist seemed to wash away the last layer of mud to reveal the engraved words: Maura Delaney, 1901-1934. My lips moved and I heard her name again; more-air, more-air, more-air—Maura. With my cheek pressed against the stone, I curled into a ball and sobbed like a child.

I would have stayed at that spot forever. But the moment I began to fall asleep, a strong hand took my shoulder and pulled me to my feet. It was Harrigan. He had followed us up the hill, had one again been watching out for me. Ruth stood beside with the umbrella, smiling like a loving mother and wiping the mud from my face with a handkerchief. With Harrigan on one side and Ruth on the other, we walked to the gravel path and back to the world.

When I awoke, the first thing I sensed was the sweet smell of pancakes and steaming coffee. I was naked under a heavy wool blanket. Ruth peaked into the room with a long bathrobe and wide smile.

"I hope you're hungry."

"I'm always hungry."

The lights were off and the shades down, creating a false darkness, disturbed only by faint sunlight that crept through the cracks. As if awoken from a coma, I had no recent memories and wasn't sure how long I had been there. All I knew was I had awoken from the dream once again. I was running alone, with raindrops smacking my face and eyes, wandering dark streets that stretched without end. When I approached an intersection, I turned on an impulse, left or right, driven by an imperative more lingering than lust and more precious than gold.

When I was ready to collapse, I saw her figure in the distance, beckoning me with outstretched arms and a longing smile. I ran towards her, faster and faster, as breathless as an athlete at the final mile, fearing she would elude me once again and vanish into the mist. But as I got closer I could see her clearly. When I was within yards, I squinted to see a face that grew more visible each second, a figure coming to life. After all these years I finally could see her eyes! She didn't vanish, she didn't flee. Then it happened. I ran up to her and stood in blinding wonderment. I could at last see her. It was Ruth.